The Showcase

George Ovitt

Fomite
Burlington, VT

ISBN-13: 978-1-953296-31-9
Library of Congress Control Number: 2022936230
Fomite
58 Peru Street
Burlington, VT 05401
www.fomitepress.com
04/18/2022

Also by George Ovitt

Novels

Stillpoint

Tribunal

Essays

Trotsky's Sink (with Peter Nash)

For Brigid and for my daughters

When this is, that is.

From the arising of this comes the arising of that.

When this isn't, that isn't.

From the stopping of this comes the stopping of that.

-Buddha-

Contents

Disclaimer

Why write a book in the third decade of the 21ˢᵗ century about the woeful 1980s? And a book set in what was at the time—but most certainly isn't now—a seedy and unhappy city? I stood on my front porch on Hazel Avenue in May, 1985, and watched a police helicopter drop an incendiary device on a house full of men, women, and children. The block of Osage Avenue where the MOVE house was located burned all night and into the next day. This is what I mean by "unhappy." And why write about a group of people who, let's be honest, weren't themselves especially "fulfilled" or "successful" in the ways that matter so much these days? The answer to these questions eludes me. These stories, based in some measure on the facts of my own life in that place and time, have proven irresistible, needing for some reason to be told. Nonetheless, the standard disclaimers apply: this isn't really Philadelphia, these aren't real people, and, as they say (but they are seldom serious), everything that follows is the product of my imagination.

Part I

A View of Water

William O'Donnell purchased the Circus Lounge from Carmine DiSanto in 1983. DiSanto was at that time a *capodecina* in the Tony Carmelo organization, which was a satellite of the Giuseppe "Knuckles" Tomaso family, the one that had Anthony Bruno killed at Tony's Napoli Ristorante in South Philly during the drug wars of the late 1970's. Bruno had been working his way through a chicken cacciatore—"blood-red with gravy" as the *Daily News* put it—with three of his associates when two men, never identified or apprehended, burst through the emergency exit and pumped the old man (he was seventy-two) full of buckshot and hollow point .45 slugs—the *Inquirer* said Bruno was shot twenty-seven times, which has to be untrue—just think about it—in any case Bruno was DOA at Jefferson Memorial, as was "Lucky" Frankie Borelli of Camden, and the officious wine steward who, unfortunately for him, was standing at Bruno's side listening (reported the *News*) to the gangster complain about the twenty-dollar bottle of Chianti he'd ordered. After Bruno's demise control of his assets passed via the intercession of half-a-dozen lawyers and no tax collectors to Carmelo and his gofer, DiSanto. As far as anyone knows Carmelo lived only another year—he disappeared after a Christmas party at the New York Playboy Club in 1984 and was never seen again. Though he wasn't bright, DiSanto detected a trend. He decided that Miami might be a restful change of scenery, and he was happy to unload the Circus Lounge for one-quarter of its assessed value—twenty grand—along with the liquor license and protection from the neighborhood association. Or so everyone said.

Stories of the sordid history of The Showcase were passed on to regular customers in dribs and drabs, usually on slow weekday afternoons, by Billy O'Donnell himself. Billy renamed the bar *The Showcase Lounge*, in italics and red neon under a Rolling Rock sign in the front window, tore off the "guinea wallpaper"—fuzzy red felt with splotchy olive trees and off-kilter Coliseums faded to a dirty brown—put in a new floor and cleaned up the bathrooms, installed a jukebox with his favorite tunes, bought two pool tables, and reopened in time for

St. Patrick's Day. The place was a hit from the start. It was the yuppie era even in gritty West Philly, and The Showcase was a friendly, reasonably-priced venue with great tunes on the jukebox and edible burgers. Billy found himself getting rich and decided to open another bar further west, The Showcase II, but it foundered, and so, strapped for cash, Billy brought in an old friend, Augustus Toole, as manager and part owner. Gus knew bars and understood the habits of the Philadelphia drinking crowd better than Billy did. Gus spruced up the place some more, added a television for the Sunday football crowd, and introduced happy hour—the first joint in West Philly to do so. It was a great place to drink. I went there for years. It was at The Showcase that I met my ex-wife, made most of my friends, earned money as a part-time bartender, and basically passed my life from Carter until Bush the first—not the best years of our lives, but not the worst.

Gus was a bright guy—he'd been to LaSalle, though I can't say if he graduated or not, and he'd worked in a bookstore and at the Art Institute during the sixties. He fell into the liquor trade when his father died. His old man had owned the Budweiser distributorship for all of Philadelphia, which was like being given a license to print money, and Gus took the business over for a decade before selling out for (we heard) a million dollars. Gus had gone to Europe for a year. Billy told the regulars that while Gus was in Germany he had fallen for a Bavarian girl, a beauty with a Wagnerian body, but it hadn't worked out. Billy thought she was too Catholic for Gus, who had soured on the Church while at LaSalle, and so Gus had wandered around for a while, looking at art and touring cathedrals, then came home to Philadelphia hoping to forget his heartache—he'd *been in love*—and eventually he ended up buying into what was a lucrative but poorly-run gin mill. Gus never did get over that German woman. He wouldn't serve St. Pauli Girl or Lowenbrau in The Showcase no matter who asked for them, and while he could be excellent company, there was something fundamentally sad about Gus until he met Agnes and more or less snapped out of his misery. Anyway, we all thought of The Showcase as Gus's bar, and it was Gus who poured for us, comped us a couple of drafts a week, regaled us with stories of his travels, and generally provided the welcoming atmosphere that you expect from a neighborhood drinking establishment. What the blue bloods and teetotalers don't get about the drinking life is that for most of us drinking wasn't the point, what matters is sharing your memories, trading stories that are enhanced by the stimulation of alcohol. I drink every day, but I'm never drunk, and everything worthwhile I have learned about my fellow man I have learned in bars. I know this isn't true, but it isn't *untrue*.

Gus loved art, painting especially, more than anyone I've ever known. When he became the everyday manager, and when Billy moved west to run the ill-fated Showcase II, Gus took down all the Bud posters of women in bikinis lying across motorcycles and Lamborghinis, the crass shit that beer salesmen dropped off by the truckload to get you to stock their beer—and replaced them with high quality, framed prints of paintings he liked, mostly by American artists. Of course there was *McSorley's Bar*, and the famous one of the two boxers, and Hopper—*Nighthawks*—is the one I remember best, and by the pool tables there was a photograph I loved to stare at called *Snow in New York* by Robert Henri—I asked Gus and he wrote it down—it reminded me of where I grew up on the Lower East Side. We moved to Asbury Park after my father died, when I was eight, and my mother and sister and I moved in with my aunt—I loved the picture for the contrast of the snow and the buildings, tenements with fire escapes, just like the one in which I was born—the struggle of the horse pulling the carriage, the thick tracks of snow, the sense that you could feel the gray flakes swirling down to the street, which was nearly empty. There were many evenings at The Showcase when I would stare at this picture imagining a childhood that I could not recall.

The place of honor, right over the bar, was a painting by Thomas Eakins—I know about Eakins since I have read about him and gone to the Art Museum to look at his pictures many times—and his stuff was what the regulars liked best. At first when you see the painting you think: so what? Two guys rowing a boat. But then you look at it, night after night, in the summer sunlight that bleaches through the big window in the front of the building, or in winter, in the shadows cast by the overheads and fake candles lined up along the bar, and you see what the beauty of the thing really is—it's the motion, the sense of pushing against the water, the muscles of the brothers' shoulders, the clouds in a sky that isn't quite blue. Looking at it made me feel peaceful, listening to the voices around me but not paying attention to the words, drinking my beer and letting my mind dwell on the feeling of being in a friendly room, with people I knew, with nowhere else to go. I would close my eyes and imagine myself pulling on the oars, even though I've never been in a rowboat in my life. I could smell the water, which is sweet and rank in summer, brown and murky, not water you would want to swim in, not like the ocean but foul river water, and when you cut the river with the oars, when you felt the light touch of the oars breaking the surface and pulling the hull fast against the current, I would imagine the feeling was pure happiness. I was lonely then, divorced and living a meager life, without a job some of the time, or with part-time work that I didn't like but needed to do so I could live, and I would be unhappy, restless and wondering if I could keep going. But I'd sit there in the evening, on a cool night early in October, and the bar would seem like the boat and I would be the brother in the front, the one who isn't looking anywhere at all, whose oar is just out of the water, poised to drop back in, the brother who isn't thinking about anything but the next stroke, enjoying the breeze in the heat of a summer afternoon, his mind blank, living in the balance between dipping the oar and raising the oar, pulling and resting, silence and the sluice of water.

Wallace's Story/Anna's Sadness

A DECADE AFTER THE WAR, when I had arrived in Philadelphia as a kind of afterthought—at the end of a restless period I had spent traveling and working at odd jobs—I started to hang out in West Philly bars, salty corner taverns strategically placed on every other block on Baltimore Avenue as it wound its way over paving stones and trolley tracks and through the dying sycamores stretching from the University of Pennsylvania to Fairmount Park. I wasn't drinking much for fear of awakening the dark thing that had resided in my heart for a long time, since the last campaigns I was a part of, the ones near the end of the thing that proved to anyone who cared to think about it that we'd been wasting our time. I drank a few beers and smoked a few cigarettes and kept to myself, but I was grateful for the friendly voices and for the chance to ask the bartenders questions about sports teams I had no interest in following and in politics that appeared to have embraced a greater madness. I was living alone, working at Met Life in the mailroom, still collecting my six-hundred and sixty-two dollars and forty- seven cents every month—an amount so precisely calibrated that I couldn't help but wonder if someone had made an error. Precision, I had come to believe, was always a mistake.

One wintery evening in The Showcase Lounge (definite article optional)—a lovely Irish joint with a good juke box and cheap drafts that attracted an interesting crowd of teachers, writers, artists, and one defrocked priest, I struck up a conversation with a young woman. She had a pleasant, open face, small hands and feet, maybe a good body under a long, baggy dress. Her hair was brown and reached her waist. She wore a turquoise ring where a wedding band would have been, and had a tiny rose tattoo inside her left wrist. Starry eyes, full of the kind of happiness you want to believe exists but doubt you'll find. Her name was Annabel, but she instructed me to call her Anna—"just plain Anna." There was nothing plain about her. She was a third-grade teacher in West Philadelphia. I told her the truth about myself—that I had been overseas and was stuck in a dead-end job, and was thinking about my next move. I bought her a beer.

She asked me my name and I thought about lying to her, but she wasn't the type I'd waste time lying to— she's see right through me.

"Wallace? I like that. Are you named after someone? The poet maybe?"

"Not the poet, though I don't know anything about him. My father liked Henry Wallace, the politician, so it's him, at least that's what they told me."

"You probably don't like any of the nicknames. Wally I would guess you'd hate."

"And you'd be right."

"Wallace it is then."

"Another beer?"

"Last one," she said. "I work early and need to be righteous."

"It must be exhausting, spending the day with little kids." I knew nothing about children. How old was a third grader? Were they toilet trained? I didn't ask.

Anna smiled full bore. She had a hundred teeth, pink gums, lines just edging out from blue-green eyes. Tiny white studs like snowdrops plugged into the tops of her ears. She smelled like cinnamon and something vaguely musky—honest sweat. Anna put her hand on my shoulder, "If there's anything better in this world than teaching little children I'd like to hear about it."

That was Anna. She lived in the superlative. If I said something—I tried not to say much for fear of making a fool of myself—she listened in a way that suggested I might be the wisest man in the world. We finished our beers and she said goodnight. When she put on her pea coat she lifted her hair and twisted it into a knot on the top of her head. She was shorter than me, which is short, with good legs. I breathed her in, wondering if I was being obvious.

We saw each other once in a while in the neighborhood, at the Korean market with the hostile owner and the rotten vegetables. Once or twice I would see her on the trolley, but she only rode a stop or two and I had to trek downtown. I never sat next to her—it would have been too much for me. I wasn't someone to chat with a beautiful young woman. I started taking an earlier trolley so I could avoid seeing her. That's a simple truth. Some things put a stone in your chest, like your heart has seized up, like what I felt at night smelling the South China Sea, a briny aroma that made you want to stay alive.

I saw her half-a-dozen times at the bar, but she was always with people, young men and women who talked with the intensity of those who have their illusions intact, and I could see she laughed a lot. I wanted to sit with them, but how could I? Anna would wave to me when I caught her eye, and once she got up from her table to say hello, but that was all. I liked to look at her when she wasn't paying attention, the way she gestured when she spoke, how she'd flail her hands, drawing pictures in the air.

I had a lot of free time to think about her. I tried not to think too much, but the empty hours stretch out sometimes, and you can't stop you mind from going to places you wished it wouldn't go.

In early November I was walking along the Schuylkill River, near the boathouses, watching the strong kids from the college pull their racing sculls through the dirty water. Thinking some about Thomas Eakins, about how he'd set up his easel right here on clear days and paint the lean boys gliding in their boats. He painted with an eye for the male body, but what I liked most was the water, the way the flat browns mirrored the willows that hang over the mud flats and trail their green branches in the still water. Eakins paid attention to the light, and the light was the same then as now. It was reassuring that something could stay the same for so long.

It was cool, verging on cold, but the sun was trying hard. The few rays that broke the clouds felt good on my face, like the touch of someone who has been away for too long. I walked for a long time, letting my mind wander across the water to the blocks of row houses in Mt. Airy, and down the river toward the temple of the art gallery, glinting yellow stone in the weak light.

A couple of joggers came toward me. I paid no attention. It was two women, ambling along in the loose way some people run, not making a big deal of it, smiling, talking. One of them was Anna. She saw me and stopped and said hey and introduced me to her friend.

I said, "You two look like race horses." It was a dumb thing to say.

"This is my friend Jenny." Anna mentioned my name to her friend. Jenny was whippet thin, maybe an athlete. She nodded and started stretching her hamstrings. Next to Anna she seemed inconsequential.

Anna had her best face on—not her bar face, which was good, but her daytime face, better yet. Jenny was jogging in place, anxious to get moving.

I was gawking like a high school kid. "It's good to get out. I was ambling along the path here, thinking about Eakins and his lovely boys. You know the picture of the two brothers in the boat? The one in the bar? He painted it right here, right where we're standing."

"They're not boats. They're sculls."

"Sure, that's right. Never been in one myself."

"I've seen the picture. The original is in D.C. at the National Gallery. It's smaller than you'd think. You almost miss it."

Jenny walked off.

Anna was a little out of breath, perspiring in the cool air. The thought crossed my mind that I could lick her face and she might not mind. Instead, I reached out and wiped the sweat from her forehead. She smiled and told her friend that she'd catch up to her. Jenny nodded and took off. She might have been upset, and it made me like Anna even more that she didn't care.

"Your friend's a quiet one."

"Jen? She's okay. We aren't friends but co-workers. She likes to jog with somebody and I'm it."

"Anyway, it's good to see you. Better venue here, better light."

"You're pale, you know that?"

"I've been inside mostly."

Then she surprised me. "Listen, let's go have something to eat."

"Seriously? When?"

"Now. I mean, today."

"Yeah, sure. I'd love to. I'm free." I didn't even have to think about it.

"We'll go Dutch."

"That'd be good. I'm a little short on cash."

"Okay. Let me go home and clean up. We could meet at one, downtown if that's cool. Tony's on Ninth. Do you know it?"

"Sure."

"Can you get there okay?"

"Yeah, I'll get there."

Tony's isn't a restaurant but a house, with the former living and dining rooms stuffed full of tables and chairs. Tony is also dead, of a heart attack at age sixty-two, but his widow Gloria and her mother do the cooking, probably using recipes from Tony's grandmother—manicotti, ravioli, lasagna, and world-class ziti—all done with perfect gravy, thick, rich marinara, no desserts but big bottles of cheap Chianti. Gloria's daughters—tall, olive-skinned beauties—take your order.

I was early so I waited for a table, then took a seat and ordered wine. Anna showed up a few minutes later, her long hair tied in a braid, dressed in a corduroy shirt and jeans.

"Did I keep you waiting?"

"Not at all. I've been drinking wine and listening to a lot of yelling in the kitchen. You know what *vaffanculo* means?"

"Sure. 'Go fuck yourself'. I heard that all the time growing up."

"You grew up here?"

"No, in Boston, in the South End."

"Never been to Boston."

"It's not bad. But Philly's better."

"Why's that?"

"Because here I have no past. I moved here after college and hit rewind. I like talking to my mother on the phone, but I don't want to live in the same town as she does. I don't want to spend my weekends eating family dinners."

"I feel the same way. I grew up in Jersey. Imagine living in New Jersey?"

Connie came over. We got Anna some wine and ordered.

"You think this place is legal?" I asked.

"Tony was connected. You'd have to be in this neighborhood. That's why no food inspectors or liquor license or fire marshal."

"You're paying right?"

"*Vaffanculo.*"

We drank a toast to something.

We talked about her job, my career sorting mail and running errands.

"You plan on staying in the mailroom?"

"I was thinking of going back to school. The last refuge of the unemployable."

"You could be a teacher."

"I don't think so. I'd like to be a painter, a writer, a telemarketer. Something where I can stay home."

"Not much on people, are you? At the bar I notice you look morose, sitting by yourself. You never come over and sit with me and my friends."

"You seem self-contained, pleased with yourselves. I mean that in a good way. I couldn't impose."

"We're blowing off steam. Teaching is pretty stressful sometimes."

"I bet. I don't know how you do it."

"It's easy. Listen, I want to tell you something. This isn't like me, okay? I don't want you to get the wrong idea."

"It's not like me either, to do this. I've been mostly alone since I got back, by choice."

"Why is that?"

"I couldn't tell you. Just the way it worked out."

"Fair enough. And the way it worked out for me was I had this urge to talk to you. Because you so obviously had no interest in talking."

"I've been thinking about you some of the time.

And I'm not like that, not liable to be infatuated. But then, half of what we think about ourselves is false."

"So that's settled."

"Absolutely."

Anna was a storyteller. She liked oral traditions, cultures that sent their heroes off into the otherworld with seeds on magic ships. She knew about farming, weaving, riding horses, baking bread, making pottery and jewelry. She played the mandolin. Bluegrass. Ralph Stanley, Jim Lauderdale, Doc Watson. She could sing, and she did, a little, right there in the middle of Tony's, unembarrassed, in a sweet alto. She could juggle, blow glass, and toss a football or Frisbee. I took her word for this. She had eyes like diamonds.

We ate. We drank wine.

"Can you tell me a story now? I mean, do you have one handy?"

"I have lots. How about this: The Divozenky, 'wild women,' live in the mountains. They are beautiful beings with square heads, long hair and long fingers. They live in underground burrows and have households like humans. They know nature's secrets, and they can make themselves invisible. They love music and singing and when they dance, they create great storms. They once got on well with humans, and even intermingled with them. They sometimes marry human boys. They exchange their offspring for human babies and raise the human babies."

"Why?"

"What do you mean *why*? It's a story. The whys are hidden."

"I thought folk stories were metaphors. You know, expressing the cultural aspirations of people."

"You're kidding me."

"No."

"That's like asking what the blues are about. You know about the Odyssey, right? Beowulf? Poems and stories and songs are patched out of riffs, set pieces. Little half-lines married together. Alliterated words, easier to remember when they rhyme and when they're from a fixed repertoire. Words that charm, a deep narrative, lots of history and tradition behind it. I guess all stories have psychological importance but so what?"

"Different ways of getting at the truth."

"What I do when I tell a story is take chunks of tales and patch them together. Like sewing a quilt. The Divozenky go to a village and kidnap a girl, make her into a slave. The villagers get together to rescue her. After a while telling a story's like playing music."

"So what happens next?"

"I don't know. What would you like to happen next?"

Anna had a second-floor apartment on Baltimore Avenue, just across the street from a run-down park. The stairs were steep, and the house smelled of mildew and cats, but her apartment was comfortable and well furnished. There were books piled on every surface, original art work, weavings, and children's drawings on the walls.

We had driven in her VW. I followed her up the stairs. At the top, she turned around, shrugged, and kissed me.

I said, "You taste like ziti."

And she said, "You're hairy."

We undressed one another in the hallway that connected the living room to the bedroom. The late afternoon light was breaking through the tall windows that lined the front of the house. We made love, got up and had drinks, talked a little, then made our way back to bed. Gradually the light went away and the streetlights came on. The rush of traffic subsided and the room became quiet, as if it were a room in the desert, lit by the stars, miles from anything.

Anna fell asleep. I didn't.

She slept deeply, silently. I've always imagined that I would love watching a woman sleep. I watched her most of the night, and dozed a little near dawn.

The sky brightened. I could make out the tips of the oak leaves firing up for the day, the birds—sorry house sparrows and pleading doves—began their complaints at the noise of incessant traffic. I couldn't be there when she awakened.

I got up, scribbled a note, quietly dressed, and left.

I didn't see her again for a long time. No doubt about it, she was too good for me—I'm sure she still is—but that wasn't why I wrote an elaborate lie about needing to go out of town, or why I snuck off to work every day and then hid in my room at night, not answering the phone. The reason was that I needed to be sure—not of her, but of me. Somebody lovely and good pays attention to you it makes sense to pause long enough to make sure there really is something in you worthy of attention. It's bad to make a mistake about another person; it's worse to allow someone to make a mistake about you.

In those days Philadelphia was a busy place, an industrial city, blue collar on the fringes and professional downtown. Nothing like the gentrified, white-collar town of today. Back then, the port was one of the busiest in the country, and men and women with Irish and German surnames rode the train from Northeast to make machine tools and durable goods and auto parts and lots of other things that people seemed to need—it wasn't a wealthy town, or a pretty one, but it was a decent place to live, aside from the crime and drugs and hard feelings between whites and blacks. Its problems were considerable, but on a scale that allowed people of good will to think about ways of solving them. Not like now, when the rot of things has gone too far to be patched up, and solutions aren't really of any interest to the people who could provide them. My hobby outside of work and reading was walking around the city, mostly along the two filthy rivers that cut the town into thirds, the Schuylkill and the Delaware, one windy and narrow and the other broad and slow, one Dutch and one Indian, one headed to the sea and one seeming to come from the hills and go nowhere at all. After the night with Anna I increased my walking, setting out on my odd days off for Germantown or the bird sanctuary in the south end of the city. On Sunday I would go to the Quaker Meeting on Cherry Street and sit in the quiet, unadorned room for an hour with a hundred peaceful souls. Or I'd go to the Congregational Church in Society Hill and sit on a hard bench with the other Puritans, listening to a sad tale of my sinfulness and agreeing that nothing but God's good will could save me. Most weeks I liked the Quakers better, or nothing at all, just the walk along the paved trails, the smell of rot and gray water, the battered brownstones that lined the riverfront of Camden.

I wasn't thinking about Anna on those walks—maybe some—but about my own soul and the things I had done that I wished I could forget. They sweep you up into their wars without caring to know your feelings; they expect you to give up your life for them. I walked and said my prayers, asking the silent god of the rivers, the deity of ruined cities, to forgive me. It felt good to ask for something so big and impossible and to know that it was a prayer that couldn't be answered. What would I have done if I had been forgiven?

She was 'Annabel' at work. Her students called her Annie, her colleagues Ann, her intimate friends A or Anna. Her parents phoned every Sunday and asked her a great number of questions that she didn't care to answer, but that she did answer, out of what she thought of as love for them and a healthy disinterest in her own privacy. Her mother called her *Ann of a Thousand Days*, which Anna didn't like at all, and her father called her Bunny, which had charmed her in high school, embarrassed her in college (he'd use the affectionate nickname in front of her boyfriends), and now, she was puzzled to notice, charmed her once again. She was small—five feet three, one hundred and eight pounds. Her hands and feet were tiny, her breasts large, too much so she thought, and she did all she could to keep them tamed. She had the kind of body that men liked, but which seemed to disappoint them in some way once they had first-hand experience with it. She had a small angel tattooed on her lower back—a college dare, now an episode best forgotten. Her hair was long; she hadn't cut it since she was nine years old, twenty years before. Often she found the hair annoying and thought of shearing herself, but then, somehow, long hair became her trademark. She had noticed that many of the women she knew had a single distinguishing feature—an affectation. Jennifer, her jogging partner, had a tiny turquoise star piercing in her nostril—Anna thought it looked sexy, but unsanitary. One of her colleagues, Rochelle, was a large woman with a beautiful face and tight dreadlocks; she looked like Tracey Chapman and had a style Anna admired. Anna lacked style, or so she thought. She wore no make-up. Her hair was tied back with ribbon and invited pulling—her eight-year-olds tugged on it as if it were her heart. She had a scar on her upper lip—it wasn't small, and it was often all she saw when she looked at herself. She thought of it as a disfigurement, and her teeth below it were capped, broken in half by a rangy jock girl from Holy Cross with a lacrosse stick and shitty coordination. Her legs were still muscular from college athletics and jogging; her arms were tan much of the year, her eyes were blue and clear, her soul, she knew, was pure. Anna loved her job, adored the children she taught, got along with her fellow teachers, had a dozen talents that she consistently underestimated, enjoyed reading obscure books, hoped to marry before it was too late, often craved sex with people she hardly knew, and wanted very much to find out if she believed in God.

Why was this? Her father was a Jew who became a Lutheran who became a Quaker who then began to attend service at the First Church of Christ, Scientist, in Boston. He looked like Bronson Alcott. Anna admired, feared, adored, and worried about her father. He was, she thought, exceptionally odd, a man who talked to himself incessantly, who often went to work—he was a professor of history—wearing different shoes or unmatched socks, who sometimes forgot to come home or who wandered around the house in the silent depths of the night arguing with his long-dead father about the New Deal or Joseph McCarthy. And yet he could be, when lucid, kind and attentive—he was that, and Anna believed her father's slipping into eccentricity and perhaps benign dementia was connected to the cruel turn politics had taken after 1968. Jonathan Garmin had been a pink diaper baby, a not-quite Brahmin whose own father worked as a foreman in a ladies clothing factory in Revere, and who had gone to Harvard not to study history, but to justify his belief that the goodness enshrined in the working class would ultimately win the argument with greed, egotism, and violence. Discovering that this belief was not only untrue but farcical took a toll on Jonathan, a man whose own nature was benign, generous, and cosmopolitan. Anna loved her father fiercely, then ambivalently, and, after she left for college, conditionally—the condition being that he not be in what her mother called "a state" over some crime of the ruling classes. Anna's mother was a calm, precise, rather cool professor of philosophy at Tufts—a student of Rorty's, an analytical thinker who addressed her husband and daughter in clipped tones and precise diction, a person so rock solid that even though Anna found her unlovable, she did rely on her for advice and the kind of steadiness that becomes increasingly important as one realizes that life is rather full of contingencies—rife with opportunities to fall flat on one's face.

God was a problem for Anna. Not 'God' as in the meaning of the term or the implications of a life with or without one, but God as the alleged personal confident who is in a position to offer in his silent way guidance and clarity. Her parents were no help on the question of the divine, nor were they asked to be, and, as is often the case, the issue of divinity wouldn't have arisen but for an unhappy episode in her life that exhausted all of the resources of her secular view of things—her own moral views, and those of her happy-talking psycho-babbling friends. Her parents were the kind of humanists who thought every horror of life is best managed by running it though the machine of reason. But reason is unreliable, or worse.

Anna had been raped. The Horror, as she thought of it now, years after the fact, had been subsumed into the realm of ineffability, and yet at the same time was physical and immediate in memory. Everything about it: the smell of the man, the heat and humidity of the night, the hours before with friends, the walking home alone, the hand on her arm, being pushed, being knocked down, the tearing of her clothes, the pain of him forcing his way between her legs, the sickening smell, crying out, his hand over her mouth, bucking her hips, his long hair, his grunting, the feeling of his wetness in her, on her thighs, his cock pushed deep into her, the stink of cigarettes on his breath, the feeling in her stomach, her crying as he spit on her, the rasping word *slut* repeated over and over, the kick into her raw, bleeding self, then, alone, crying and bleeding, blood and sperm running down her legs. Then nothing. Weeks in bed and seeing nothing and feeling nothing. Hoping to die. All of her in pain, her skin filthy, scrubbing herself in the shower, the smell in her nostrils at night, a stench that made her vomit. It went on for weeks, the wanting to die. And then there was a change in her body, a slowing down, a new kind of emptiness. And at night, when she was lying on her girlhood bed in the house where she grew up, her mind blank, she prayed that she would die or forget. But she didn't die and didn't forget. She tried every God she knew: her father's Yahweh, Jesus hung on the cross, kindly Buddha. She didn't blame God or hold him accountable, or expect the universe to cease its pointless whirling or persons she met to care in the least that she had been turned into nothing—no, all she asked was a moment's comfort, and it never came.

She had been in college when it happened. It was years ago. She saw someone twice a week for a few months but it didn't help. Talking to a stranger about what had happened eased some of her pain, but when she brought up not pain but emptiness, the feeling that the world had been washed of color, the woman had asked what she meant and was she going to hurt herself and didn't she think having loving parents and good health would help her to pull back from the edge of something terrible, and she had said to the woman, you don't understand, I'm not ungrateful and I won't kill myself, but something that was inside of me, my faith if you want to call it that, is gone. And the woman didn't say anything but made a few notes in a black moleskin notebook with her expensive pen, and Anna thought maybe the woman was planning a menu for a dinner party—you know when someone isn't paying attention, even though people don't know that you've caught on to them.

Now Anna is better. Teaching has made her better. When she thinks of how she is she thinks 'I am well,' or 'Everything is going along smoothly for me.' She knows that this is only true in a relative sense; she knows that if she puts the 'horrible thing' back into the forefront of her mind for just a moment it will leak like acid into her whole body and then she won't be fine any longer, or perhaps ever again. Life has become an effort to strengthen her will, her ability to be introspective, but not to open the tomb in which the bad thing is buried. When she meets someone new, they often think that she is glib and doesn't have much of an interior life— she knows that people think this about her, but the only basis she has for belief in herself is her conviction that she mustn't probe the wound that will never heal. Not remembering. If there were only a drug one might take to not remember the horrible thing. It is as if she has another scar that itches every minute of the day, and the annoyance and distraction of this hidden scar has become like a ringing in her ears, a piece of herself that has to be ignored.

Perhaps this new man, this Wallace, this wounded, empty man, will help her to forget. But probably not.

Ned, A Bit of a Sadist

Ned has a little of the sadist in him.

At The Showcase he always sits at the end of the bar, nursing his Scotch and water or rye straight up, or maybe a shot and a beer, munching on the free peanuts that are, for him, one of the few attractions of the scuzzy place, silently mocking the sad sacks lined up on the stools—regular regulars, unlike Ned who comes in for a few pops on weekends and Monday nights for the football, and occasionally if there's trouble at work, which happens, but at no other time, and never at lunch or at eight in the morning like Lane down there, a rail-thin, chain-smoking rummy who by this time of night—it's nearly eleven—has been at it for eight hours and is now only allowed coffee or coke. Gus over-serves as a matter of policy, but there are limits.

Ned has his own view of things—who doesn't? He thinks, *this is America; I'm entitled to my opinions.* At fifty-something, Ned didn't make the cut for the greatest generation, and though he often talks of the privations of the Depression (he was born in 1934), the truth is his family was reasonably well off. His father worked as an account for First Federal here in Philadelphia, and though Ned's old man took a pay cut in '32, he didn't lose his job or house or car, nor did he ever fail to "put food on the table," and for the Rankin family "putting food on the table" was the heart and soul of life, the reason one goes to work and votes Republican, supports the American Dream, etc. Ned's "worldview," as he calls it, a phrase he picked up at Temple, majoring in finance but not quite finishing, included an opinion he had culled from Ayn Rand—he didn't get far in *Atlas Shrugged*, but he quickly internalized the core message—which was that the world was organized so that the ruthless and selfish invariably triumph over the altruistic and sociable. Ned wasn't a brave man, nor was he especially energetic, but he was single-minded in his pursuit of success, and he had in fact acquired a modest fortune and a degree of notoriety in the field of forensic accounting. He had testified in many of the high-profile bankruptcy cases that resulted from the restructuring of the tax codes under the Reagan Administration—he had moved from a low-level position at Reynolds and

Nolde—a small Center City accountancy firm—to the City's largest firm, Brown, Bristow, and Allen—to establishing himself as a consultant, a professional overseer of the dissolution of companies large and small, up and down the Northeast Corridor. He was well off, but cheap. His business associates—he had no friends—thought of Ned as tightfisted, competent if unimaginative, and just a little too fond of facilitating the ruin of companies whose only real offense was sloppy bookkeeping, capital over-investment, low profitability, or a less than maniacal view of the bottom line. Ned was all bottom line.

Ned was *thinking* on this chilly late fall night in West Philly. It was Saturday, and The Showcase had a good crowd—the regulars at the bar and locals who mostly gathered in the back rooms around the pool tables, jukebox, a tiny dance floor, and the fireplace—the only fireplace in a bar on this end of Baltimore Avenue. From his perch on the end of the bar, Ned could survey the rooms, and what he most enjoyed considering was how much better off he was than everyone else in the joint. It was important to be the smartest person in any room, the wealthiest, the one with the most interesting job. He saw a lot of students from Penn shooting pool—they were spoiled rich kids—a table surrounded by half-a-dozen black men and women who were well dressed and probably worked downtown but lived in West Philly. Ned wasn't a racist, but he didn't enjoy the company of *African-Americans*—he used this term with a sneer—for reasons he couldn't have specified. There was a nice-looking woman sitting with another woman—she was a regular, and not, Ned knew, a lesbian, since he had seen her making out with an older man just a few weeks before right at that same table— Ned enjoyed watching this girl, who was, in fact, nearly thirty, and he had, once or twice, masturbated while thinking about her blond hair and long legs. She was an artist, he had heard her talking about a show she was working on, and Ned had plans to attend the opening and maybe buy one of her paintings, if they were any good, which he rather doubted since, in his experience, women who were attractive lacked talent—he was so sure of this that he probably wouldn't go to the show after all. One guy at the bar was a veteran and hung around the place all the time, nursing a beer. Ned had bought the guy a drink one time and told him that he, Ned, was a vet as well, of Korea, which was a lie, and the psycho started asking Ned a lot of detailed questions about his unit and MOS and deployment, questions that Ned didn't understand let alone have an answer for, and he'd bullshitted the guy a little more but could tell the vet knew he was lying so Ned had avoided him from then on. Ned knew better than to sling the shit in a bar, but he couldn't help himself—he enjoyed lying to strangers, or doing little things to mislead them, inflating his own ego in the process. He got caught. So what? Most of the time Ned could tell a person he'd been in the service, in the infantry, had seen combat in Korea, and that would be enough to get him a little jolt of satisfaction because whoever he told believed him, and sometimes, once anyway, a woman even offered to go home with Ned due to the fact that he was a hero. But Ned was afraid the woman would have AIDS—it was the '80's and half the low-life's in the town were walking around with the virus, waiting to infect whoever was stupid enough to insert his worm in them. 'Insert the worm' was Ned's witty term for intercourse. He had a lot of unique (as he saw it) ways of talking about sex— he thought of himself as clever and interesting and took pride in phrases like 'chewing the pole,' 'munching the clam,' 'flapping your jack,' and 'lapping a reamsicle,' which he knew wasn't entirely original with him, at least the reamsicle part of it, but, hey, it was still usable, though with whom was an open question. Ned wasn't exactly a chick magnet, and with the help of porn films and dreams about women he spotted at The Showcase his sex life consisted in furtive self-stroking which he pretended not to enjoy. Anyway, it was mostly gays who got AIDS and Ned knew for a fact he wasn't gay, not even close, so maybe it wasn't a worry after all. It goes without saying that Ned hated gay people.

One thing about assholes like Ned is that they never seem to know that they *are* assholes. The real bastards of the world appear oblivious to their miserable personalities, their ugly way of treating people, their crudity and vulgarity and stupidity. Ned, for instance, thought he was a charming, funny guy. Once when he was just starting out as an accountant, making his bones on small potatoes violations of tax codes that were too esoteric for anyone to figure out, too full of inscrutable loopholes and wormholes and black holes to make any sense to any one, too hermetic for your average schmuck who for sure wanted to cut some corners on his return without being out of compliance in a such a way as to draw the wrath of the IRS onto his poor dumb head, a good thing for a guy like Ned who had taken the time to follow Ariadne's thread through the Code, or who just didn't have a life outside of Rules and Regs, no life at all—so this one time Ned was explaining to a client where he, the client, had screwed the pooch, hiding-profits-wise, and why he, the client, was going to get whacked by some constipated IRS-compliance-type agent, and that he, Ned, was the only hope the guy had to escape five to ten in Loretto or McKean and that while he, the schmuck, wouldn't have to get fucked in the ass every day by a gangbanger, he would have to eat Wonder Bread and mustard sandwiches and jerk off into his prison jump suit if he, Ned, didn't save his felonious butt…and so forth. It was the standard hook-the-client speech, exaggerated of course since the chances were the fish would pay back taxes and a small fine, or maybe not even a fine since it was his first offense and came via his, the schmuck's, error in relying on a commercial, store-front, chain-type accountancy firm's good faith promise that they, the small potatoes firm, had accountants with actual tax experience who could parse the legitimate depreciation schedules and complete the 4562's without forgetting to carry the one, or some such…anyway *in media res,* the guy, the fish, the schmuck, stops Ned cold and says to him, in a voice that was resonant with hatred, or so it seemed to Ned, the following words:

"I've been in business for twenty years. I've run into *all kinds of assholes* in twenty years—take it from me, every kind. Guys who'd fuck a squirrel to get its acorns, you know, cheap, miserable pricks, of which there are plenty, take it from me. But you, you arrogant miserable little pissant, are the biggest scumbag I have ever met in my life. I would no more let you represent my interests than Adolf Hitler." There was more, all in this vein. Ned was flabbergasted. The man walked out and filed a complaint against Ned with the Chamber of Commerce. Nothing came of that, of course. But still, Ned didn't get it.

The guy meant nothing to Ned, but his words stung. Ned felt humiliated at having been caught red-handed. He decided to do some soul-searching. "Soul-searching" had nice ring to it. Did he have a soul? Ned had no idea. He assumed he must because if he didn't he wouldn't have a life after death. Like everyone else, Ned was counting on eternal life. He believed in God. He was sure he believed in God. His parents had sent him to Catholic School—they were Lutherans but believed that Catholics were better at discipline—and he's gone to one or another Church for most of his life. He'd eased off recently, given his other obligations, but, yes, for sure he believed. So, yes, he had a soul. And the soul was what exactly? His moral self. His inner voice. His conscience. The part of him that gave permission when asked, and, once in a great while, withheld that permission (he'd then ignore the voice). The soul, he figured, looked like him, but better. "More perfect and eternal." It was everywhere inside of him, but mostly, he knew, in his heart. The heart was the part of him that felt things, which is why the soul took up its lodging there. Ned could see all of this as clearly as he could see his receding hairline (at 40!) and the paunch that inexorably distended his mid-section and caused his shoulders to slump. The soul. Now he would search it. Which meant—what? Would he ask "it" questions? Not at all—this searching was a metaphor. What he really needed to do was to sit quietly and ask himself if he was really an asshole. Which, he supposed, meant was he an unpleasant person, unlikeable? The charge seemed far-fetched. He had, after all, several friends, none of them of them close, but still. His parents were both dead, as was his sister, so he couldn't confer with them, and he had quarreled bitterly over a small inheritance (under 10K actually) with his only cousin, and they no longer were on speaking terms. Ned believed with all of his heart and with the limited but rational brain God had given him that he was the sort of man who did his best in every circumstance—he was, he knew, a "decent human being." Ned repeated this phrase to himself over and over for a week— "I am a decent human being," and it seemed right and it made him feel better.

This was all before.

Understanding Ned requires understanding Hegel. Ned Rankin had heard of Hegel in college, but never read him and couldn't have told you the first thing about the *Phenomenology of Spirit*. But watching Ned sit at the bar in The Showcase, watching him sneer into his Wild Turkey on a recent Saturday night, knowing exactly what he was thinking (I was reading his mind, with a pen and my notebook handy), I understood that Hegel was the key to Ned. In the spirit of full disclosure, I should say that I wasn't sitting in a booth at The Showcase to observe Ned Rankin, a man I dislike intensely. I was hoping to ambush Agnes, but she hadn't been around for weeks, wasn't answering her phone, and never was home, at least when I rang her doorbell. It's a free country, and I know we will run into one another sometime, but meanwhile I have to pass the evenings somehow, and my apartment has become depressing, and The Showcase provides many opportunities for me to practice my profession—I am a writer. Not a writer who writes, but a composer of strings of words that can be imagined as delineating modes of consciousness experienced from inside a person who is undergoing periods of stress. I am a projector, or maybe a portal, available for use by others, to ease them through psychological trauma. I do this privately, as a kind of hobby. I don't *write*. Stories are of no interest to me, nor do I enjoy poems or song lyrics. I like jingles and ads sometimes, lightness is a quality I appreciate. Real writers have subjects; I have only objects. Writers try to create; I only transcribe. Hegel, mentioned above, believed that human beings embodied self-consciousness—that they were vessels of the spirit of consciousness. This is true.

I am a Hegelian. Probably it is important to be something—especially now. Having a compass for one's life, a source if not of inspiration (Hegel is *not* inspiring) at least of guidance. Why Hegel? A fair question, to which I reply, why the Bible? Why the Qur'an? Why the Bhavagad-Gita? The point being: why anything at all? Some people believe that every single word of the entire Bible was inspired by God and is therefore true. You don't see too many fundamentalists plucking out their offending eyes or cutting off their own hands. And the virgins in paradise—not likely. Or a god with a bow and arrow, with four arms and extra heads—a shape shifter? I'd say not. At least with Hegel you find yourself on familiar if turgid and pedantic ground. And his phenomenology covers all the bases, just like any other book that pretends to explain it all—from the origin of human consciousness and desire to the cunning of history to the transformation of religion into self-consciousness to the arrival of the Final Man—Hegel himself. It's a stretch, I know, to take any of this with less than a grain of salt, but show me the holy book that doesn't bend the truth to the point of madness.

Ned is my subject in the notes I am making. He was selected based on a set of parameters derived from *Phenomenology of Spirit*, trans. A.V. Miller, pages 248-252, sections 410-418, where Hegel considers individualism, consciousness, and *the matter at hand*. I should mention that I am fluent in German, but prefer the clarity of Miller for my own analysis, especially in the case of Ned, who is, frankly, among the most difficult of subjects.

I have read *Phenomenology* thirteen times.

A year ago, eleven months and nine days ago, I was sitting in my usual position in the third booth from the front door. In the winter, when the door is opened, freezing air flows unimpeded into the otherwise body-warm The Showcase. I was able to ascertain that the third booth, a two-top, narrow worn oak, chipped and knife-scratched, gum-encrusted, with a bottle of Heinz 57 (it's really an AP brand manufactured just down the road in Lancaster, but poured into premium bottles), a bottle of Gulden's (ditto), salt, pepper, sugar—no saccharine—that this booth is the optimum place to watch the other customers at the bar, at the tables, in the back. There is also, at each of the booths, a mechanism that allows you to select songs from the legendary juke box that, let's face it, is the principle attraction of The Showcase, a none-too-clean gin joint with average food, worn pool tables, and, aside from Agnes, misanthropic waitresses. Yet it is always full. Night after night, every stool, all the booths, half the tables, are crowded. It's the music. Down the block, at Crandall's Pub (*Pub!*), a fern-strewn yuppie hellhole, the box is all country, which makes no sense in West Philly where Al Green and The Four Tops rule and nobody in his right mind would play Chet Atkins or my namesake George Jones (not my real name).

I don't care for music myself, but the crowds are appealing, a good place to pick a subject, Ned in this case, a classic case of self-consciousness concerned solely with "the matter at hand," a willed Self that has converted itself to its purpose, subsumed itself in the negative moment and incited others to do so as well. When Ned told me that he came here to study the people, especially the women, I knew that he was enacting what Hegel called "making something its own affair," or "opening up the subject" by uncovering Being itself. *Being* is the key here. My transcription of Ned is *the capture of Being*, the Being that is self-consciousness.

"George," Ned said to me, "you see that lady over there, the one with the long hair, the purple fingernails?"

He was pointing to a woman whose features were unremarkable.

I pointed.

"Yes, her."

I pointed again, more demonstratively.

"Don't point. That's the best-looking woman in West Philly. And if you see me in here nursing a drink, you'll know I'm studying her."

"Okay." What could I say? That was his business, but the unremarkable nature of the woman he proposed to study suggested to me that he had an ulterior motive. He wasn't looking *at* her, but *through* her. Hegel shows in his chapter on "Reason" [231ff.] that the single indi-vidual consciousness is the *Absolute. Looking through* is looking directly at Being, at God. We call it "empathy" sometimes, or "compassion," but those aren't Hegelian terms. The woman was a *portal to the Absolute* for Ned, and Ned was a *portal to Consciousness* for me. I look *through* him looking *through* her. I know this seems complicated. Why not the Absolute? Obviously I was at a lower stage than Ned—this was all his idea, not mine. You can think of me as an understudy, preparing myself to make my own study, to make my own *opening into the Truth*.

I know a lot about Ned.

When Ned was ten, his father had gone out back into the shed where he stored his lawnmower, his rakes and shovels, and shot himself in the head. Ned heard the shot and the synchronized sounds of body and gun hitting the aluminum floor of the shed. Ned was playing on his tire swing at the time, and his father had walked past him without a word. After a few seconds, Ned could smell burnt cork or perhaps smoldering charcoal. He kept playing his game. The game went like this: Ned was a prince and the tire was a great eagle. When the prince wanted to go to one of his other kingdoms the eagle would carry him, up and over, slowly easing little Ned over the trees—the dying elms and the ash tree that had been struck by lightning the previous summer and had a black line seared into its trunk—up and over the garage, the alley, the shops that lined Commerce

Street—the cobbler's shop where an old Negro replaced Ned's heels each September, a Jewish bakery that Ned's father wouldn't patronize, a Bank with a great green clock that had for years informed the town that it was 10:04, the Five and Dime where Ned had been caught shoplifting gummy erasers that he enjoyed chewing during math class (not for the taste, but for the cut against his teeth as he bit into them), the Sub Shoppe and the florist's, stores doomed to bankruptcy on a street destined to be by-passed by the Interstate, just a few blocks south, a wide, loud thoroughfare that would carry eager townspeople to the first shopping center ever built in Lansdowne. Ned kept playing for a long time. The Eagle was named Sally, after his sister. Ned loved Sally very much, and when he climbed onto the thin, worn tire his mother had hoisted up and over the bare limb of the dying elm, he always said to himself 'I love you Sally,' and then the Eagle would move and Ned would close his eyes and imagine himself in the places Sally had once shown him on the large torn map in the basement. It was a map, inexplicably, of Brazil. No one that Ned knew had ever been to New York or Washington let alone to Recife, but Sally told Ned that Mom had liked the enormous green blotch across the top, the lines of rivers and the empty patches without contour, a place where people lived, Sally said, who didn't know Jesus or have television, the Amazon she called it, and on his Eagle Ned asked if he could go there, if Sally would take him to the Green Place, as he called it, not being able to remember the word "Amazon," and she did. Ned knew he would never see his father again. He knew it as he rode with Sally to a place that was far away but which, strangely, seemed very close by, right there, over the sagging, broken roof of the detached garage that was full of spiders and mice and bits of broken wood. After a little while, Ned stopped Sally from moving—he would drag first the toes of his shoes, and then, for more traction, his brand-new heels, and gradually Sally the Eagle would slow and he could jump off. He jumped off and went into the house and asked his mother, who was quilting, if he might have a glass of milk. She said yes.

When Ned thought about Anna he was respectful. There were many women who visited The Showcase, and women at his job, and women walking on the streets, about whom he had lurid fantasies. But Anna was different. He never undressed her in his mind, or thought about anything other than having a long, searching conversation with her. Ned could be romantic. Not in the candies and flowers and candlelight sense, but in the reality-is-best-approached-through-the-will sense. He knew the limits of reason. He didn't think about what he was doing when he covertly cast a glance over at the table where Anna and her friends from the local elementary school drank and talked—it was, he knew, Samuel Huey, just west of Malcolm X Park, a part of town Ned usually avoided, but which he had driven past to see where Anna worked—he just did it, out of an irrational (his word) desire to maintain some kind of connection with this woman who seemed to Ned to be the embodiment of all he imagined a woman could be. He even used these words to himself— *"she's all that a woman should be"*—as he splashed on aftershave and reapplied deodorant before setting out for the bar. He said these somewhat odd words— *"she's all a woman should be"*—aloud, while looking at his graying goatee and bald head, at his deeply circled eyes, his jowls and misshapen right ear, the one his step-father had accidentally nearly severed with a pair of shears as he angrily chopped at hair he had thought was too long. Ned's wasn't, overall, a promising face. His teeth were straight, but brown; he had broken blood vessels in his nose and upper cheeks—he looked like Stanley Holloway in "My Fair Lady." But Ned knew he had some good qualities, and he wasn't out to marry the woman—she was twenty-five years his junior—he only wished to observe her and, with any luck, talk to her. What he wanted, to be honest, what he wished for more than anything, was for Anna to think about him.

What's wrong, Ned asked himself, with obsessing about someone? He had plenty of money, a nice little house downtown, a secure job, was accorded (grudging) respect for his knowledge and skills, had no real vices apart from drinking a little too much and sometimes behaving badly with women. His mind was clear despite half-a-dozen events better left unscrutinized—he was a man who might be permitted this one indulgence— serial obsession with unobtainable women—without having to explain himself or feel ashamed. He actually had spoken to Anna on three occasions, twice at The Showcase, and once at the downtown MVD office where, due to an incredible stroke of luck, he had happened to be renewing his driver's license at the same time she was registering a car. They just happened to be standing in adjacent, and unmoving, lines—think of that! —Ned could hardly believe his luck, ten minutes of conversation during which he managed to be witty, articulate, and uncommonly considerate of another person's feelings. He had introduced himself as someone who (rarely) frequented an "establishment" on Baltimore Avenue, and, he thought, if he weren't mistaken (yes, he had used the subjunctive), he had seen her there. This after a moment's banter about the line and the legendary incompetence of MVD personnel. Said with compassion rather than pique. It wouldn't be politic to mock the tired black women who processed the paperwork at the MVD with this young, no doubt liberal, teacher. Yes, dryly ironic was perfect for the circumstance. He was surprised at how friendly the lovely girl (in the dull light of day he could see that her face was unlined, that she was fresh and youthful) behaved toward him, acknowledging at once her fondness for The Showcase, her employment as a teacher nearby, the frequency with which she would stop in with colleagues to have (one) beer and shoot pool or darts.... it was almost overwhelming for Ned to take her in, to look into her blue-green eyes, to watch her tongue (tiny, pointed) flick across her lips as she spoke, to study her scar—so feminine!—to get a close-up look at the onyx earrings and the dagger-like silvery spike that poked up from the top of each ear; he could smell her breath when she laughed—he made her laugh by quoting one of the bartender's jokes about a regular who had put the moves on a nun out of uniform—and her breath smelled of wintergreen and clove. He was stirred, not sexually, but in his "soul." He felt serenity lift him nearly out of his body as they spoke in low tones, spoke so amicably, and with such sudden intimacy (or so it seemed to Ned) that people in the line turned to smile at them, or at Anna anyway, whose vivacity and charm were extraordinary. And then the lines moved, out of sync, and she did her business, bid him a friendly goodbye, and left the building. Ned was so bereft by her departure that he walked out a few minutes later without having completed his transaction. How hopeless it all was—he knew he was a fool, but his folly felt so much better than any of the reasonable things he spent his time doing that he wondered, in a sort of dizzying moment of clarity, why it was that he had only now—too late—uncovered what it was that he wanted from life, the thing, at last, that would make him happy.

I don't think that Ned really understands himself. Watching him stare into space, noting the cautious way he looks around, the haunted empty eyes he casts on the world, I see a man who Hegel would say had not learned how to *transcend the Self by embracing non-being*. Ned suffers. Non-being is not *not being*, but the fullness of being, just as an empty glass isn't empty, but waiting to be full with anything that might come to fill it. Ned has no receptivity to Being. He came over to me a few days ago—it was Friday—and he asked me, in an unfriendly way, why I kept staring at him and writing in a book as I did so. Was I sketching him? I said *you are mistaken*, or *if I looked in your direction it was at someone else.* I was quite perturbed and embarrassed—how could I have been so obvious? The method of recording I use requires delicacy and tact; here I had gone and ruined my project, undone weeks of work. Anyway, Ned gave me a hostile look and said he hoped I would respect his privacy. The way he spoke to me carried overtones of violence. I felt as if he might hurt me, or that he was capable of doing so. I apologized twice, and then stayed at home all weekend—dejected and uncommonly agitated—before returning the following Monday. My glances at Ned have since been covert, so I have to speculate more than I would like to about his mental state, and, I admit, I have had to make a few things up to fill in some of the inevitable gaps in my account of Ned's inner life.

Hegel wrote the last words of his great book on the day of the battle of Jena, the day Napoleon captured the city in which Hegel resided. And Hegel asked the question, "*Has anyone understood Napoleon before me?*" Not until Consciousness overcomes Desire and becomes Spirit can there be any true understanding. If one can understand one person fully, not a friend or a lover, but a stranger, then one can break through the ice of our ignorance, then one can penetrate to the secret that lies at the heart of human consciousness. This seems mad, of course. But if I were to sit in a church instead of a tavern and pour through Scripture every day of my life, looking for Truth, I would be a saint instead of a madman; or if I were to gaze at the stars and ask what the black emptiness of the universe meant I would be a scientist or a mystic or a poet. There were those who lived long ago who believed that every letter of the Bible contained all the truth that exists in this world. Kabbalah teaches that the mysteries of God and of Creation are written in symbols hidden before our eyes, and written down in the Secret Books. There is no madness in this. It isn't even eccentric to believe such things. To pursue wealth and power and fame is madness. Hegel is my *portal to the truth*. My own consciousness, not yet honed to the point of Hegelian clarity, is my real subject—Ned Rankin, chosen more or less at random, is a suitable object whose unraveling, like the unraveling of the meaning of Napoleon, will allow me to break through the bondage of history. Thinking is the only means of freeing ourselves from time; only thought endures—the rest is chaff.

No one gives much thought to his own death. Ned understood that one day he would die in the casual way that we all do, but the distance to his passing from this world was unimaginably far removed from his present life: acquisition, self-absorption, voyeurism, day-dreaming, auto-erotic sexual activities, wistful regrets, conflicting emotions centered on the loss (of Sally) and hopes for future—always future—happiness. He wasn't a melancholy man. That would have required a degree of self-awareness that Ned, for reasons deeply embedded in his past, was incapable of possessing. But he was moody and sometimes immobilized by sadness—what he called "his funks." He believed in heaven—he had been taught to do so—and he envisaged it, vaguely, as this same world, seen through a gauzy film, cloudy and bright at the same time, slightly out of focus for being unimaginable. No one, certainly not Ned, could believe that upon dying he would simply vanish, not only from this world, but from everyone's memory—that he would be extinct, as meaningless an entity as a passenger pigeon or a dodo. No, this wouldn't do. Ned sat in The Showcase on Saturday nights, covertly watched by a tidy older gentleman wearing pressed coveralls who appeared to be scribbling in a notebook—Ned assumed he (I) was a writer of some kind, and he didn't care for the man, though he wasn't sure why—Ned Rankin sat at his usual place and drank whiskey, ate a cheeseburger, watched the many pretty women who came and went, and thought that he would be spending his time in just this way forever.

When his sister Sally had "passed on," passed through the thin air of earth and into the ephemeral spheres of the planets and stars, as if, Ned imagined, the girl—only a child—was a probe launched into space in order to send back a report on what was out there—when she was gone, Ned believed with all his heart that she was still alive, that she was, if anything, more alive, and that he would one day find her in the *precincts of heaven*. Perhaps he would. No one can say for sure, but the odds appeared to be against it.

Sally had been hit by a car while riding her bike to school. These things happen. It isn't as if God can watch out for every child in the world—who has the time? Hit and run, thrown from the seat of her little pink bicycle, still decorated with streamers on the handlebars, a bike she loved to ride to school. The car that hit and killed his sister hadn't stopped. No one had seen the actual accident, or at least no one came forward. Ned's mother said,

"She went straight to God, right into the arms of Jesus," and when Ned asked why, his mother had said nothing. Ned hoped it was true, hoped that his beloved sister had been repaired and given a new, transcendent body with which to enjoy eternity. Though Ned didn't realize it for a while, he was drawn to Anna because she resembled his sister. When he did at last come to understand that this was the case, Ned was ashamed of himself; he felt as if he had committed incest. But there was nothing wrong with the feelings he had, nothing that Sally wouldn't have understood and that Anna wouldn't have forgiven.

Some time after the revelation of the MVD, after more "soul searching," Ned believed that he had at last seen more deeply into his character. Perhaps, he should take some time off to amend his flaws, if they were flaws. He closed his office—money wasn't a concern—and thought about taking a trip—to Mexico perhaps, or to Portugal, a country whose geography appealed to him. In the end he spent weeks drinking at The Showcase, brooding about his family, about Anna (who had, unaccountably, been talking to the psychotic vet)—the sheer disaster of his life—and then, on a brisk November morning a few days after Thanksgiving, he packed his car and drove to the West, to the place where people went to save their lives.

A Walk in the Snow

Constance, never Connie, was translating the poems of Vicente Aleixandre. She was the poetry editor of two Philadelphia poetry journals—*The Inconstant Bride* and *Crystal Nocturne*—and a lecturer at the Community College downtown—two sections of dreadful freshman composition, though she did sneak in quite a bit of Gregory Corso and Denise Levertov; and, of course, she wrote her own poetry when she could, and conducted an active social life. She worked on the Palestinian Solidarity Committee and volunteered at the Committee for the Homeless, sometimes attended church or synagogue or Quaker Meeting, depending. She took trips to New York for concerts (*Dead Kennedys* and *Circle Jerks* last weekend), and the *de riguer* but, let's be honest, idiotic Whitney Biennials. She walked her neighbors' dogs for pocket change, dealt a small amount of hash to her poet friends, read one book a month without fail and conducted a lively circle of flash and smash poetry readings at local bars and clubs. Constance enjoyed her many commitments, and the idea of being a poet appealed to her a great deal. She read many biographies of women writers—Woolf, Akhmatova, and Gertrude Stein were her most cherished literary idols—and each day as she arose in her untidy West Philly apartment, ten long blocks from Penn, her first thought was "Cool, another day of being a poet." Not really. But there isn't any question that Constance Bello, neé Constance Bellamano, born and raised in the great Northeast blue-collar enclave of Torresdale, right there on Audrey Avenue, not half a mile from Michael's Diner—regionally heralded for serving the best eggs and scrapple in the city—and not far from the rusted-out factories and abandoned warehouses that sit along the railroad tracks that now lead to nowhere—was quite content to be who she was. Constance had needed to escape her place of birth, and she had done so, on her own, without the blessings of her unfortunate family, all the way south and west to Hazel Avenue and the corner of Forty-Ninth Street, a lovely urban block where Constance owned a one-third interest in a triple decker, a pre-war twin, a hulking brick monstrosity impossible to heat or cool, whose roof didn't leak so much as ooze water and tar into the attic, where any item left on the porch for ten seconds—say, a bag of groceries—would disappear into thin air as if the laws of physics, of materiality, had been suspended on that particular block, on that sagging porch. But to Constance, the house, the commitments, the friends, the complications all possessed the sweetness of freedom—this was what she wanted and she had earned it the hard way.

I am writing an account of Constance's life for those who knew her.

We all liked Constance for her will power and illusions. She was our aesthetic and spiritual leader for almost a decade. We were poets and musicians and novelists and critics, filmmakers and painters. We were a dozen friends, all from Northeast, escapees to West Philly, denizens of the Half Moon Café, Harold's All-the-Time Diner, Lulu's Tropical Bar and, right down the street, The Showcase. Some of us had jobs; some lived at home with parents (me), a few of us made a living from our art. Constance showed us the way, she was the one who told the poets about entering small contests for cash prizes, the artists about start-up galleries off of South Street and North of Market; she went to City

Hall and applied for the micro-development grant that allowed the founding of both the Sansom Street Little Theater and our signature magazine, *Crystal Nocturne*. It was Constance and no one else who called everyone up to see how they are doing, how their work was going, if they needed anything. It's been like that since we were together at PCC, taking art classes or creative writing, working on the newspaper or the literary magazine. All of us were into the arts but, for good reason, unsure of ourselves. We weren't living in New York, we weren't going to Penn or Temple, we weren't from wealthy families, we weren't connected or published or exhibited—we were hungry, and, in my opinion, not without talent, but we didn't believe we should be taken seriously. That's a Philly problem: thinking that since Philly isn't much of a city—not Gotham and lacking the arts funding of D.C., a funky working-class town associated with blight, crack, asshole mayors, MOVE, and bad weather—Philly artists like ourselves had a natural inferiority complex that crushed us even before we failed. I was like that. And everyone in the group except for Peter Siliato and Constance came from families where reading and learning, let alone art and literature and music were despised. There wasn't a single book in my house growing up except for the Bible. Most of my friends at PCC told the same story: their parents were "letting them" go to Community College to get job skills, not to learn how to write poems or short stories, or, worse, how to paint or act or dance. Art meant nothing to plumbers like my Dad, or to shop owners like Sal's family. Sal's father had a corner store that sold groceries and beer and deli sandwiches, a place where you could buy light bulbs or toilet paper or nickel candy. And his father, Sal's grandfather, had folded boxes at United Parcels for thirty-six years. My father had quit school to join the Marines in 1940. My mother had worked a switchboard for the Signal Corps. In their hard-earned leisure hours they watched TV, 'Bonanza' and 'Gunsmoke,' and 'I Love Lucy'—those were the shows I remember growing up. When I walked into the living room of our narrow duplex and announced that I wanted to go to CC to learn how to be a writer, well, my parents weren't supportive. My father told me he wouldn't give me a nickel and that he sure as hell wasn't going to let me live at home while I wasted my time. I did get to live at home, if that can possibly be thought of as a good thing, but only because I earned money waiting tables and could pay rent for my childhood room. Self-confidence, as you can imagine, wasn't my biggest problem.

Constance wasn't an attractive woman in a stereotypical way, but she was magnetic, and drew people to her. She *was* attractive. Tall and well-proportioned and with astonishing legs—long, shapely, and on full display. On the other hand, her hair was never combed and looked like a bird's nest—I have to be honest here, and since Constance is now gone (see below) I feel it is important to tell the truth about my feelings and impressions, which, I can assure you, are objectively true. Her skin was rough—probably from girlhood acne, and her weight fluctuated, depending on how busy she was and, I would guess, on how many reds (amphetamines) she used on an average day. Many of us loved and admired Constance, and supported her in every way we could. I know I did. My boyfriend Jimmy used to say that there are two kinds of people in the world, those who have something to offer others and those who depend on that offering. I'm embarrassed to admit to being among the latter. It would be easy to blame my parents and siblings for undermining me, or to say that the teachers I had at St. Jude's weren't of the highest caliber, but nobody was keeping me from studying harder or using my "natural gifts" to get ahead. Constance spoke quite a lot to all of us, either singly or in our informal get-togethers, about "natural gifts," it being her contention that everyone has them, and that sympathetic friends and teachers can help us to discover and develop them. The last thing I ever wanted was to be a wastoid—one of those drugged-out pseudo-hippy types in the 70's who smoked pot all the time and read comic books and watched too much TV. I had drive, but I lacked direction. Jimmy had direction, but lacked drive, so we complemented one another, right from the time we met in high school. He wanted to be a musician, not in a rock band, but a real musician, a jazz drummer, and he was pretty good, but not great, and things always seemed to conspire to keep him from putting in the time needed to get better. And I wanted to be a writer from the time I was a little girl—nothing made me happier than making up stories and imagining conversations among people—but I had no idea how to go about putting this passion of mine to work. So I drifted. I had this idea right after high school when I was still living at home and waiting tables, thinking about the next chapter of my earthly existence, that great writers were great because they had a lot of different experiences. They lived in Paris or London, travelled, as Graham Greene had— he's my favorite writer—to Africa and Latin America soaking up exotic locales and observing with acuity the lives of unusual people. Greene's *The Quiet American* is the pinnacle of what writing should aspire to, and I wanted to visit Saigon and walk the streets and visit the cafés that haunted my dreams of Pyle and Fowler and Phuong. But of course this was impossible in that there was a war going on there. Also I was nineteen and living with my parents, and I made about fifty-five dollars a week in tips on top of my one-seventy-five per hour minimum wage. Travel was out. Instead of French Indo-China, my drive, my desire to write, was channeled into the quest to talk to every interesting person in West Philadelphia—to seek out strangers and listen to their life stories. I'd engage people at Quill's Bar, where I was working at the time, but when I did so, the men would think I was hitting on them and the women would think I was angling for a bigger tip. Anyway, the stories I heard were usually just like mine: these were people who grew up in Philadelphia or South Jersey, went to high school, lived at home, or went to college, which was even less interesting as a narrative since all college people appeared to do was go to beer parties. Jimmy and I had long conversations all during this time, and we still do, but Jimmy is just one person, and he's pretty one-dimensional.

I'm still young and hardly wise, but what I've learned from Constance and the others is that life can be cruel and people are indifferent, but that having a purpose, doing something that is fulfilling, can redeem you. Most people whom I have met, people my own age, born in the early 1960's and therefore children of the 70's—that lost decade—care only for worldly success. After Jimmy and I parted ways for a few years, I dated other guys, but their preoccupation with the accumulation of objects—cars and second houses and high-end stereo equipment—were often the topic of (one-sided) conversations I found myself engaged in on lonely Saturday nights, bar crawling on South Street, listening to men whose idea of happiness was flying to Aspen in their own private plane, who wanted sex and couldn't understand my preoccupation with writers and films and paintings. What was the point of art, they would say, and mean it. What I learned from Constance and Sal and Peter and the rest of them was that you don't have to buy into the material culture, the presuppositions of what Doug called (a little self-consciously) "late capitalism"—you *can* be an artist, or you can spend your life doing work that benefits others, you can volunteer at an animal shelter or feed the homeless, and not have to hang your head around the hustlers and con artists who dominate our culture.

I used the word "redeem" here, and I want to say more about that idea. Redemption has religious overtones, and it isn't a word that gets brought up in ordinary conversation all that often. The presumption is usually that redemption is attached to atonement, to paying for sins you have committed, offenses against the moral law, the one within you or the one imposed on us from without. But the type of redemption that interested me—I won't speak here for any of my acquaintances or even for Constance, especially given the way her life ended—was the type that *validates* who you are, or how you see yourself existing in the world. In other words, I never thought of redemption as freeing me from myself, or releasing me from some punishment I deserved for the mistakes that I made—and I made plenty—rather, redemption was an affirmation of my existence, of my belief system, of my hopes for myself. I was redeemed, if anything, from what other people expected of me. Constance showed me the door to redemption, but I had to walk through it myself. My parents never believed in me, or, for that matter, in the importance of believing in anything. We tend to think that nihilists are young people in black clothes with bad posture and long hair, but there are plenty of nihilists in suburban homes with manicured lawns who go to church and despise the kids in black clothes. My father was a nihilist. I didn't know that when he was berating me for my ideas and dreams, but that was what he was—a person who believed in nothing, who believed that nothing matters, except maybe pleasure. But putting your faith in pleasure is a terrible mistake. This isn't about my parents, or about me, but it is important to say that the only happiness we can ever achieve in a world that is, I am convinced, skewed toward heartache and tragedy, comes from affirming that we have worth, that our ideas are not foolish and that we aren't 'inherently' anything, certainly not evil.

Constance. A typical day in the life of Constance included writing and editing, talking on the phone to friends and contributors to the journals she helped to edit, teaching at the Community College, spending time with the printer, trolling the bookshops and boutiques for advertising, writing grant proposals and giving advice to her many friends. If she was in a relationship herself, Constance would spend time with whoever he or she was, and, if not, she would end the day with some of us at either The Showcase or Lulu's.

We had a large booth at each place and Constance would "hold court," as we called it, sipping gin and tonics and talking about writers we liked or Reagan's disturbing policies, or the latest outrage of the Mayor's, or her own writing and the trouble she was having with this or that line or stanza of *Sombra del paraíso*. Constance believed that every poet needed to translate another poet in order to learn something about form and metrics, but she confessed that Aleixandre—an unknown whose book she had found in Miami and which she had valued for the "clarity and rigor" of the Spanish verse—Constance was half Puerto Rican and her mother had taught her Spanish growing up, but of course idiomatic spoken Spanish is a long way from formal poetic Spanish, so the book gave her fits, and she complained endlessly about the poet's overuse of the names of obscure (she said) flowers, his over-indulgence in anthropomorphism, the mawkishness of some of the images ("water's breasts" was one I've never forgotten), and the expressive (read: romantic) tone of the collection as a whole. So why not translate someone else, someone for whom you feel an affinity? Constance seemed aghast at this suggestion because Aleixandre was not only a great poet, but had won the Nobel Prize just a half dozen years before—I didn't know this—and that her "criticisms" weren't complaints but observations about the temperament of a great and now renowned, Spanish-language writer.

"At last the Spanish literary tradition is receiving the recognition that has eluded it for so long." She said this often, in direct proportion to how many drinks she had consumed.

Constance could be forceful on topics that were dear to her heart, like, for instance, "the Spanish literary tradition." She seldom spoke Spanish, and I suspect her command of the written language wasn't up to the complexities of Aleixandre's aestheticism—I can say that with some confidence because I have since read the excellent Hugh Harter version of the poems and can see the difficulties Constance must have faced in making readable translations. The few that she finished and that I read seemed unsatisfactory to me—they were wooden and, I suspect, literal—but the whole point of this story about Constance and Vicente Aleixandre hasn't much to do with translation, rather it has to do with the fragility of poets, of people like Constance, when faced with the beauty and importance of art. Yes, I know that sounds foolish, but there's no clear way to put this, and my eulogy for Constance consists in this single, all-important point: during her brief life, my mentor and friend Constance Bello, a lovely girl from Northeast Philadelphia who believed that beauty could save her, who worked to create and preserve poems that stirred the soul, who moved me to become a writer—this young, doomed woman, understood that language is not simply a means of communicating, it is the means through which we create ourselves, though which we express that self and make it known to others.

That's the end of the formal eulogy; the peroration needs work. I've not written a eulogy before and Constance is the only person I've known, aside from my grandfather, who has died. Grandpa Bill was buried in Florida and my Mom flew down by herself for the service. I suppose there was a eulogy, but she didn't say anything about the experience except that it was awfully hot in Sebring in February. Constance's mother asked me to speak at her daughter's service since I was the only one of Constance's many friends and acquaintances who she knew well enough to ask, and who, in her opinion, "didn't have her head in a cloud." I wouldn't argue with that characterization of me, though my head was here on earth mostly because of the problems I was having with my parents, with Jimmy, with money, with school, and with my own so-called life. Unfortunately, not everything I wrote above, intended as it was for public consumption, was entirely true. When I think about Constance, not just the person, but the force she became, briefly, in the lives of our circle, I find other things that need to be "put out there," though where "out there" might be I have no idea as I am writing this account—not the eulogy, but this appendix to my remarks (which were delivered long ago and rather embarrass me)—not for anyone but for my own peace of mind. One of the reasons my stories, have not done well (understatement) is that I have no sense of audience. I write for myself. Constance used to read my pieces and say in her patient way that she liked them, but…and then I would of course ask what the 'but' was and she would say 'nothing' and I would ask again and finally, after much negotiation and a promise that I would not be offended by her probably correct view of the matter, she would tell me that it was as if the story were a diary, a wholly private and therefore uncommunicative collection of thoughts, a memoir perhaps, but too idiosyncratic to have broad appeal. She was right, and I appreciated her honesty, but her opinion hurt me, as, of course, she intended. Yes, I believe that. Her own boast was that she understood what people needed to hear. Not wanted, but *needed* to hear, and that was what I aspired to as well—to be read and appreciated. I've sold only three stories so far, and have written over fifty. Constance was perceptive, but I couldn't help but think that my failures, which proved I was no rival, made her feel superior. This is a thought unworthy of me, but I know I am right.

What do other people mean to us? Think about it: we have 'friends,' and we embrace them for their embrace of us; those whom we feel 'close to' are generally people who flatter us, who affirm our view of ourselves, who endorse our folly and applaud, however insincerely, our successes. Those who have many friends are the most insecure; each person 'gives' them something for which they are grateful, and they 'give' something in return. But this giving is suspect. It is a stay against our fear of being alone, our terror of not being constantly validated in other people's eyes. It is said—I've heard it said—that we are social animals, but does that mean we are *capable* of being social or that we *must* be social? All of this sociability is allegedly rooted in some kind of biological altruism, some deeply encoded sense that what we give we get back, that friends are better than enemies, and that the solitary individual stands no chance of survival. But we aren't living on the *veldt* any longer; we aren't arboreal primates, we're no longer chimps—we have created the tools of solitude out of the callous, empty heart of nature: fire and agriculture and divisions of labor and birth control and printed matter and micro-waved dinners and TV and psychotherapy . . . it's a long list, but the point is, we aren't social animals any longer—we are solitary entities who drift around other solitary entities, like rogue planets far from any star, way out in space beyond the orbit of Pluto, chunks of matter swirling about for no good reason.

Take Connie.

Connie. Constance was an affectation, a sort of pen name adopted in the interests of high seriousness. How else could a girl with a Puerto Rican mother and an Italian father, a girl from a part of town where furniture is wrapped in plastic and statues of Jesus and Mary are perched on either side of the bird feeder, where drink is the only sacrament, and everyday life is a struggle with boredom—how else could such a girl make herself into anything except by making herself into something she wasn't? Connie was good to her friends, but they repaid her many times over; Connie worked hard, but always for her own benefit; Connie was the center of things wherever she was, but she never would go anywhere if she weren't the center. With Connie, the game was always rigged.

Connie was pretty, but, more than pretty, she was carnivorous. She took away Jimmy, but that was easy since Jimmy had the character of February sunlight. Sorry. I don't mean to reach for poetic lines, but the hurt I still feel is so deep and viscous with bile that I can't help myself. She took Jimmy and used him and spit him out. This was something I wasn't supposed to know. And Jimmy wasn't the only one. Connie was not only a carnivore, she was an omnivore—she slept with men and women both, but sex was never the point—the point was adoration. Connie was remarkable in the way that all true narcissists are remarkable. She believed she was the center of the universe and did all she could to demonstrate to others that this belief of hers must override any sense they had of their own worth. Narcissism isn't conceit, it isn't being "self-centered" because all of us, except for rare saintly types like Dorothy Day or Mother Teresa, are centered in ourselves. The narcissist, like Connie, cannot feel empathy, does not have a capacity for compassion, and does not admit the validity of any ethical system, values, or taste apart from her own. The narcissist believes that she is the only person in the world, the only standard of measure by which any judgment can be made. When Connie was nice to someone, it wasn't out of sympathy or altruism—there was always an ulterior motive, one that advanced her program for her own life. And her program was adoration.

And yet, since I have practiced projecting myself into other people's lives, I offer this insight: Connie was in hell throughout her brief adult life. The trouble with narcissism is that it precludes the possibility that what you think is true isn't true. But what we think is true is *never* true, at least not entirely. And the non-narcissist, the average person with average gifts and run-of-the-mill morality, people like me, and Jimmy, and Sal, and the rest of us, we have the advantage of believing that other people might also have valid ideas about how one should live. We recognize that we can be wrong, something Connie was incapable of doing. Sartre, whose writing appears to me to be puerile and unreadable, had it backwards when he offered that "Hell is other people." Hell is living without other people. Hell is the black hole of the greedy, self-devouring ego.

On December 6th, Constance and her friends—including me and Jimmy, who had recently been exiled from Constance's intimate regard—were at our usual table in the back room of The Showcase, celebrating Doug's appointment as Director of the West Philadelphia Marxist School, a surprisingly successful workingman's bookstore and educational cooperative, a storefront where union laborers, black radicals, Penn and Temple undergraduates, hippie housewives, and general malcontents could take classes like "*Das Kapital* and 'Trickle-Down' Economics," "Organizing in the 80's," "Trotsky and Modernist Fiction," and, one I had taken, "Women's Literary Voices from Nicaragua." The job paid like $2000 a year, but Doug was ecstatic—it was his first job since graduating from CC three years before, and even on two grand he could move out of his parent's Havertown house and find a room in our part of the City. I'd baked a red cake and Sal had made a cassette mix of Victor Jara and Woody Guthrie tunes that Doug liked. We were drinking shots of Wild Turkey and schooners of Miller, enjoying one another's company on a bitterly cold Friday night. Constance was quiet, which wasn't unusual, but she seemed preoccupied in a way that she seldom ever was. She must have done most of her serious thinking when she was alone since none of us (later on that is) could recall ever having seen her so glum. When someone asked her if something were wrong, Constance had shaken her head and said only "Not a thing." We let her be.

At about 11 p.m., when all of us were drunk and loud, Constance abruptly got up and said, "I have to go." And without another word she pulled on her jacket and headed for the door. I was worried about her, so I told Jimmy I'd be right back. I followed her outside where a light snow was falling and the sky was a whirling eddy of gray light reflected from the street lamps.

Since no one is going to read this account I may as well be honest. The trouble with writing stories is that after a while you lose the knack of distinguishing the truth from the near-truth. As Isabel Archer would say, "It's just like a novel," meaning that sometimes life blurs over into the distortions of imagination, just the way, when you are sitting alone and writing, you find yourself slipping out of the fictive mode and into straightforward truth-telling. I hate memoirs for that reason—they're neither fish nor fowl, neither fiction nor, let's be honest, truth. Most of my life has become wrapped up in stories, and I sometimes get a case of vertigo when I'm put on the spot and have to tell the unvarnished truth. My first-year French teacher at CC called me in for an office visit—I had a C- at the time, not because French was difficult but because my Writing Workshop wholly preoccupied me—and when he asked me what academic subject I most enjoyed I said "More than anything in the world, what

I love is Literature." The capital 'L' was implied by my tone and serious expression in pronouncing the word. I thought this was both a wise and truthful answer, one that would be appreciated by a man—an older man by the way—who adored Balzac and Flaubert and could recite long passages from Paul Valéry from memory. But Professor Rodig's response was to shake his head and say, "You don't love literature, you love *stories*," this last word pronounced with the intonation one would use to say "green snot." And he was right. It turned out that I don't love Literature, or literature, half as much as I enjoy stories, The proof of this is that I can read romance novels and Agatha Christie's Hercule Poirot novels with as much pleasure as Virginia Woolf (more, to tell the truth), James Joyce (much more), or that old fussbudget Henry James. But, so what? Where's the shame in liking stories? All Literature is, when you come down to it, is High Cultural stories, stories for those who prefer brandy to beer and canapés to appetizers. I wish I could have thought to say this to my French professor back then, but, of course, I didn't. Now, when I'm all alone with my thoughts and my pen—actually my IBM Selectric—I want to stress that the following paragraph is the Truth.

Connie and I had a sexual relationship, a really heavy-duty, full-speed-ahead, take-no-prisoners, raw, satisfying and gratifying sexual affair—a long one, nearly a year's worth of regular, thrice (or more) weekly groping, kissing, and fucking, her place and mine, in Atlantic City at the Trump Tower, in Manhattan's bars and in Brooklyn, in Connie's friend Audrey's brownstone bedroom which I can see at this moment, the bed flat against the slanting roof, long narrow windows looking out toward the East River, the World Trade Center phallic and strangely fragile in the center of my field of vision; there it was, in the midst of my tenth orgasm, and we giggled like schoolgirls and tried things I'd never imagined—all of which worked out far better than Jimmy's awkward attempts at "inducing ecstasy," as he put it. Ten months of pleasure and sisterhood (no irony, honest), and, I thought, love.

As it transpired, there was no love, nor could there be—remember, Connie was all for Connie, and there was none, not one drop, left for me.

Constance walked out of The Showcase and into what was shaping up to be a heavy snowstorm. I liked the snow, especially walking in the first flurry of white, the purity of it, the clean smell of wet that coats the grime of the streets.

She turned east and began to walk briskly toward Penn, a dozen blocks away. I called her name, but too softly for her to hear. I might have caught up if I'd wished to do so, but I was curious to see where she was going. There were exactly two people walking on Baltimore Avenue, crossing at Forty Third, then turning onto Walnut. Constance had to have known that I was twenty feet behind her. The snow, just beginning to accumulate, muffled the sound of our boots, but not entirely. When I think about that night now I realize that she wanted me to follow her, wanted me to see where she was going and what she was about to do. If she had wanted me to interfere, to stop her, she could have said something, she could have turned around and opened her arms to me and I would have gone to her. But she didn't do that. She just walked, block after block; the snow coming faster, the wind picking up force and blowing the dry flakes into my face. I wasn't dressed for the cold, but what could I do? Constance was wearing her black leather jacket, the one she always wore, but a block or so before the river, on the edge of the lovely old art-deco bridge that crosses the Schuylkill and links the University with downtown, Constance shrugged off her coat and let it fall to the sidewalk. And a moment later her long black scarf—her winter trademark—that had been trailing down her back fluttered in the wind and swirled into the empty road. I remember thinking that the scarf, seeming to cartwheel in the wind, looked like a bird that couldn't rise up into the cold air. At the bridge, Constance disappeared from view. I knew where she was and began to jog to catch up with her. There was a small enclosed space under each of the lamps on the bridge, like diving boards. Connie and I had stood on these several times, hiding from the world, watching the water thirty feet below us. When I came to the platform, the "secret square" on which we had once shared a half-pint of blackberry brandy, Constance was gone. I called her name but there was no answer. I looked down into the water but saw only snow tumbling into blackness. I was shivering in the bitter cold and turned around and walked as quickly as I could back to The Showcase.

Everyone was still there, drinking and talking and smoking, just as if I hadn't been gone at all. I half expected to see Constance, my Connie, sitting among them.

"Hey, Agnes, where'd you guys get to? Where's Constance?"

"We just went for a walk in the snow. I guess she went home."

We stuck around until last call, and then said goodnight. Doug wanted to go home with me, but I wasn't in the mood. Sometimes a person needs to be alone.

The Biglin Brothers

"You see that painting there?"

"Which one?"

"That one, over the bar, between the lights. The guys in the boat."

"There's a lot of guys in boats, but yeah, I see the one."

"I love that picture."

"What is it, like a copy of a real one?"

"Yeah. The original is probably worth millions. It's by this guy who lived in Philly. Thomas Eakins. He was famous. There are lots of his paintings in the Institute."

"Huh. A long time ago right?"

"A hundred years at least."

"It's good. Simple and calm. I don't much like modern stuff, smears of paint."

"See the way the tree shows up in the water? That's what I like. I can't imagine how hard it must be to do that. I can't draw anything."

"Me either. I like the clouds. I've always liked clouds. The way they trail off, it's just how it is in life."

"It's fall there in the picture. Can you see that?"

"Maybe. Or maybe that tree is dead. The bare spot there on the left."

"No, it's fall. The leaves are brown, and the cattails are dead."

"You're probably right. There's something about the light. It's not summer but there's no clouds."

"I hadn't noticed that."

"And now that I look at it more, it just *feels* like October. The smoke is going straight up in the air, the water is flat. You ever see the river that flat?"

"I don't see it too much. We live in West Philly now. I grew up over there in Mt. Airy and my dad took me fishing every Saturday. Some days the water was just like that, flat and brown. It looks sort of green in the picture, but I remember it as always brown. We'd catch catfish and sunnies and maybe once a month a small-mouth bass. Always threw them back of course. Dad said the water was polluted."

"I was born in Mt. Airy too. On Lynnwood, right near the cemetery. Ivy Hill. We'd go over there to sled in the winter. Never did go fishing. But we would skate on the river. Can you believe that? The Schuylkill froze every December and thawed every March, just like clockwork. Now, hell, you get little bits of ice under the willows and that's it."

"I grew up on Chew Avenue. That's something. We live over on Fifty-Third now, big house, picked it up for $60,000. Four bedrooms and three baths. There's just four of us. You can get lost in the place. My wife has a little garden, grows tomatoes and basil. We can vegetables every September and she makes pesto for the freezer. My kids love the house. Three floors, wrap-around porch, even a little back stairway up from the kitchen to the second floor. The lady who sold us the house said it was the servants' staircase. Imagine that? Sixty thousand."

"Chew Avenue? Hell, I know that street. We probably ran into each other. Well, probably not. There were so many kids over there. We'd have two full teams for football, baseball, two leagues for basketball, I knew like twenty kids my age."

"Yeah, it was nice. My dad worked downtown at Northwestern. He was an accountant. Lots of my friends left the neighborhood after college. My best friend, maybe you knew him, was Kendall Schmidt. You ever hear that name?"

"Ken Schmidt. Sure, of course, he was the best

running back to ever graduate from LaSalle. Big guy. I never saw him play, but my old man was a football fan."

"All-State in '61, '62, and '63. First team All American. Profiled in *Sports Illustrated*—just in the high school section, but still. Broke every parochial school record in the state his senior year. One thousand one hundred twenty-seven yards rushing."

"Didn't he get drafted?"

"Yeah, twice. By the Browns and Uncle Sam. Same year in fact."

"I didn't know that. So you guys were buddies?"

"All through school. His mom was my mom's best friend, since before the war. They grew up in Germantown. My family moved to Mt. Airy the same year they did, we lived a block apart. We went to the same schools, to LaSalle, the works. We did everything together. I was a pretty good student and Ken was an athlete, but we got along. He was a good guy."

"So, what's he doing now?"

"Oh, he's doing nothing. He got killed in Vietnam. Nineteen sixty-eight. He's buried in Arlington."

"That's tough. I'm sorry to hear that."

"Yeah. I didn't go myself. I mean, I was in the Reserves. My old man got me in, which I feel pretty bad about with Ken and all. He could have gotten out but didn't want to, you know, take advantage."

"I have bad asthma. Never went at all."

"You know what I think though?"

"What's that?"

"These things happen for a reason. Not like a big plan or anything, but for some purpose. Like maybe something worse would have happened to Ken, or maybe I was supposed to get married and have kids and work at Raytheon and die in bed. Who knows?"

"Raytheon? The defense contractor?"

"Yeah, I work there."

"What do you do?"

"I'm an attorney. I handle government contracts. It's pretty routine stuff, but it pays well."

"That's a big place. Where is that, Plymouth Meeting? A long commute."

"Yeah. I take the Turnpike, four exits. Maybe a forty minute drive, less if I can get going by seven."

"I work downtown. We have a little shop on Lombard and Sixth. Antiques. Though most aren't technically antiques but old things, valuable for the craftsmanship."

"Huh. That's nice. How'd you get into that?"

"It was a hobby of mine. Of my wife's. She passed

away two years ago. And still I talk about her like she's alive. Anyway, we'd go on drives out west, like Lancaster or up north to Williamsport, stop at garage sales, pick up nice things, furniture, books and records—I love old records, 78's and 45's especially—and then we put them in our house. Then we couldn't fit any more stuff so we rented a storage locker. And we kept at it, years and years of buying things for a song. Finally my wife says to me, 'We could have a shop,' just kidding, but I say, 'Why not?' And then we did it. We got a place further west on Lombard, but that was no good, so we took a lease on a storefront, six thousand square feet, not cheap, but we do fine. I was working for the City doing inspections. I retired on a partial pension and now I run my own life. Open at 11. Antique people don't shop early in the morning. Stay open till 7, six days a week. Some weeks I sell two or three things, other weeks, like last week, somebody will come wanting to furnish an apartment, one of those nice new ones at Riverfront, and I'll make a month's worth of profits. It's funny how it works."

"I'm sorry about the Mrs."

"Yeah, thanks. Breast cancer. Four years it took to kill her."

"Jesus. My wife had cancer but they fixed her up, operated on her. It was a tumor in her stomach. She had radiation for nine months, lost her hair. She's in the clear now."

"They can cure a lot more cancers these days. I take three or four drugs every day. Asthma. Blood pressure pills, two cholesterol pills."

"Me too. How high is yours?"

"High. Two-ten."

"That's high. Mine's one sixty."

"Where do you go?"

"Dr. Goldstein. Been going to him since right after college. He's an old man now, but thorough."

"I just switched. I have a woman doctor, which is all right, but it makes me a little uptight sometimes."

"Call my guy. I'll write the number down."

"Thanks."

"You want another?"

"Sure. Pabst is fine."

"What do you think of the new bartender?"

"Alice? She's a looker. What do you think, thirty?"

"If that. I don't like the tattoos though."

"Me neither. Her's are pretty arty, but still."

"My boy got one. He's nineteen. I about killed him, but what can you do?"

"They look trashy. That was what my father used to say. Now I say it and I think how every year I get more like him. Hell, I look like him now, bald and paunchy, just like he was, at least after he turned forty. He was a good-looking man when he was young, then he hit forty and he started to fall apart. Course he was a big smoker. You ever smoke?"

"For years. Two packs a day. I could kick myself now. They say your lungs heal after a while, but I don't know. They never said back then how bad it was for you."

"That's corporations for you. I mean, they run the country now."

"I suppose."

"Not all of them. I mean tobacco companies."

"Raytheon is all right. They treat me well. But I see what you're saying. I'm pretty conservative I guess, but I'm not crazy about politics. My father loved Ike and hated Kennedy and Johnson. I'm okay with Reagan, not a big fan, but he's all right. Carter, I didn't care for. All that born-again stuff. Hey, listen, I'm sorry if I offend here. This is not really the best bar talk."

"No that's fine. I'm a Democrat, been one my whole life. My father was one, his father. My mother's father was a shop steward at Penn Central. All of them loved FDR, had his picture in the kitchen if you can believe that. Imagine having LBJ's mug staring at you while you're eating your pot roast? But, look, I don't get upset. It's just like if you go to one high school and your buddy goes to another one. You root for your team, but you're still friends, right? We might disagree about Reagan. I don't like him, but so what? He's president and I support him."

"That's a good attitude. Some of the guys I work with aren't like that. If you don't worship Ronnie you're basically a piece of shit. I don't get into that."

"Too much money in it now."

"For sure."

"Thanks for the beer."

"You're welcome. Can't drink beer myself anymore. Too bloating."

"I prefer bourbon."

"I'll buy you one if you'd like."

"Thanks, but I can't. After my wife died, I went a little crazy. Drank too much Jim Beam. That went on for a year or more. Then I quit altogether. Now it's just three or four of these things a week, just to get out of the house."

"I was the same way for a while when the wife was sick. I was home all the time, going crazy with worry, drinking too much. It's easy to fall into that. I was never one for drugs in college, or even drinking beyond socializing. Then all of a sudden I was going through a fifth of vodka every other day. My wife said to me one night when I was three sheets to the wind, 'You know if you kill yourself there won't be anyone to watch the kids,' and that woke me up. I only come out here on Wednesdays now, and at home I don't drink at all."

"I can't go to bars because of the smoke. This is about the only bar where the ventilators work well enough that I can sit for an hour. Downtown it's like walking into a fog bank, especially around South Street. Anyway, the crowds there are too young for me. I like this place, nice folks, good music, not too loud."

"I been coming here since it was The Circus, since the mid-70's. It's way better now. Used to be a real bucket of blood, guys sitting all day, half dead with drink. You still see some of that, but not so much anymore. Prices have gone up for one thing, and they don't over-serve anymore. Christ, the sky used to be the limit in the old days. You could be passed out and the bartenders would put another one on your tab. This Gus fellow knows how to run a tavern."

"I do like a good bar. I live alone now and that's hard. I have tickets to the symphony and I like to go to the movies, but still, you like company."

"Ever think of remarrying?"

"No."

"Sorry, that was sort of personal."

"That's all right. I just can't consider it. You know what I mean? I was married twenty years, and happy every one of them. That was lucky. You can't duplicate that kind of luck."

"Yeah. I understand. I'd be the same way. When I was in my thirties I used to look around some, you know, not with intent, but just out of interest. What would she be like or I wonder if she's available. But it was all bullshit. Fifteen years and I've never strayed. I mean, marriage is funny when you think about it. When I was at LaSalle and then at Fordham, I dated all the time. I'm not exactly Don Juan, but it was the sixties, even a mutt like me could get girls. But then in law school, first year, contracts class, I sat next to Barbara Tatum. And that was that."

"Lucky. I had to work to meet Julianne. This was after college. I was with the City and she worked in that bookshop on Chestnut, 'Blue Sky Books.' I must have bought fifty books I never planned on reading so I could talk to her. And I was shy, which didn't help."

"That was a nice place. I used to go in there for the Civil War books. That's my hobby. The Civil War. Probably I saw your wife in there, what, in the early seventies?"

"I think '66 to '70. She was two years older than me. I was a psychology major, of all things, and they didn't even have a psychology section, aside from Freud. I started buying genre novels—Westerns, Sci-Fi, English detective stuff—and darned if I don't read the same books today. One after another."

"I read history. Majored in it in fact. I always loved books about battles. My wife is a big reader. That's where she is tonight, at her book club."

"My wife too. She read everything that came along. We'd sit some nights after dinner, leave the TV off, and just read our books. Zane Grey for me and some bestseller for her. Those were good times."

"Where'd you go to college?"

"State College. It was okay. My parents didn't have a lot of money. I didn't like it so much. I wasn't into football or fraternities so I just kept to myself. I was hoping to be a counselor when I graduated, like in a school, but I couldn't get a job, I mean I tried all over the area and came up zilch. A cousin of mine worked for the Mayor back then, this was maybe '68, a year or so after I finished college, and this cousin fixed me up with a part-time job. Inspections of property. It was easy and paid well and you were a lock to stay on if you didn't mess up. I said, 'Sure, but just for a year.' I stayed for eighteen, overlapped with the shop. Left with a little pension. It wasn't what I'd planned to do, but it was all right. I always felt I was lucky to have a regular job, you know? Those years in the seventies with so many people out of work, '78 especially, and here I was making forty grand, putting in thirty-five hours a week, driving a city car, going to two conferences a year in places like New York and Miami. A beautiful wife, a nice apartment. I had it made. We were happy. I never looked for that job I thought I wanted so much. Life just goes on, and so fast, that it makes no sense to have regrets about any-thing, as long as you're happy."

"My parents had some money, which made it easier. My father wanted me to be a lawyer. That was it. He let me study history at LaSalle, but then I was going to Fordham, where he went, no matter what. It's funny how I just let him push me into my career without a word of protest. He'd hand me twenty bucks on Fridays and give me the keys to the car and say 'Two years from now you'll be in law school,' and I'd smile and say 'Sure Pop' and off I'd go, never thinking that someday I'd be reading boring precedents so I could save Raytheon some money on their taxes. But, yeah, I can't complain. It hasn't been exactly interesting, I might have liked to be a history teacher, in a high school maybe, but so what? I would have been a lousy teacher as I don't even like my own kids to tell you the truth. I mean, I love them, but I don't want to hang out with them. You do what you do."

"You do what you do."

"I'll drink to that."

"One more? My turn to buy."

"Just one. My wife expects me at ten. I got a meeting tomorrow at eight sharp."

"Vodka and tonic?"

"Sure."

"She is a looker."

"Yes she is. Reminds me of a girl I dated in New York when I was at Fordham. Rene something. French girl. American French. Reddish brown hair and a great body. Her old man owned this perfume company in Nyack. She lived up there. I'd ride the subway up on Saturday afternoon to see her. Her father was a nice guy. He liked me enough to let me borrow the Mercedes to take little Rene out for dinner and a movie. Which I did. But she wouldn't let me touch her, I mean, beyond making out in the car on the street adjacent to her house. It was early fall, still warm, and we'd park the car after our movie and roll down the windows. We'd be under a big old tree—those neighborhoods were full of elms back then, hundred-year-old trees—and she'd scoot over on the bench seat, no buckets then, and we'd kiss and talk. She always smelled like the ocean. Her father had all kinds of scents in the house but Rene liked this one that smelled like salt water and fresh summer air. Her hair was long and braided, in a shape that has a French name."

"Chignon?"

"That's it. And I'd pull it loose and let her hair tumble out onto her shoulders. She had beautiful arms and shoulders. And then I'd twist her hair in my fingers as I'd kiss her, hoping she'd, you know, or give me a sign that it okay to go further. But she didn't. She was a good kisser, not great, but she was so beautiful, and so touching in her beauty, I couldn't push myself on her, and later I'd think maybe she wanted me to force things, but I knew she didn't want to go all the way, at least not with me, and I knew she didn't like me well enough, I was just a Fordham law student, first year, a rube, and she was this French girl who would go through life breaking every man's heart she ever met. But I remember those nights like they were yesterday. The cicadas in the trees, the warm breeze, the smell of fresh-cut grass and dampness from the creek that ran down into the neighborhood, the still silence of the night while everyone in the world watched Walter Cronkite and I kissed the best-looking girl in New York. After a while I couldn't stand it anymore and broke up with her. Just mailed her a letter saying I was moving back to Philadelphia. Never heard from her again."

"Jesus. That's quite a story. I can't top that. I was a klutz, lucky to get any dates. The only woman I've ever kissed was my wife."

"Nothing wrong with that. It's quality, not quantity that counts in love and friendship."

"I agree. Though I don't have many friends either. None actually. One, but he died, five years back. We knew each other growing up in Mt. Airy, and then we were out of touch for years. One day he walked into my shop looking for a lamp. And I said, 'I know you,' and I did know him, sort of. It turned out he was gay, and his life had been difficult. His parents disowned him when he came out. They were Catholic and couldn't accept that he hadn't just made a bad choice, like taking up smoking. He moved to New York and struggled—he told me all this in the shop that day and then later on we'd meet for coffee once a week or so and he told me his life story, which was pretty grim. In New York he'd worked as a copyeditor for a magazine. Sounds okay, but he said it was boring work that paid poorly. And he had a lot of male friends. He said he'd made bad choices out of a sense of guilt. We'd talk for hours, not all of it sad. A lot of our talk was about the past and growing up in a nice neighborhood with good people. He'd never seemed odd to me, you know, unlike the rest of us. But that of course was the problem. He was hiding who he was. And then he got sick. He was living with his aunt back in the old neighborhood, not working, living on savings. He died when he was thirty-seven. I was there in the hospice room when he died. He weighed like a hundred pounds and was covered with sores and yet he kept up the chatter as if he were just fine. I honestly think he was relieved to die."

"Man, I'm sorry. That's terrible."

"Thanks. A lot of people I know wouldn't care about someone like him. But he was a good person."

"Makes you think. You know, how your life could turn out like that."

"He told me that no one chooses who he is, not really. And I thought that was wrong, but then I understood later on that he was right. All of us get pushed and pulled in ways we don't understand. We think we choose everything, but we don't choose what we can choose."

"Like Kendall. He had a choice—big money playing in the NFL or the service. But did he really have any choice, being who he was, how he'd been raised? I'd say not. He was going to do his duty, and then, if he came back, he'd take the million bucks to play football."

"He was a hero."

"I suppose. I don't put much faith in that word anymore. Turns out my friend probably died for no good reason. The lies they told us at the time, the bastards, it makes a mockery of heroism."

"And it continues, I'm sorry to say. We might not agree on everything, but, yeah, shame on us for falling for the same lies again."

"Yeah, well. You see that guy down the end of the bar, the blond guy? He looks pretty gone. Sat next to him one night, three, four months ago. We got to talking, just like us, and he had a story to tell, a terrible story. Lost his little girl, his wife divorced him. He started drinking, lost his job. I was about to cry listening to him, counting my own blessings, and then I thought how you can't escape it, the suffering. One of the things about Kendall in high school—I don't know if you remember this—was he never missed a game, or even a snap. And he told me he had a secret place inside he went to when he was sore or hurt, his 'pain-free zone,' he said it was his fenced-off refuge from whatever he felt. I think about that a lot. If you don't have something like that you suffer all the time. I've been lucky, forty-two years of life and aside from my wife's being sick, I haven't had to suffer. But you know you *will suffer*. I can't imagine what you went through, losing your wife. I don't know if I would have fallen apart like that guy down there. Probably I would have."

"I did. I fell apart. I didn't have a place to hide. My mother would have called it 'inner resources,' that was a big phrase of her's. 'You need inner resources in this life,' meaning you have to be able to endure. Which is what she and my dad and grandparents all had to do, just get up every day and do what has to be done, no complaining. I'm not like that. We got spoiled by having everything we wanted for so long. And when my wife died, I thought, 'What kind of world kills a forty-one-year-old woman'? Which was pretty stupid since the world had nothing to do with it. But I thought her dying proved something that I couldn't face up to, which was what you said—we suffer. That's it, end of story. You're okay a lot of the time, but mostly, you're not. Things aren't set up to placate us, to attend to our desires. Just the opposite."

"Yeah, well, on that note. I'm sorry if I opened the wound again. Don't know how I got on this topic."

"No, it was me. Bringing up Tom like that. I'm sorry. Alcohol makes me maudlin sometimes."

"You know what?"

"What's that?"

"Look at the guy in the picture there."

"Yeah, in the boat."

"Scull. They call them scull's, which is sort of weird."

"I think I knew that."

"Anyway, what do you see?"

"You mean the guy? He has a mustache; you can just sort of make it out. He's pale for someone outside, but I think we decided it was autumn. What else? What am I missing?"

"His eyes, where is looking?"

"Back? To see where he's going?"

"Maybe. But I think he's looking down into the water. See? It's so calm and peaceful on the water. And he's thinking how lucky he is to be all alone on the water, away from the city and the problems he had. You see it?"

"I do, now that you mention it. He sees his face in the water. The picture is like a mirror."

"There you go."

"I love that picture."

"Yeah. It gives you something to talk about."

Falling

The baby began to vomit at breakfast, right after ballet class. She wasn't a baby anymore, she was two—Rosalyn still used months when asked the age of her child—so, exactly twenty-eight months. The child was small, vivacious, already walking well, uttering some phonemes that Lane and Rosalyn had yearned into words. It wasn't really ballet but 'movement for preschoolers', ten girls and boys with fleshy legs and faces that weren't formed enough to be thought of as belonging to full-fledged human persons except, of course, to the Moms and Dads who stood three deep in the tiny room with the narrow window looking in at their children (No photos allowed!) and at the lithesome and, to the Dads, unbearably lovely twenty-something who with a patience the Moms envied but knew couldn't be sustained beyond the thirty minutes of the class, charmed the tottering children into raising and lowering their arms and legs while Tchaikovsky's 'Dance of the Snowflakes' blasted away on a cheap DVD player, horrid music, music synonymous for many of the parents with worries about the upcoming holiday season and the impending arrival of doting and mildly demented grandparents, child fatigue and tantrums, mandatory shopping in hellish toy stores, and maxed-out credit cards. Adulthood had come to some of these stylish Moms and their chubby husbands like an October snow storm. Most of the women were still attractive, with tattoos on their ankles that suggested carefree years of safe sex before settling on some now-disappointing guy who was a CPA or a high school guidance counselor to engender the baby whose arrival made it in under the genetic counseling wire before they hit forty, forty with its statistical spike of a dizzying array of diseases and congenital disarrangements of DNA, as if God Himself had set the timetable for procreation—no more Saturday nights chugging tequila and going home with strangers, no more, that is, if you didn't want to end up a lonely lesbian with cats and a Ford Focus, talking to the frozen food guy at Smith's. Kids were heartache for sure, but what else was there?

Roz herself had been a dancer, a star in college theatrical performances, an understudy for the part of

Eliza Doolittle at the Havertown Dinner Theatre, and then Mariam in "The Music Man" at the Walnut Street Theatre—she still had great legs and a thin but touching voice. She'd played soccer and swam the butterfly; her shoulders were broad and she had the poise and residual grace of someone who had stood in front of too many mirrors. Her husband loved her backside, the way it jutted up in her Mom tights, the pony tail that wagged in counterpoint to the sway of her now temporarily expanded hips and abdomen, temporarily because Roz was busy *working on* herself. Like all the other Moms, Roz pushed Kristen furiously up and down suburban streets in a three-hundred dollar Swedish stroller, panting and listening to Kansas on her iPod, sometimes dragging Millie the short-hair pointer/poodle mix along as well, burning calories and anxiety, "doing something for herself," as she put it to Lane when he asked about her day, which, truth be told, she didn't enjoy as much as she pretended. On Wednesday nights, with the baby asleep, Roz went to a spin class at the Sports and Wellness downtown, a place she loathed for all its trim teens and weirdly-muscled old men, people who appeared to work out for a living, hot blonds stuffed into skin-tight bun huggers whose contours attested to a life spent eating mixed greens while Roz, famished around the clock, chomped down bagels and veggie subs, fighting not to eat pints of Häagen-Dazs chocolate. In her desperation, Roz flung around ten-pound dumbbells while the baby napped. She did all of this, she said, for the baby and for Lane. This wasn't true. She seldom gave her husband a thought and what she felt for her baby was beyond any feeling she could reasonably describe. She knew her husband adored her, and though he had admired her pre-pregnancy body with the zeal of an idolater, he had made it clear that he was equally comfortable with the post-gestational Roz as well. He loved her *engorged* breasts (his phrase—not her's)—she was only going to breastfeed for a few weeks then switch to the bottle—and the tiny purse of reserve cellulite nature providently laid on as the pregnancy had progressed. Lane himself had put on weight during the nine months of his wife's "being with child." He had loved those nine months more than any other in his life, excepting of course the twenty-eight since the *miracle*—Lane used this word, without irony or embarrassment—of his daughter's birth. He had loved the fact that he and his wife could eat whatever they wanted, that they slept half of the weekend away and did very little aside from visit the doctor and cuddle on the couch. Roz had been weepy for a full month, but then, after morning sickness and maternal *angst* had evaporated, around month four, she had become gentle and happy and attentive to her husband in a way that was brand new. Her competitive side gave way to nest building, and the weeks spent decorating the little spare room for their daughter (they'd had the ultrasound and yes, they wanted to know), the wallpapering and tearing up carpets and assembling cribs and changing tables and shopping on hot Saturday afternoons at Babies R Us for just the right car seat, the one that received four stars from *Parents Magazine*—a publication neither Roz nor Lane had ever heard of but which they now read, devotedly, from cover to cover, tearing out product reviews and discussing over French toast the pros and cons of breastfeeding, of inoculations (they knew people who believed fervently, with the conviction of Jehovah's Witnesses, that the DPT shot caused autism, epilepsy, and retardation), of the fifty kinds of strollers (they ended up with three). On Thursdays after Lane returned from the gallery they went to the hospital for a two-hour birthing class. No way were they going for home birth—Roz had taken Anatomy and Physiology in college and had a pretty clear sense of the biology of childbirth and the mind-numbing array of ways in which things could go awry. They would go to the hospital and be attended by real doctors and not by some gray-haired holistic midwife like the one who had botched the delivery of Roz's cousin's best friend's son—the umbilical cord, that astronaut appendage that threatened strangulation if mispositioned, had choked off the little boy's oxygen supply for just a few seconds too many—none of that for them. Let childbirth be thought of as an ailment instead of an epiphany—who the hell cared, so long as the little girl, whose birth weight was going to be on the low side anyway, arrived in one piece and attained the maximum Apgar score ("What You Baby's Apgar Score *Really* Means!"), and just so long as—to be honest—Roz could have all the drugs she wanted (and she wanted the maximum amount, within reason) and not bleed to death or have her insides arrive wrapped around the baby or end up needing a Cesarean that a menopausal unlicensed natural childbirth person couldn't, or, for baroque ethical or philosophical reasons, would not perform, preferring to see the Mom die than the baby be traumatized by the heartless, patriarchal system of corporate medicine. Lane had his worries too, and many of them were focused on the health and safety of the woman whom he had married because she was beautiful, sexy, and funny, but whose new role as bearer of his child had enhanced her worth in his eyes to the point of idealization: Roslyn was his alpha and omega, brave, selfless, deeper than he could have imaged any jock party girl could be. Lane was worried about himself now, wondering if he possessed comparable stores of character to help him become a Good Dad.

Lately, as she lost weight, Roz was having trouble with her *self image.* She was 'cute,' with clear skin and liquid-green eyes that teared up once a day as she sat hovering over Kristen, the miracle baby whose fragile perfection Roz could never quite accept. In the park, strange men would talk to her, ask directions to the Starbucks that was in plain sight, or make a fuss over her daughter—Roz found this creepy—a ploy Roz suspected, without vanity, was a means of letting her know they would tolerate the kid if they could have a closer look at the Mom. Roz was a girl and a woman, unformed and yet fixed, as full of certainty as her own mother, or any mother who understood what was entailed once a person—helpless, but a person nonetheless—was removed from her body.

After movement class, at eleven each Saturday morning of the clear, dry autumn days, with shifting breezes and yellowing cottonwoods making the beauty of the world unbearable, with the occasional flyover of Canada geese or migrating songbirds, the contrails of jets etched like tears in the sky, right at eleven, the little family, happy in the way that Saturdays empty of obligation make one feel, steeped in love for their slightly irritable little girl, full of tender regard for one another, drove a mile to a favorite restaurant for an early lunch. On the agenda for that day were domestic chores, perhaps college football on television, a trip to the park and its child-safe swings, early dinner, a light comedic movie for Roz and Lane, sex if they weren't too tired—all the things they had come by silent agreement to treasure, their "family time," the life they had made when, just a few years before, after less than a year of marriage, they decided it was time to "get serious" and start a family.

Kristen had scrambled eggs and orange juice. A few minutes after she started to eat, the little girl, attired in a lovely pink dress just arrived from L.L. Bean, stood up and "upchucked," all over herself, the table, and the *huevos rancheros* that her parents had been splitting. A few seconds later, in a second great heave, little Kristen puked all over her mother and father. Roz was horrified. She was usually the calm type, not a worrier, but the intensity of the retching, the volume and the orange-brown color of the vomit threw her into a panic. She lifted up the weeping little girl—small and fragile—and moved toward the door, saying, not softly, 'Pay the bill.'

Lane, having had less experience with children's effluvia than his wife, was more aghast and jogged over to the cashier, unmindful of the state of his clothing, and simply dropped some bills on the counter, pointing stupidly toward table and apologized for the mess.

The vomiting didn't cease. All afternoon and into the night the little girl threw up with metronomic efficiency—at thirty-minute intervals, water, Gatorade, applesauce, and bits of dry toast reappeared, unaltered by the child's digestive system. Lane knew about dehydration; Roz got on the computer and searched the American Society of Pediatrics site for advice. At eleven, near despair, Lane packed his little shivering girl into two blankets and her car seat and drove with Roz to the emergency room at Central Hospital. There was no alternative. Doctors did not answer phones; answering services picked up and promised a call back that never came. The emergency room was packed with teenagers who had been stabbed and shot and beaten at parties and in gang wars. It was Saturday night; the entire underbelly of the city was slumped over in the orange plastic chairs, bleeding into towels, nodding with druggy insistence toward the candy machine that didn't work, cursing and even fighting—the ER had three cops just to keep the wounded from doing further damage to themselves before the triage nurses could attend to them. At midnight, Roz began to weep as Kristen vomited for the third time on her mother's wet and reeking Penn State sweatshirt. Lane was ready to commit violence himself. He began to yell at the nurse behind the great barrier of the front desk. The nurse ignored him, and then called one of the burly security cops over. Lane shut up. At one a.m. Roz and Lane and their daughter, were finally taken into an examination room, where they waited another thirty minutes.

"This couldn't happen in Canada," Lane said.

"Why not? You think socialized medicine is any better?" Roz wasn't in the mood for a political discussion.

"I didn't mean that. There are thirty people out there. Half of them have been wounded in some kind of violent confrontation. That isn't happening in Canada. I know they're doing the best they can, but Jesus, we've been her for two hours."

Roz didn't need to be told how long they'd been waiting. She had Kristen clutched to her chest; she hadn't put her down in five hours, apart from the car ride. She wouldn't put her down. The baby's skin was pale and felt dry. Roz knew this was bad and was close to losing control, but that wouldn't help anyone, so she held on, repeating to herself, as she often did, that this too would pass away.

The doctor looked about twenty-five. He wasn't rude or officious; he took his time, introduced himself to Roz and Lane, and tried to calm them down. His name was Banerjee—he had thick black hair and liquid brown eyes. Roz thought he looked kind, and Lane hoped he knew what he was doing.

Banerjee peeled Kristen from Roz and made a little joke about the condition of the latter's clothing. He undressed the girl and listened to her heart, her respiration. He asked them a lot of questions. Lane answered, at too great length, but it made him feel better to speak of the ordeal his daughter had been through. He knew better than to think doctors would care about how he felt—they couldn't, he understood that—but Lane choked up as he spoke of the relentlessness of the vomiting, the helplessness he and his wife felt, their fears.

Dr. Banerjee noted and said nothing. He wrote out some instructions and got up.

"First thing, she's dehydrated. We'll get an IV started and then, when she's back to normal, we'll do a couple of tests to see what the problem might be. It sounds like a simple virus, but we need to be sure."

"What else could it be?"

"Oh, I couldn't say. We need to give some tests—blood first, perhaps an x-ray, depending on the blood work. You'll be here for a while, I'm sorry. I will put you and your daughter in a private treatment room here in the ER, and then we'll see about admitting her."

"Admitting her? To stay?"

"Just for tonight. We'll see. But you can't stay in this room, you see?" He gestured hopelessly out toward the waiting room and its queue of wounded and dying. "We're very busy tonight. It's party night." He said this with a sad smile, as if to confirm that he too found the mayhem distasteful.

"Is she going to be all right?" The first words that Roz had spoken.

"Oh, yes, of course." Dr. Banerjee smiled at them, and then, without another word, he was gone. It's only an infection, a virus, nothing to be concerned about.

They waited some more, a very long time, and then were shown to a small room still in the ER. It was loud with compliant, with detoxing addicts and drunks. Kristen woke up, vomited, and fell asleep again. Roz cried, softly. They waited until the night was nearly over. They never saw Dr. Banerjee again. At some point, perhaps it was 4 a.m., the thought occurred to Lane, his brain addled with sleeplessness and stress, that there had never been such a person, that he, Lane, had hallucinated the youthful Indian doctor, or perhaps he was Pakistani, or Bangladeshi, or a jinn.

He fell asleep and dreamed he was falling out of the sky, perhaps from an airplane that had split in half, falling from a plane into the blackness of the ocean, bodies not plunging but floating among the debris, gently, for longer than he had ever imagined anyone could ever fall.

Rosa

I'M NOT EXCEPTIONAL IN ANY WAY. I'm like everybody else. When people ask me about my life I say to them—why ask? My biography would be five sentences: Carlton Dunbar was born in New Jersey in 1945. He grew up in a warm, loving household, and he attended both public and parochial schools. He graduated, without distinction, from a decent Midwestern liberal arts college where he spent far too much time engaged in politics, unfulfilled sexual longings, hedonistic self-destruction, and general time wasting to have received a good education. He became a high school teacher, not much out of wanting to, but out of a general inertial sense that nothing much mattered more than anything else. He took up the reading and writing of poetry in a serious way when he was far too old to be especially good at either; he probably drank more than he should have.... that's five and a clause. The sixth is yet to be written. He, I, settled about twenty miles from where I grew up in Haddonfield, settled right here in the City of Brotherly Amour, and, out of laziness, seldom left. I was known by my friends in college as Carl Doobie, and am now called by my "friends," who are all wry and ironic high school teachers just like me, Cal Dumbbell.

The school is named after a famous Philadelphia person—that's all I can say. Literature and history both since the staff is small. Good pay, or, not bad pay, given the fact that I never finished my Master's degree. I might have suggested that I did finish and forgotten to send the transcript that didn't seem like such a big deal during the interview. I'm personable, or at least can "sell myself" as my Dad used to say. He was an insurance man. Life insurance for the most part, but later on all kinds, any desperate way to hedge one's life against the inevitable. Of course, life insurance is a losing proposition since you have to die to collect—ha.

What I would say about my boring life was that it was wonderful. There is no other way to describe how lucky I am to have lived. I know, I sound bored and cynical a lot of the time, and a lot of the time I am—bored and cynical—but like most people I have another side, or, more to the point, I have an inside, and that inside, the genuine Carlton Dunbar, is grateful for his life.

Think about it. My parents were born in 1919 and 1922—father and mother. They're both still alive by the way, which is lucky I think since it means that my past is still with me, even if I don't live with them—I couldn't bear that—or even see them that often, at least they're *here*, which means there's continuity in my existence, memories still living of my early years, those lost events of childhood that remind you of the duration of your existence—the fact that, for example, I was born on the day FDR died, on April 12, 1945, and my parents can tell me how they laughed and cried almost in the same moment as I came into the world and as the president whom they loved—adored—left it. When my mother tells me this on the phone, I sometimes yawn and tune her out, which is foolish, since it is a fact of great importance. To have a life that is rooted in history seems to me important. You can imagine yourself, as I do, arriving on earth in the midst of a roaring torrent of events, as if you were dropped into a river swollen with the debris of other lives. You know what I mean. I don't want to sound like an egotist or anything, but I like to think of where I belong in the grand scheme of things, so to speak. So, April 12th is a day when I think about our greatest president and my own luck at arriving at the very beginning of our Golden Age—I mean it. We're so jaded now that I'm almost embarrassed to say it, but it's true, we Americans ruled the world for a while, and if you were born in '45, you won the lottery.

Most of the people I know claim to have had terrible childhoods. It's a badge of honor for middle class people, those who comfortable lives, to say they were unhappy growing up. I don't begrudge anyone his unhappiness, but it does seem to me improbable that, among a particular socio-economic group of educated white professionals, a majority claim to have been "abused" (psychologically, for the most part, but not only) or to have been deprived of something whose possession would have guaranteed their happiness but, in whose absence, there is only anomie, self-loathing, or the kind of terminal cynicism that is the leprosy of liberalism, liberals, by and large, having taken utopian promises of universal human progress as covenants entailing their personal fulfillment. The split came with Hegel—everybody who has taken basic philosophy in college knows that liberals want society to meet their personal needs, to reflect *them* as unique, atomic individuals. History becomes a kind of monumental egotism, and all of the communal values that made the classical world great—the idea of the *polis*, of duty and honor, and character—all get boiled down to "the pursuit of happiness" for this one selfish person—the liberal. And liberals don't want churches or religion—aside from Rousseau's civil religion—because religion cramps their style, their monomaniacal pursuit of pleasure. This was *before* Hegel. Then he wrote a great book about how to reinvent the social world without sacrificing either the individual's consciousness or the social good. A lot of Hegel comes from Herder. I read all these books a long time ago at my pricey liberal arts college in Indiana. I wasn't a strong student in high school—the opposite really. I was a jock, a wrestler and shot putter and for a couple of seasons, until I broke my leg, a linebacker on the Haddonfield state-champion teams—I was quick and big, not fat like now, I was muscular, I could bench 325 as a junior. Then something happened to me. Something terrible and I quit sports and started to read and study in a serious way; my grades went up and it turned out I was smart, or smart enough to get into a good college.

I don't like to talk about it. Between my sophomore and junior years I worked at a restaurant in Haddonfield, a place that's called "The Edgewater," on Fremont Street, on the north end of town where there's now a big empty lot. They tore down the restaurant after the recession in '74 and built office space, but that flopped too, and in the late 70s there were three or four business on that spot—a frame store, a used comic book store, a consignment shop, then St. Vincent's was there for about two years, then nothing, then it was bulldozed for the Mayor's planned municipal center—remember? There was going to be a pool and community center for the elderly, but Talbot lost in '82 and the Republican, I think it was Murdoch, didn't appropriate the money so now Haddonfield has a big eye sore, a bombed-out lot full of dumped appliances and broken concrete instead of a pool. Whatever. Anyway, in the early 60s, right after JFK got killed, I had a summer job at the Edgewater, which was a nice place, white table clothes and good steaks and seafood. My Mom and Dad were proud of me—they used to drop in to say hello, maybe sit at the bar and drink an Old Fashioned, or, on a special occasion, usually their anniversary, Dad would put on his best gray suit and Mom her red dress with the flouncy skirt, and they would come to eat dinner and I would stop by their table just for a few minutes to say hello, as if I were a stranger who just happened to be the head bus boy at the best restaurant in

Haddonfield. It's hard to describe to anyone how perfect a time this was for people like me. My Dad was a "good provider," that was how he described himself, and when Mom would talk about him to her friends over coffee, if you were eavesdropping that phrase would inevitably be mentioned—to have a husband who was a "good provider" was more important than his being handsome or loving or even his being around. My father was seldom at home. He left for the office early in the morning, came home at six for dinner, and then was gone again every night until long after I was in bed. That was what a "good provider" did, or so I assumed. Dad sold insurance, as I said, and he had to meet with people all day to try and make a sale. And he had to drive all over New Jersey to visit his clients. Later it turned out he wasn't only visiting clients. My mother's and father's failures—if you want to call them that—mirror my own, or mine mirror theirs, or every marriage ends in the same way—I'm not sure what I want to say about this topic, but I do remember that talking to my parents at the Edgewater when I was sixteen years old was the best moment of my life.

Then there is the one bad thing—the worst thing imaginable—the source of suffering.

The one thing left in the world about which there is nothing to say is love.

All the books and songs and plays and movies: what original thing could I tell you about Rosa and me? It's best to keep quiet about our inner lives, about our failures of heart. I can tell you this much: Rosa was the only woman I've ever loved. My wife was a good person, but there was no passion in our relationship, or not enough to sustain it. The formula for a successful love affair and marriage is as complex as the equations that purport to describe the origins of the universe, but the one constant, non-variable, is passion. Passion being the irreducible and indescribable yearning that one person feels to be in the presence of another. It isn't sex, or just sex, though it *is* sex; but passion carries on long after physical relations cease or become less important. Anyone who has ever been in love understands this, and anyone who doesn't understand it, well, they need to live more deeply.

Rosa and I were inseparable for a year—it was like a dream for me, the one thing I'd always wanted was to be fully immersed in another human being, in just the way the mystics professed to lose their identities in God—that was what I wanted from a woman. I had gone through casual affairs and even a few serious relationships, but nothing that was sufficient to fill the emptiness I felt, the fundamental loneliness that never seemed to grow less, but only deepened as I got older, as if I were sinking into the black hole that lived inside of me, the one I had felt ever since I left home and encountered the world. You can see that I'm not good looking, not tall or well built, not witty or especially smart or ambitious. But she loved me, she seemed to adore me. It was a miracle that this beautiful woman would look at me as if I were the best thing in her life.

Rosa *was* a beautiful woman. Her mother was Mexican, and Rosa had long black hair and dark brown eyes, skin that was cocoa-colored and flawless, as cool to the touch as the ocean she loved. Her father was German. We met at a party, some charity thing at the Hilton put on by Penn. I was there with someone else, someone I hardly knew from work; I remember it was for ALS. A co-worker's husband had died of Lou Gehrig's disease and she asked if I would go to a fundraiser, a dinner and dance, if I would mind escorting her since she was reluctant to go alone. She was a nice woman, pretty but worn out, about fifty. She didn't like me much, just enough to spend a sociable evening with. So we're there, Grace and I, that was her name, Grace, which was a name I liked a lot, and I had picked up a couple of drinks for us, and were standing among a sprawl of a dozen people, making the kind of disconnected conversation that you make at fundraisers, listening to this guy play flamenco guitar, a kind of music I've never much liked, a sort of technical set of runs up and down the guitar whose total sound was strangely unsettling, aggressive and not at all suited to be background music at an affair dedicated to the most horrible disease I could think of. I was smiling in the kind of rictus way I have when I'm totally uncomfortable, when there appears next to me this stunning woman with shimmering hair wearing a modest green dress—a color green that evoked not lush rain forests but the patchy dull green of the desert, and a strand of onyx beads that set off her thin neck. I know—too much detail. You don't need all this detail. And for all you know, Rosa was dumpy and sallow and brittle. Take my word, or don't, it doesn't matter, I'm not saying this for you.

Green dress. Brown eyes. There isn't an easy way to tell this story, or a short way—some stories could spin out forever, every nuance of feeling, each supposition about the beloved. If you think about it, being in love is tiring, given all the time one wastes trying to penetrate the impenetrable mind of the person you love—and, let's face it, it is probable that you love yourself as much as the person whose face you never can quite recover, whose voice remains indistinct, whose smell you catch a hint of now and again, but each time you wonder if that really is her smell.

Did I ever know Rosa? I thought I did, but then it turned out that I was mistaken.

There is nothing in the world quite like that first stirring of attraction. It's hard to say that with a straight face. But Rosa was special, and when I finally worked up the courage to speak to her that night I found that she was not only beautiful but intelligent and vivacious—yes, she was full of life. I asked for her number and she jotted it on a matchbook—so romantic really, to have a beautiful woman write her number on a matchbook cover and hand it to you, not at all the sort of thing that happens more than once or twice in your lifetime. I called her after a full day of wondering if I should call her—there's a risk in *making contact* with another human being, and for someone like me, so average in every way, the risk was greater—I supposed she would find me tedious and unattractive and I would have opened myself up, once again, to disappointment. Am I tedious? I suppose I am, but then why should it be that unattractive people have to suffer for something that is hardly their doing?

I called and we went out for dinner—I think it was that Italian place on Lombard Street, the *atmospheric bistro* as the *Inquirer* put it, as if the place floated ten feet above the ground. We didn't hit it off at all. I was nervous, and you can't blame me. Rosa wasn't especially interested in being with me—I could feel that at once. She nodded when I spoke, but offered little in return and gazed at the other diners in a way that said she would have preferred to be any place else but with me. But then, when I could feel her attention slipping from me—and usually this wouldn't matter and I'd chalk the experience up to another bad decision—I decided to make an extra effort to be *worthy of her attention*. I hate the idea of having to grovel, but one does grovel with women, with bosses, with so-called friends. I told Rosa some stories about myself that weren't true. They were lies. For example, I told her that I had a law degree, which was plausible since I had attended law school, though only for a single semester. And then I mentioned being on the board of PNM and a couple of banks in the tri-state area, my interests in skydiving and deep sea fishing…. there was a lot of talk about my family that was wholly spun from invisible thread—all lies.

Was she impressed? Curious, I would say. She started to listen to me, and as I felt her attention shift

I stretched things a little more, telling her about my service in the U.S. Navy (I'd been disqualified from military service due to poor eyesight) and the farm I owned in Lancaster County. Rosa wasn't materialistic, but I spread the lies about, touching not only on my imaginary wealth but also on my imaginary sensitivities to art and music, my imaginary interest in the "less fortunate" (her term—I prefer "poor"), and my imaginary hopes for the future. The truth is that lying is fundamental to any relationship. My lies were bold, shameless. Rosa, though an honest person, told a few of her own: that she cared about me, for instance, which was, when you consider the matter, a far more hurtful bit of mendacity than my stories of serving on a destroyer in the South China Sea. She also told me many things about her family—all, it appeared, paragons of selflessness and achievement—that turned out not to be true.

Well, none of that is important now. She's gone and I'm still here.

We started to *date* after than first, dishonest evening. What is a *date*, exactly? A planned meeting that serves as a preliminary to sex. Rosa enjoyed going to the movies, and that first romantic winter I found myself sitting through dozens of tedious popular films—"The

Elephant Man," "Ordinary People," "The Shining," and many others even less memorable. After the *cinema* Rosa would be *famished,* I suppose from all the vicarious events she had participated in, and so we would go to Mel's Diner or to Rosie's on South, or, if the movie had been *screened* closer to home we'd come here to The Showcase for a beer and a burger.

Then, of course, sex.

Rosa enjoyed sex. I did too, but not in the same way. Rosa was of the school of thought that sex was primarily a means of "*getting to know someone*." My own view was that sex provided a release, a means of escape, a kind of controlled oblivion. There was a lot of talking during the act with Rosa, *meta-sex* as I came to think of it.

"Oh Carl, when you touch me there I remember lying in bed as a young girl . . ."

You can see why I would tire of this. It was as if the simple act of coitus had become a form of autobiography for my partner. With my hands and mouth I was stirring up powerful memories, associations, and sentiments—Rosa purred when she wasn't talking, and I felt, at first, that this sound was complimentary, an indication that I was learning my way around her lovely body, but later on the mewing began to seem contrived, rehearsed and disconnected from what we were doing.

On several occasions, at the moment of *apotheosis*—that was Rosa's word—she would call out to a fellow named Larry (Larry!), and I was upset, naturally, to think Rosa had someone else in mind just then, but then she would reassure me that I was the only man in her life, etc.

Why did she spend time with me? As I've mentioned, I'm average. And of course, one by one, the lies I had told her came to light. That I wasn't actually a lawyer but a high school teacher, or, when she asked to visit my farm in Lancaster County and I had to say the family had just sold it in order to invest in computer stock—something called Apple. Rosa seemed to take these little disappointments in stride. She had a resigned air at times, as if being with me was her fate, or penance.

Beauty, of course, is a burden. She confessed that she had tired of fending off men who were only attracted to her *perfect face* and *hourglass figure*. Of course, I took this information to heart and never commented on her physical appearance, focusing instead on her sense of humor (non-existent) and intelligence (as it transpired, limited). The truth was, Rosa was the most beautiful woman I had ever seen—imagine Natalie Wood in "Rebel Without a Cause" or, even higher up the scale of perfection, Liz Taylor in "A Place in the Sun." Dark, sultry, sensuous, but refined; not flaunting her loveliness, not able to disguise it either. And I was then, as I am now, ugly. Big nose, big ears, dull eyes, bad skin. It was a miracle that Rosa enjoyed my company, and I was willing to put up with a great deal to be able, night after night, to unfasten her clothing and run my hands up and down her long, muscular legs. She was, as my friend Benny used to say, *a dish.*

Does this story seem implausible? You're thinking, the guy's a liar, and this is just another tall tale. But consider: how many times have you had a bit of luck, had something undeserved, even remarkable, happen? Once? Twice? Up until Rosa nothing especially good had ever happened to me. I don't mean that I hadn't enjoyed good fortune, but no *epiphany of joy* had come to me—that was also Rosa's phrase, and not used in relation to me, I'm sorry to say. Lovely women some-times like average men, and, as I learned with Rosa, there is a price to be paid, some psychological costs to be extracted. Jealousy, it goes without saying, became my daily fare. I stopped seeing my friends socially since they couldn't keep their eyes off of my girlfriend. Or their hands. Benny, that asshole, ran his hand up Rosa's leg right in front of me, here, in the booth under the picture of the boxers. I saw him do it. I was across from Rosa and next to Caroline, Benny's wife, and I saw Rosa stiffen and sure enough there was his hand, halfway up her thigh. That was it for me and Benny, even though I still see him at work we never exchange a word—he apologized, blamed the vodka, but I'd had as much as he had and kept my hands to myself. And then Rosa was a problem, the way she dressed, her manner, which wasn't modest, despite her being a *churchgoing woman*— "You know I'm a churchgoing woman" Rosa would say if I asked her to do something a little kinky in bed—meaning, "I'm above all that." But she'd leave the house in a dress that left little to the imagination—or in those black jeans I still have hanging in the closet, the ones she wore the day of the accident.

Rosa, what happened to us?

When I asked her to marry me, after six months of dates and five of near cohabitation—we kept our places but *slept over*—she said no. I wasn't surprised, but the ring had cost me a month's pay, that cheap Greek wouldn't give me a refund. So we broke up. I was devastated. For weeks I'd sit in my tiny third-floor apartment staring at the phone, willing it to ring. It never did. She was out with someone else. I knew that she was going to bed with "Larry" or to an art opening with that creep Benny. Or she was sitting at home wishing I would call her, which I wouldn't do, ever—how can a man crawl back to a woman who has rejected him? I took to walking around West Philly at all hours of the day and night, hoping to run into her. I never did. You never meet someone casually when you want to—you have to *not* want to see someone to see them.

I talked to myself a great deal. "You dope, you fool, what did you expect? She's too good for you. Nobody will ever want to marry you; you're a loser…" And so forth. Everyone except priests and rabbis and the deformed goes through this at some point—having your heart broken five or six times is just a normal part of adult life.

Rosa, Rosa, Rosa.

I even went to the Catholic Church on Walnut and lit a candle, knelt on the velvet cushion, nearly choked on the smoky, waxy smell that was trapped in the alcove that held an enormous rococo statue of St. Elizabeth and her wheel: I prayed: *Please, Elizabeth, let Rosa love me.* A month after my proposal, Rosa wrote me a note. I still have it. It was short:

> *Dear Carlton:*
> *Leave me alone. I don't love you.*
> *Rosa*

I was discouraged. It seemed clear from the note that Rosa didn't love me. I missed her terribly—there were days when I could think of nothing else but how lonely I was for her voice, the look of her hands—she had beautiful hands, thin fingers, nicely manicured nails—I took to walking past her apartment at all hours of the day and night, peering up toward the curtained windows, imagining her in her kitchen drinking tea or sitting in that red chair of hers—I still have it—reading poetry or *Vogue*. Sometimes, if it wasn't cold or raining, I would stand across the street in the small, litter-strewn park and ask the gods if they could have Rosa come to the window and wave me upstairs. I imagined that this happened, that she had parted the thick blue curtains and gestured to me, that I opened the door—a heavy oak door whose knob was in the center, in the style of the 70s—that she buzzed me up—*buzzed me up*, what a lovely phrase—and that she was waiting for me at the top of the stairs in her black jeans and a white tee shirt, something like that, the details are little unclear, but what follows was vivid—a glass of wine and then a kiss and then.....I would spin through this vision for half an hour, become lost in my imagination, aroused under a tree that smelled of dog shit. I made note of the paradox of this: that here I was, *lovelorn*—a sad, but apt word—roiling with deep feeling, surrounded by garbage.

After a few more weeks I stopped stalking Rosa—what was the point? I resumed my life, not that I had suspended it, for I had to work and eat and sleep, despite the heartache that accompanied each of these acts. I still had dreams about her, but then they might have been dreams about anyone—no one has a face in my dreams, no one is identifiable in them, and if I thought I had dreamed of Rosa it was only because when I woke up I said— "What a lovely dream about Rosa!" But I usually couldn't hold these images in mind for more than a few minutes; real life would intrude and I would have to go to the bathroom or brew the coffee, dress for work. Then, every fifteen minutes, Rosa's face would float into my consciousness, as if a little door were opened and a tiny Rosa, pretty but indistinct, would walk onto the stage of my consciousness, take a bow, or smile wanly at me, and then go back into her little neuronal room, stuffed among the other debris of my thoughts. I liked this image. Soon Rosa had little strings attached to her boney shoulders, to her legs, and I was the puppet master, at least in my imaginings; the feeling of control was soothing, as if I had walked from the hot sand into the cool, refreshing ocean.

Months passed. I tried not to think about Rosa. There were days when I didn't think of her, but there were days when I didn't think of anything else. I dated a few women, ones I picked out who had at least two of Rosa's features—that was my criteria—hair and eyes, or shape and size, or style of dress and carriage. But these surrogate Rosas felt wrong, facile or empty of what made Rosa unique. A person, after all, is just what she is and nothing else. The cut of her hair, the amount of eye shadow she wore, the shape of her lips, her scent—my nose knew Rosa well, dressed and undressed, perfumed and not—the way she laughed (does she throw her head back? Close her eyes? Giggle or let her sense of humor flash, full bore?). Rosa had tics. She would, for example, keep her watch loose on her thin wrist and, when she needed the gesture or the time she would spin the watch up so that she could read the face of it. Or she would tug at the knee of her dress as she sat (it was hopeless; the dress was too short). Or she would chew her food with a look of enjoyment that I had not seen on the face of a woman before, as if food weren't the enemy of her waistline but something to be savored. Attraction is complex, based as it is on many cues, on little gestures that seem empty when taken out of context, but when allied with a flow of movements and words and flashes of sexuality (the pushing up of hair, the holding of the chin in thought, the half-smile, a slight tug at the ear, that flourish as she brushed a bit of lint off her clothing—the number is infinite) prove irresistible. Unless, of course, the person has nothing to do with you, cares not in the least for the depth of your feeling, sees you as a cipher, an annoyance, invisible.

One morning, after months of yearning for Rosa, I woke up from an especially deep sleep, a dreamless nine-hour hibernation—it was winter—a Saturday—and there she was, perched on the edge of my bed. She looked radiant. She was wearing a white dress, and her hair, longer than it had been when we dated, was unfurled, spread across her shoulders and over her forehead like a benediction. She was smiling. I woke up from a dream—of her, I think—and leaned on my elbow. I was surprised to see her. She said: "Carlton." That was all. Then she leaned forward and kissed me, kissed me deeply, and then lay down on top of me—I could feel her body under the dress, her breasts and stomach pressed against me. I fell back and dreamed her as she gave her body to me.

It seems to me that the wedding was at St. Cecelia's Roman Catholic Church, though apparently there is no such church. It was most likely one of the other large, gothic-looking downtown parishes, probably in South Philadelphia, that part of Philadelphia where Italian Catholics shared alternate blocks with black Baptists. Or we may have been married by a Justice of the Peace at City Center. Yes, I think that's how it was. It was a nice ceremony, with someone, probably one of Rosa's brothers, reading from St. Paul, the business about love and seeing face to face. Our honeymoon week was spent in New York City. We stayed, I think, at the big Hilton at mid-town, near Central Park. I know it was the Hilton because that's where I stay when I go to New York. It's expensive, but worth it. Then we moved into Rosa's apartment. She had the bigger and nicer place. It was on Walnut, I think Walnut near Spruce Hill, so maybe 45th Street. I remember the front porch was newly painted—white, with gray trim—and there were baskets of flowers hanging from the eaves, a couple of nice rocking chairs, and a small charcoal grill—they call them hibachis—on the edge of the porch. I remembered I enjoyed sitting on the right-hand rocker, the one farthest from the neighbor's house, all during that spring and summer we lived together. There were stairs to our apartment—quite a few—and the rooms were light and airy. One thing I remember clearly is the bathtub.

I enjoyed taking long, hot baths, and the tub was one of those where you could comfortably lay down without bending your back in an unnatural way. I could turn the hot water on with my big toe—I remember that distinctly, reheating the water with a few gallons of hot, slipping down into the steaming bath until the water was right up to my lower lip. I spent hours in the tub, with Rosa in the kitchen, doing something, cleaning I think, or having a glass of white wine—she loved white wine, though I never did develop a taste for it. And I'd have the radio on in the bathroom, the window opened a crack, even in winter, to keep the steam from choking me, maybe a book to read if I felt like it. I think Rosa was upset that I spent so much time in the bathroom, but she never said a word to me—she was patient. We worked, I think, at our same jobs. Rosa was employed briefly at an art gallery. That was why she was able to come and go as she pleased, and to dress the way she did. We were happy, most of the time.

What is it about marriage? The intimacy is pleasant at first, but later on becomes difficult. The clothes lying on the chairs, the dirty coffee cups. I remember that Rosa was attentive to me for those first blissful months—*blissful months*—that phrase has a melancholy sound, the sound of what is transitory, passing like the seasons. That was what I learned during my marriage to Rosa, that time is a thief—it takes away what we love. I wore my ring to work and showed my co-workers. They asked if I planned to have a party to celebrate my wedding, but I had no such wish, and I know that Rosa felt as I did. We always agreed; we seldom fought.

Then there was the accident. Something about stepping in front of the trolley. It was quite terrible, as I recall.

I still think of Rosa from time to time. But I learned from my relationship with Rosa that suffering is best avoided through forgetting.

The Hurricane

AGNES HAD BEEN NAMED after a hurricane, which was backwards and odd, but Agnes told anyone who would listen that her mother was like the person in the mirror— "Everything with her is reversed, left is right and right is left." Agnes was pretty backwards herself. She slept most of the day and stayed up most of the night; she was fifteen and had quit school, left home, and started waiting tables—she was fifteen but looked ten years older, not in a worn-out way, but in the way of those kids whose hormones work overtime, the boys with the full beards in high school, the girls whose breasts and hips were womanly at thirteen.

While she had been in school, Agnes had been a wayward child, a D student, not a troublemaker, but friends with the troublemakers. Once she stopped going—and she'd just stopped—she'd taken up reading books and writing and visiting the Art Institute. She had a full set of fake I.D.'s, even a decent birth certificate, but for most part never needed them. She waited tables at The Showcase when she wasn't supposed to be able to walk through the door. But neither Gus nor Tommy doubted her photo ID—the kid looked twenty-three if she looked a day, and she was cute and sassy— "vivacious" was Gus's view—and a sure bet to bring in some business from both the college and dirty-old-man demographic. Anyway, West Philadelphia in late 80s was hardly the most law-abiding place in America—no cops were checking driver's licenses in the bars—for that matter no cops were around to pick up the bodies on the street. "Live and let live" was the mantra west of 30th Street Station, and so Agnes walked out on her mother, rented a room, took a job, and started her life over again, living it just in the way she had imagined she would, doing what she wanted, and when, and with whomever she pleased.

There was a little of the nag in Agnes, a trait she had probably inherited from her mother, who was a world-class nag, the sort of woman who could empty a room with worry, regret, recrimination, and sourness of disposition. Agnes hadn't been able to endure her mother's "ragging on her" but then discovered that she, Agnes, had not only her Mom's red hair but also her fondness for "getting on everyone's case." The thing was Agnes knew better than anyone else. At fifteen, when she should been soaking up the so-called wisdom of her elders, she was dispensing wisdom to friends, co-workers, and strangers alike. After a week on the job, Gus was ready to fire the kid for her officiousness, but she was cute, and already she had three or four tables of regulars—underage kids, but they had good paper—the kind of kids who drink and eat a great deal, pay in cash stolen from their parents' wallets, and make no trouble out of fear of being 86ed. So Gus let Agnes the know-it-all bullshit about the menu, the tap-beer selection, the music on the box, and the art work—Agnes hated Eakins and wanted sports photos, but no way was Gus taking down his beloved art, removing Motown charts from the juke, switching from Miller to Budweiser ("cat piss"), or adding mozzarella sticks and onion rings—"yuppie food"—to his straightforward offering of burgers, fries, and pizza.

"You're making a mistake, Gus," Agnes said, "people in this town love mozzarella sticks and everybody knows Bud is better than Miller."

"Everybody? Who is this everybody? You mean those punks from Penn?"

"They drink a lot Gus, and eat like they're starving. Give them what they want."

"Listen Aggie," Agnes hated to be called Aggie, "I've been in business about as long as you've been alive. One thing I know about bars is once it's working you don't change *anything*. People who go to bars want dependability, the sort of thing you don't get in your job or your marriage. I have regulars, not a bunch of transients who drop in once and never come back. These guys are here night after night, and they want the High Life and my bland pizza. So that's what they get."

And they did. Agnes didn't really care. Her "thing" was being "free" in the sense of "not giving a shit" about anyone else. Maybe there's a gene for selfishness; it's widespread, endemic even, and American, though not only. Agnes went her own way. Once in a while she'd pay attention to what someone was saying, but not often. It was too much trouble to have any real friends, and her boyfriends were always young men who were passing through—Agnes herself appeared to be a person who could vanish in an instant. But she didn't. She came to work six days a week, complained a lot about the clientele, the food, the slow bartenders, the art work, but then went on to do her job with style, as if she were a rock star, a glamorous waitress, a chick with good moves, great hair, a sexy smile, and big teeth. The tips were good and Gus loved-hated her, called her "The best damned pain-in-the-ass waitress he'd ever seen," and they were all pains in the ass as far as Gus was concerned, the cost of doing business, not as bad as drunks and deadbeats, but the next worst thing.

People can get under your skin in all kinds of way. Gus disliked Agnes, and the feeling was mutual, but there was feeling, and like any bit of black dirt in the city, indifference can support life of some kind, however blasted and doomed that life might be. So after three months of being around an annoying, under-aged but oversexed girl—not yet, in Gus's view, a woman—Gus, inching up on forty himself, a bright guy with no pretensions to being anything but what he was, namely a bar owner, a drink mixer, and a confidant to drunks, began to think about Agnes more often than was required, as in, on her days off, asking himself, as if by accident, *I wonder what Agnes is doing today,* or, worse, *I wonder who Agnes is with today?* He wasn't invested enough to feel jealousy, but there was a nibble of that destructive feeling around the edges of his thoughts, an itch he couldn't locate or scratch. Gus was one to say that opposites attract—it's the sort of thing people say to one another in bars and elsewhere when they are trying to make sense of the human heart—but the truth is that what appear to be opposites are often not, what is felt in common is sometimes hidden, but present nonetheless. Gus was as opinionated as Agnes, as stubborn, as drawn to what was then being called "low-level conflict," as in, not many casualties, or not as many as there might be. The first few times that Gus thought of Agnes in an intimate way, that is, as a person and not an employee, he shook off the feeling and laughed at himself for (what he thought of) as his charming way of growing attached to strangers—it's what barkeeps do, after all. After a month though, he began to worry about himself, the state of his feelings. Gus knew enough to understand that attraction is usually a dead end. Most of the time the person you are attracted to won't reciprocate, or, if they do, the attraction, once come to fruition, will prove to have been a mistake. Real love, if there was such a thing, falls into your lap—that was just how Gus put it when asked: "Love? Don't go looking for it; if it comes, it falls into your lap." Which it hadn't, not for Gus or any of the other barflies who bent his ear on the subject of women—it just didn't work that way.

And what did Agnes think of Gus? I hadn't a clue. You never are allowed to look inside the minds of two people at once. I was Gus's friend, sort of, he talked to me, but Agnes never did—why should she? But I can guess what she thought: she wasn't interested. We had no idea back then that Agnes was seventeen, honest to God. And despite the bodies some seventeen-year-olds get (hormones in the milk?), they don't know much about the human heart—you can't know much about the human heart until you've lived. Gus was a big, hairy, gregarious but quick-tempered Irish-Italian blue-collar guy, my type, but not the sort of fellow who would attract a callow person like Agnes.

When I was on the same nights as Agnes she would ignore me—she ignored all of the other girls—but once in a while we'd have a moment, like, she'd ask me for a cigarette or to help take care of a big party, and I'd say yes, and we'd work together, but as soon as the table was cleaned and party was gone we'd go back to our regular way of being, which was—nothing.

Gus was taking longer looks at Agnes all the time. Men think you don't notice, but you do. I wanted to mention to him that she was underage—I thought eighteen or nineteen—but Gus would have been upset with me so I kept my mouth shut.

I knew what Gus was thinking—anyone who has ever been infatuated knows how those in love suffer.

He was wondering what she was thinking, wondering if she thought of him, or, if she did, *what* she thought of him. He was big, on the heavy side: was she thinking he was too big, too heavy? Did she wonder if he were thinking of her—you see the loopiness of this line of speculation, thinking about what someone is thinking about what you're thinking? And what did she look like? Even though Gus saw Agnes nearly daily, when she was out of his sight he couldn't quite capture details—yes, her hair was red and short, but *how* red and *how* short? He wondered if he'd seen her ears—her ears? Gus was surprised at this question which he asked himself day after day—why her ears? Gus was an ass man, going in for hips and the curve of thighs, for a flash of bare abdomen, breasts—of course—a pretty face, vaguely defined as such, might be an afterthought. Agnes wasn't Gus's type in any of the ways women had been his type before—she was pretty, shapely, busty—but when Gus imagined Agnes it was her face, her hair and eyes he tried to conjure up, her ears—were they pierced?

"Hey Tam," Gus had asked me, "you ever notice if Agnes has pierced ears?"

"She does. Why? You going to buy her some earrings?" I was teasing him, but he didn't catch on. He was dead serious.

"Nope, I was just wondering is all. I mean, I know yours are, but you wear your hair back. Hers is like, what, down?"

"Jesus, Gus. Yeah, it's down. I didn't know you were so observant."

Gus gave me a look—it said— "Don't fuck with me" and I knew not to. Gus is a nice person, but he's got a temper. I shut up, but I knew what was going on.

The thing about love that most people don't understand is that it doesn't always appear in the same way—there's isn't one type of love but many, as many as there are people who feel love. We use the same word to cover a million varieties of a feeling that is more elusive than any other. Gus *fell in love* with Agnes, not in the way he'd fallen for his long-lost German girlfriend (Erika?), and not the way, years later, he'd fall in love with Patsy and marry her and have kids. But this thing with Agnes was love. And you *can* love more than one person at a time—no question about it. Our feelings are big and complicated so why pretend otherwise?

Trouble was Agnes didn't even like Gus. I know this because I finally got around to asking her.

"No, I don't like him."

"Why not? He's a good guy."

"So, *you* like him. Doesn't mean I have to."

"You're a hard ass, you know that?"

"What of it?"

"And you're underage. I know it and you know it. But Gus, he's pretending not to, for some reason."

Agnes didn't say anything. She walked into the back and lit a cigarette. There was something not right about her, not her being too young, but the exterior, the anger. I was going tell Gus that she was trouble, to get rid of her, but what business was it of mine? I was a waitress and part-time bookkeeper. I wasn't Gus's wife or mother, or Agnes's friend, so, I let it alone.

There's no better place in the world than a bar for taking the measure of people. A few drinks ease a person's inhibitions. My father never took a drink, though my mother did, once in a while. I can't stand the stuff myself—I take after my father in most ways—I'm quiet, shy, and under control at all times. When I graduated from high school down in D.C. my father thought I should go to college, but I didn't like school, didn't like the rules and sitting still all day, so I started working as a waitress, and then later on I tended bar in Cleveland Park at Four Provinces. It was there that I met my boyfriend Christopher, and, after a year or so we decided to move to Philly since it was cheaper. Christopher was a carpenter, still is I suppose, but where I have no idea—we split up after a couple of months of living together in West Philly. I'm not sure why, or rather I am sure why, but I no longer care. There really is such a thing as "heartache," and I had it for a long while. Now I don't. But I did learn something from my bad experience with Chris, which is—never trust anyone with your heart. Armed with this piece of folk wisdom, I was able to take the measure of the people around me—of Gus and Agnes, of Ned, of that poor guy who lost his kid and ended up stepping in front of the subway in Center City, of Anna and her weirdo friends—all of them mysterious to me, each with their own stories that they would tell you at the drop of a hat. I liked all of them, some more than others, but I never trusted anyone with my own business, never flirted with the teachers or the frat boys who'd slum through on a busy Friday. I was always "that cool customer," or "the quiet one." And that was fine with me, since I liked to listen and wanted nothing more than to go home to my cats and sit in my favorite chair and stare out the big wraparound front window that looked over Clark Park, maybe watch the kids playing if it were light, but mostly it wasn't ever light when I was home, so I'd end up staring into the black glass at my own face, the one that got a little more worn looking each year, but the one I was used to seeing—and I had no other plans than sitting and staring—no place to go, no one to see, and nothing much to do. I was happy living in just this way and would do so, I thought, for as long as they'd let me.

I watched it happen. A train wreck, a two-car collision, with neither person wearing a seat belt. Gus went after Agnes, or rather he let himself get obsessed with her, lost control of his emotions—what is the way of putting it that doesn't sound foolish? —he didn't do the thing that most avails us in matters of the heart—how's that? He made the mistake I made with Christopher, letting down his guard too much, and thereby inviting the kind of cruelty that some people love to inflict. Agnes played him, I'm sure of that.

It was late December, near Christmas, I remember that much, and Gus asked me to go with him to the license hearing. The Showcase had two violations, one over-serve and one underage drinker—that dope Nick who worked ten to two every Saturday had a heavy pour and was too busy chatting up the ladies to look at anybody's ID. And there was a guy from ACB in the place, just for the express purpose of catching Nick, who came with a reputation, serving a drunk that one extra drink that put your business in jeopardy. Gus fired Nick on the spot, the minute the subpoena came in the mail. He picked up the phone and told Nick that if he, Gus, ever saw Nick's ugly face again he'd bust it—and Gus was serious. The fact is, with the loose mob connections that Gus had, he could have done some damage to Nick if he'd wanted, but he wasn't like that. He fought his own fights.

What they make you do is go to the Alcohol Control Board office downtown in the City Hall Annex and attend a hearing. There was no way that The Showcase would lose its license on account of two tickets, but they liked to show you who was boss, and the ACB Director was a political appointee of the Mayor's, an old Army buddy, and he enjoyed busting chops on behalf of the administration. So I tagged along with Gus so he'd have someone to rein him in during the hearing, and somebody to talk to while they kept him waiting half the afternoon for his turn. It was a busy, overcrowded, gray steel and florescent lit hole in the basement of the Annex. The windows opened onto the alley and the air smelled of cigarette smoke and piss. Gus and I were told to take a seat by a clerk who appeared to be half in the bag.

Gus didn't say anything for a while, then he started

asking me questions about the other bartenders—who else might be bending the rules, that sort of thing—then he asked me if I thought Agnes was okay.

I just looked at him for a minute and then I made a mistake and said: "Tell me."

And he did, right there in that crappy bunker of an office. He was half whispering, but I heard every word.

"You've known me, what, four years? Okay, five. And I'm a regular guy, down to earth, head *not* up my ass. Right? But I got to tell you Tam, this girl's got to me. It's chemical. I mean, she's not pleasant, not especially bright, pretty but not my type as far as that goes, but, what can I tell you, I can't stop thinking about her. The way she is—that's what I think about—half the time I can't even see her face, but the way she moves and laughs and even the way she bitches at me—you see what I'm saying? It's as if she weren't a person but a force that's taken me over, like an alien being. I don't sleep well anymore, and when I do fall asleep I dream about Agnes."

I didn't know what to say. I said the only thing that made sense to me.

"Nothing's going to come of it Gus. You've got to see that. She's not even twenty-one, you know that right? She's a kid. And I know for a fact Gus, and I hate to tell you this, but she isn't as crazy about you as you are about her. Okay? Don't make me spell it out."

"I know that. You think I'm stupid? This isn't about her being my girlfriend Tammy, or us going out on a date, or having a conversation—it isn't about anything even slightly in the realm of how men and women get along or don't get along. This isn't even about Agnes. I mean, it is, but not in the way you think. The problem is with *me*. I'm the one who's fallen into a black hole. My feelings aren't *my feelings* anymore. I don't love her Tammy; hell, I don't even like her half the time, but she's done something to me that I can't undo. I don't understand, but there it is, and I'm only telling you because I have to tell somebody and I know you'll keep quiet."

I did keep quiet. But it wasn't easy. I could see Gus falling apart right before my eyes. It got so he wouldn't come to work when Agnes was scheduled—he couldn't stand to see her. I thought about the meaning of "obsession." Never have I felt drawn to anyone strongly enough to distract me—not once. Gus told me—I was now his only confidant, that he wasn't sleeping or eating—he was *ill*, his word, and Agnes was the reason. I told him to fire her, but he said that he couldn't stand to lose the chance to see her, if he could stand to see her, which he couldn't.

Usually when I have a problem with a customer I talk to Gus about it. Billy, the co-owner, is too much the tough guy to waste time on the likes of me. But I couldn't talk to Gus obviously since it was his problem that was bothering me, and the ex-priest had gone off someplace and I didn't trust him, and Ned would listen to me, but he was a creep and not someone I'd trust, and he was in LA last I heard, so I thought of having a little talk with the sad Vet Wallace who everybody called Ace, though not to his face, but I'd promised Gus not to say anything to anybody, so I made up a story about myself that was like Gus's story and sat down at the bar with Ace on a quiet Thursday, late afternoon, just as the sun was setting and the bar was in that sleepy late-afternoon mode where the bartender is polishing glasses and changing the taps and the waitresses are going off for the afternoon, and only a few lonely drinkers are relaxing, enjoying the best time of day, four in the afternoon, the languid hour before the nighthawks are up and the working folks are off, and the morning drunks are back for more. Ace is okay in that burned out way a lot of Vets fall into—staring into space, probably reliving some horrible nightmare from years before, who knows, not drunk—he never drank very much—but

still and pulled into himself, eyes half shut, clearly looking at something I'd never seen.

"Can I ask you something?"

"Depends on what it is."

"I'm going to have to ask and then you tell me if
I can, okay?" I was a little tense. But this Gus thing
had started eating away at me. It occurred to me just
then that I was obsessed with Gus's obsession, which
was weird.

"So ask."

"I have a problem and I need advice."

"And you're asking me? I'm the last person in the
world to give anybody advice. Talk to Gus, he's the
wisest man in this city."

"No can do. Look, it's simple. What do you think
someone should do if he, or she, is in love with someone
who doesn't love him, or her?"

"Do?"

"Behave. Carry on. Get over it. Short of suicide
or alcoholism, how do you get over an obsession with
someone?"

Ace smiled, but not at me. He looked up at the rowers
and made like a pistol with his left hand and shot an imaginary bullet into his head. Then he said, "Who told you?"

"Who told me what?"

"About me. Me and Anna."

I probably looked confused. Ace asked me again, just with his eyes.

"Honest, I didn't know anything about that. I was asking about someone else I know."

Ace smiled and said, "Listen carefully Tammy. '*This arises, that arises.*' Got it?"

"No. What's that supposed to mean? What is that, like a riddle?"

"Yup. How do we end suffering Tammy? How do we stop the hurt? You feel it, or your imaginary friend feels it; I feel it, hell, half the people in here any time of day or night feel it. They're hurting. They lost someone—a child or a wife or a lover. Or maybe they never had any of those things to begin with and they want it—they want a person to love them, or a baby, or decency. Anyway, the answer is the one I heard one time, a long way from here: '*This arises, that arises,*' meaning, I guess, that life goes on, and you go on or you don't. You jump off a building or shoot yourself in the head or take too many pills. But most of us just keep living. Simple, isn't it?"

I didn't say anything. What could I say? Ace pulled a five dollar bill out of his jacket pocket, put it on the bar, gave me a tight smile and a bump on the shoulder, spun on his stool, and walked out the door.

Part II

Dancing Lesson

Right around the third time my mother asked my father to move out, Mom decided that I needed to take dancing lessons. I was just twelve, it was summer, and I had been wasting a lot of time hanging around the house, working just three days a week as an umbrella boy at Loch Arbor Beach, and doing a little boxing on Saturdays at the Boys Club. My father had introduced me to the "sweet science," and while I didn't much care for getting hit, I did enjoy the adrenaline rush of sparring, dodging a punch, and occasionally landing a soft left (we wore twenty-ounce gloves) on the cloth helmet of one of my buddies from the neighborhood. Pop had done some fighting while in the Army—flyweight—and he taught me footwork, how to jab, and a couple of basic combinations. He was a small man, five-five and maybe one-twenty, but he was tough—he drove a truck for the county road department—and, unfortunately, he was also tough at home, with my mother. We're an Irish-German family, my mother's mother having been born in Munich. Grandma was a large woman, loud and fond of vinegary cabbage, fatty meat, and ice tea. My father's family was Irish, but I never knew his parents—his old man had run off right after Pop was born, and his mother, of whom I have one indistinct memory (a frail old lady staring out the window on Cookman Avenue on a rainy day), died when I was six years old. Anyway, Irish and German, lots of tempers and often too much to drink, and a Catholic preoccupation with sin whose principle effect is a lot more sinning, as if life were a curse that had to be fulfilled. Pop drank too much, but he wasn't a violent drunk—in fact, he'd calm down after a whiskey or two, stretch out on the ratty old couch in our living room and doze off. But Pop did like other women, and Mom was a tight-fisted, jealous person who was always accusing my father of "spending every last dime on some floozy," which, who knows, he might have been, but now I suspect he didn't do much more than smile at women he thought were attractive and maybe buy one or two a drink at Flanagan's Bar, his favorite place right there on Ocean Avenue.

Our neighborhood was what came to be called "ethnic," meaning all-white, all Catholic, all working class. Later on, in the late sixties, a black family moved into a bungalow down the block, and aside from some nasty comments (which I didn't hear, but which were reported to me by my sister) from Mr. Bascom, our next-door neighbor—a legless ex-Marine who hadn't a good word to say about anybody—everyone felt fine about having the neighborhood "integrated." We reserved our rancor for our "betters," for the rich people who lived on the other side of town, whose lawns I cut in the summer, and onto whose doorsteps I tossed the *Home News* on Thursday afternoons all through my youth. Black people were fine because they were poor; what upset my father was that there were people in our town who had a lot of money but "never worked a day in their lives." That was his term of disapproval; "working" meant sweating, being outside in bad weather, and not having soft hands. "That Bill Markel, I bet his hands are *soft as a girl's*" was something my father might say at dinner after having a disagreement with a guy at the motor vehicle division. Men in ties and jackets, even if they made a miserable two grand a year, which is what Pop made with the road department, were no good since they "dressed like monkeys" and "sat around an office all day." My father's resentments were broad and simple, but I don't know if they ran that deep. The truth was he got along with almost everybody—the guy at the bank who lent us the money to replace our roof, the Jewish man who ran the local pharmacy, heavy-set Mr. Siliato at whose little pizzeria we ate every Friday night—Pop hated fish and loved spaghetti—and the folks in the neighborhood, mostly Irish and Italian, who he might refer to as "dopes" but with whom he would play bocce and drink Rheingold on summer evenings, people whose walks he'd help shovel on snowy days, the people whose kids attended the same public school as me, with whom I played baseball and basketball, the kids who boxed at the Boys' Club of Asbury Park. This was the world I grew up in, blue collar and full of large passions—some hatreds, some odd affections, many friendships and some feuds that ran as deep as blood. My mother didn't like our street; she hoped I'd be different from my father, more sensitive maybe, capable of finding my way to an undefined, but somehow better life. It was these ill-defined hopes of my mother's that led to my taking dancing lessons.

Mr. Musto was a professional dancer. That's what Mom told me, though I had no idea what a professional dancer did, aside, of course, from dancing. But where? And to what purpose? I didn't ask. Mr. Musto wore pastel-colored slacks and coppery Nehru jackets and always kept a hankie in his top front pocket. He had reddish-brown hair—lots of it—and he wore tap shoes, or at least shoes that made tapping sounds as he moved, quite gracefully, across the linoleum floor of our finished basement. He wasn't the sort of man you would think my father would like, and yet my father adored Mr. Musto—did he have a first name? I never heard it—adored him because he was affordable, a "snazzy dresser," and "sophisticated," meaning he was a good dancer who was willing to come to our run-down row-house every Saturday afternoon to give lessons to half a dozen pre-teen boys for an insignificant amount of money. Looking back , I realize that Mr. Musto was probably one of those down-on-the-heels types who orbited our lives back then—the man who came around with a little cart and sharpened our knives, the black men who came each autumn to the back door to ask my mother if they might, please, rake our leaves for a dollar (she always said yes and gave them two); the grown men who shoveled sidewalks at the houses of the war widows, the tattered house painters and Italian ice salesmen, and a real junkman who bought and sold anything metal from a hand-cart. We lived, my mother and father and sister and I, on the margins—on the edge of town, on the edge of the neighborhood, right where the oldest houses gave way to the woods and the lake, where better-off people might dump tires and batteries and rusted-out appliances at midnight; the kind of place where feral dogs chased (and once caught, with predictable consequences) my mother's cats and, never satisfied, then burrowed in our trash for dessert. Mr. Musto seemed to my mother the intimation of something better or at least something less run-down and hopeless than what she had come to expect.

My mother and father had loved to dance. In their better days, before the War, they would take the bus downtown to the Berkeley-Carteret and dance to Tommy Tucker's Orchestra, to Benny Goodman when he came to the Convention Hall, to Duke Ellington's great ensemble at the Casino—a night my mother spoke of with longing, "it was magical" she told me, Ellington's big band there in Asbury Park, one night only, and my father, not yet my father, had borrowed five dollars from his aunt to get in and paid fifty cents—fifty cents!—for two ginger ales to go along with four hours of the Lindy and Fox Trot and Jitterbug. My father was a fine dancer—a nice-looking man, athletic and slender, a good dresser, and my mother was the prettiest woman in the neighborhood, all my friends said so. And yet, by the time I was old enough to pay attention to my mother's appearance, she and my father had grown apart, had come, at last, to despise one another.

Or did they? How little we know of those we love the most. They fought, certainly, but what did they say to one another late at night in their narrow bed when my sister and I were asleep? Did they make love and weep as they recalled the angry words they had spoken over dinner? Did my father promise to do better? When he would leave, the routine was always the same: he appeared in the living room with his small cardboard suitcase; he would tell me and my sister Margaret that he was "going away for a while" and that we should be good to one another and to "your mother." He always called her that, and I never liked it; it sounded too formal—"your mother" a functional description that left out all the important parts of our lives. Anyway, he'd look contrite, pathetic with his satchel of clothes, a cigarette perched in the corner of his mouth (as always). He would come over to the couch and give me and my sister a peck on the cheek, a tousle of the hair, and then he was gone. He had to leave the car for Mom, so I don't know what he did, where he stayed or who took him to work. I know he worked because we never went hungry, even when he was in exile for months at a time. He always took care of us, and I have no idea at what cost to his own happiness.

Even when Pop was gone we'd have our dancing lessons. Mr. Musto came on the bus, which would drop him down the hill from our house. I dreaded dancing, so I'd sit in the window and pray that he wouldn't show up—but he always did, week after week, for almost a full year. When I saw him I had to run next door to get Billy, whose mother was a war widow and whose son, my best friend, was a sad bookish boy, my opposite in most ways, but good in just the way my mother wanted me to be, in a way I could never dream of being. And then the two of us walked across the narrow lane to get Stuart, a blind kid who loved music and dancing and at that time had less than a year to live—and Kenny, on the other side of Deal Road, a kid who didn't hang out with us but whose Mom had persuaded my Mom to let him come over to learn the cha cha and tango and waltz.

Our family clung tenaciously to the lower reaches of the middle class; we were the only people on the block who had a finished basement—knotty pine walls, drop ceiling, linoleum floors, and a wet bar. Thus the dance lessons were at my house, which was a great burden for my mother and a source of embarrassment for me, especially since I had to explain to my friends that my father was "away on business," which was a terrible lie. I often lied about my parents, saying that my father was in the hospital or visiting his (dead) father in Buffalo—divorce was unheard of in the Catholic neighborhoods where I grew up, and Mom told me never to lie, but seemed not to want me to tell the truth either. So I lied. Lying was at first painful, then routine, and at last, after years of spinning fables about my father's long absences, lying became a part of my nature, to the extent that I would lie about my father even on those occasions when he was at home.

So each Saturday afternoon, Mr. Musto would walk up the hill and ring the doorbell. I would let him in and take his coat, which was blue and, my mother told me, "cashmere," and ask if he wanted a coke or a glass of water—he always said no. And then he would follow me downstairs into the dampness of the basement and greet Kenny and Billy and Stuart. Mr. Musto was especially kind to Stuart. He would shake our hands, one after another, and then give Stuart a hug. Mom said this was because Mr. Musto knew that blind people like a lot of physical contact—how she knew this, or how Mr. Musto came to have insights into Stuart's needs and desires, was beyond me. Stuart was a quiet and polite boy, whose face was always turned upward and who clicked his tongue constantly, as if were a bat using vibrations to locate himself in the immense and hostile world he lived in. We never talked about his being blind. I never asked him how he felt about it—he'd gone blind as a baby after a bout of measles—and I never wondered for a moment what it was like for him to navigate the five square blocks of our neighborhood. I wasn't insensitive, but it was impossible for me to allow the thought of blindness to cross my mind. This was in the days before handicapped parking or bathrooms, or cuts in the curbs or braille numbers in the elevators or any other kind of consideration for blindness or for those who had been crippled by polio—there were three such children in my neighborhood—two small girls and an older boy—polio vaccine was still a year or two off, and each summer my mother would warn me in the most solemn terms never to go swimming in the lake for fear that I would "grow up a cripple." Even the word "disabled" was nonexistent; we said "crippled" and never cringed. Anyway, I always did swim in the lake— we all did—and many summer nights I would lie in bed feeling my legs grow numb as the disease worked its way up toward my spine. I was more afraid of polio and of going blind than I was of ghosts or nuclear bombs or even communists.

But my legs never grew numb enough so that I couldn't learn the cha cha with Mr. Musto. He brought his own records in a black leather case—it looked like a handbag, and Kenny giggled about Mr. Musto having a "purse," but what could he do? My parents had a Victrola—a big white maple box with one small speaker that played 78's and 45's and 33's, but we only owned six records, including the soundtrack to *South Pacific*, which my mother had seen with her mother and whose songs she would hum or sing all day long as she did laundry or ironed my father's undershirts or cooked our meals—"I'm Gonna Wash That Man Right Outa My Hair," and she did, every six months, like clockwork, as if she were Mary Martin and my father, who reeked most days of tar and grime from patching county roads, was the exotic French plantation owner Nellie had to forget (I read the synopsis on the record jacket about fifty times). Two Glenn Millers, a Tommy Tucker, and a Guy Lombardo rounded out the collection—no cha cha's or tangos or even a decent waltz—so Mr. Musto would unpack his Tito Puente and Ernesto Duarte and Facundo Rivera discs and drop the needle and we'd be off. First he'd show us the steps on his own—"one two, cha *cha* cha"—and he'd swing his hips and smile and put his right hand on his stomach and hold his left hand up in the air as if Chiquita Rivera were right there dancing with him....then it would be our turn.

Mr. Musto would take my hand and pull me out into the middle of the room and have me count aloud as I shuffled through the steps like Bela Lugosi—I was mortified—and then Mr. Musto would take my hips in his hands and rock them back and forth all the while counting and saying "Feel it, *feel it* in your body!" My buddies would be smiling ruefully—their turn would come. And pretty soon the four or five of us would be moving around the black slippery floor, ignoring the music entirely, half enjoying ourselves, half embarrassed by the attention Mr. Musto was paying to our awkward movements, wondering perhaps why we were spending a sunny Saturday pretending to dance when we could have been playing basketball up at the Hurley's or, if it were dead winter, skating on the lake. Mr. Musto never took the time to explain the point of dancing, or to defend what must have appeared even to him to be such a pointless waste of an afternoon. He just danced.

After a half hour or so the upstairs door would open and my mother, dressed as always in high heels and stockings and a nice "house dress," would descend the stairs with a tray full of cookies and a pitcher of lemonade. Her hair was burnished red-brown and she wore just a hint of lipstick. She would smile at Mr. Musto and ask if "the boys" had worked up an appetite, and we would say that, yes, we had, and be grateful for the opportunity to eat and clown around for a few minutes before the ordeal of the tango began.

Then, on a quiet Saturday afternoon in the middle of February, a day or a week or a month after my father had once again left us, my mother arrived in the midst of Tito's *El Cayuco* (or something like it) without the tray and the cookies and big blue ceramic pitcher of hand-squeezed lemonade. Instead she stood at the base of the stairs, one hand on the railing, one hand smoothing back her hair, and watched as Stuart and I moved in half twirls and, to the best of our twelve-year-old ability, swayed our hips in time to the conga drum. She watched and she smiled at me, and then she turned her smile—it was a lovely smile—at Kenny and Billy as they followed behind us, the four of us moving almost in time with the music—*one, two, cha, cha, cha*—and then, from Tito's horn section, a blast of trumpets and his voice rising behind the brass in a staccato cadence, *cha, cha, cha,* the sound, as I imagined it, of warm sun and a white beach like the one I had visited with my mother and father—before Margaret was born—on Key West, an island so remote that in those days you took a boat to get there. Just then I *did feel* the music; I closed my eyes and put my arm on Stuart's waist—it was odd, but at that moment everything felt right. I was dancing.

And when I opened my eyes I saw my mother dancing with Mr. Musto, not the cha cha, but some slower dance, one that required Mr. Musto to have his arm around my mother's slender waist in a way, I thought, that looked calm and natural. Mr. Musto was leading my mother in small circles around the edge of our finished basement—he was as graceful as ever. The song ended, the needle swung across the empty vinyl and rose with a mechanical whirl back to its resting place. But Mr. Musto and my mother kept moving—dancing— and the only sound was the light tapping of Mr. Musto's shoes and the rustle of my mother's dress. My mother's eyes were closed, and I could see that she was crying.

Orlando Awakens

Ten miles north of Abiquiu, and ten more miles west on a dusty, unpaved road, at the end of the road and perched between an arroyo and a flat pan of sandstone and chalk, there is a lovely monastery, a place to find God if one is in search of Him, or perhaps a place to lose the world if it has become burdensome. The grounds contain a small, self-sufficient dairy farm, a dormitory for the dozen monks in residence, half a dozen tiny *casitas*—sparsely furnished cottages—and a stuccoed chapel whose bell tower leans into the azure blue and cloudless sky on a cold November morning. There isn't a sound in the compound; even the cows have taken a vow of silence. At Laud, just before dawn, as Orlando awakens, the monks recite the fiftieth psalm. Orlando has slept outside his *casita* so that he when he awoke during the night he would be enveloped by the great curving ring of the Milky Way. The male voices, a soft drone in the freezing air, stir something in Orlando, but he isn't able to identify the feeling. He sits up and pulls the coarse woolen blankets around his head—it is colder than he expected, and when he arrived at St. Thomas Monastery a week before he was surprised to see snow on the beavertail cactus and squat piñons.

Orlando gets to his feet and stumbles through the dark to the chapel. He doesn't go in, but he sits on the front steps and listens to the recitation of the psalms. He knew them well at one time, but much of what he once knew has been forgotten. His quarrel with God may be over, or the hostilities may have been temporarily suspended, but in any case, the Latin words he had loved as a younger man now evoke only a vague nostalgia, a feeling he mistrusts. Renouncing God had been easy; giving up on the culture of belief—the comforting rituals and baroque emotions—much more difficult. What better place to cure oneself of faith than at this austere Carmelite monastery?

When he had written to the prior, asking permission to visit St. Thomas, to take up residence for an unspecified period, Orlando had debated with himself as to the wisdom of misrepresenting his motives. Most visitors, the monastery's literature proclaimed, came to St. Thomas on a spiritual retreat, to deepen their faith, to test their vocation, to ease the burdens of their lives in the world. The Abiquiu site was pristine, isolated, silent and austere. The natural beauty could help one "to feel the workings of the Divine in the world and in themselves." Orlando knew that to be relieved of the burden of belief—the debilitating disease of his life, a crippling form of self-regard and self-delusion—he would have to confront the source of his despair directly, much as a patient in analysis must dredge up the trauma that had made him ill as the first step on the path to purgation and cure. Orlando thought that the metaphors of psychoanalysis worked perfectly, and that in his case they served a dual purpose: he required both the purgation of faith and the excavation of his past as a means of relieving the unease he felt. As he shivered on the chapel steps, he listened to words that still touched him: *Wash me clean.* Orlando knew that he had been seduced when he a boy, not physically but spiritually violated, convinced of his sinfulness to such an extent that he came to hate his own body and the desires he could not repress. The sweet rising baritones, perhaps forgetting how music can mock lyric, rose up through the weak morning light: *Redde mihi laetitiam salutaris tui—restore to me the joy of your salvation.* Orlando remembered the weakness he felt as he knelt each night on the side of his bed, the wooly feeling of the blanket on his face as he buried his shame in tears—*if I die, if I die.* He was ten, eleven years old, devoted to his mother and father, to his brother and sister, dutiful toward and afraid of the gray-faced nuns and priests at Holy Spirit, afraid of dying when he had no idea what dying meant, sick unto death of the flesh when he had felt nothing from it but aching and the cramping of his limbs as he prayed, sending words into the void, night after night, asking to be cleansed of sin, to be clean, to be pure. Seduction and abandonment, and then years of hiding from what he no longer believed, then the symptoms which follow from secrecy—the lies and betrayals, loving oblivion more than life, wanting, near the end of his spiritual crisis, to die.

Orlando shuddered with the memory. He got up from the chapel steps and threw off the coarse blanket, making his way down past his *casita* and into the emptiness of the desert. He loved the clarity of this place. In the East he felt claustrophobic, stumbling from his apartment to his job among crowds of people whose sheer numbers and mass weighed on him like the lowering sky. He lived stacked up in a high rise, twelve floors up, surrounded by a thousand strangers. When he spoke to someone in his building or at the school where he taught Latin and German, he watched himself as he might watch a newsreel—he imagined himself at all times as a man in suit and hat, formal and decorous, with 'old world manners' as his grandmother would say, polite and detached, perhaps like Heidegger in the twenties, before his madness, but always as someone who wasn't quite there, living in the present, having this conversation. He would sit at home in the evening in his chair holding a book and feel desire rise out of his skin like sweat—not desire for anything, only a kind of undirected will, or a yearning for someone to come and sit with him and speak to him about the most trivial subjects. He felt himself losing interest in his job and surroundings, in other people, in his students. At work he hid in his office whenever he could, and he came to resent the interruptions that his position imposed on him. It wasn't that he had anything better to do. He wasn't reading very much, or at least he wasn't reading with any object in mind, nor was he teaching well, as he once had—in fact he'd started showing movies to his language students, excusing the irresponsible practice by telling the docile children it was a way of improving their comprehension. Students would put their heads on their desks when the lights were dimmed and Fassbinder's *Die Bitteren Tränen der Petra von Kant* would begin, yet again. Orlando played the film over and over, without subtitles, and several parents lodged complaints with the chairman of his department, not because of the film's psychotic subject matter but because their children had complained of the difficulty of the language. Orlando gave up on the film after a stern warning from Dr. Channa and began to show his students episodes of German-language cartoons instead. It didn't matter. He simply couldn't continue to prepare lessons and speak out loud or even sit in the narrow stuffy room with the lights on. He was living, he knew, in a cave of his own devising, uneasy, not fully understanding why.

Here in the desert Orlando felt himself disappear. It was comfortable to be swallowed up in the immensity of the Sonora, and as he walked among the rabbit bush and cholla, he imagined this ocean of sand, once the bed of an actual ocean, imagined it stretching south into Mexico, into the graveyards full of women outside Juarez, the black sky now lightening on the bones of dead.

—Is your visit meeting your expectations?

—Are your accommodations adequate?

—Does the refractory meet your needs?

—Have you found opportunities for meditation and prayer?

In a silent world the questionnaire must suffice, and one
of them appeared in the small mailbox outside his casita
each morning. Orlando ignored them. He wrote on the
back of the first that he would appreciate an opportunity to meet privately with the prior sometime before
the end of his visit, but he had thus far heard nothing.
After his morning walk in the desert he retreated to his
cabin to wash his face and then walked to the refractory
for coffee and a roll. There were half-a-dozen retreate-
ants on hand, sitting one to a table, scattered around the
tiny dining room, hunched over their meagre breakfasts,
praying or reading. Three of the men were in Orders;
one was a Franciscan who wore his brown robe as he
sipped tea, and the other two were probably Domincans.
There was a Buddhist monk whose shaved head and
thick glasses reminded Orlando of the Dali Lama, and
two lay women, both younger and more attractive than
Orlando would have liked. He nodded to each of the
six in turn as he gathered his food. It would have been
pleasant to sit with one of the women and to chat about
the beauty of the day, but their brisk way of moving and
downcast looks precluded any sort of approach. The
only words he had exchanged since he arrived were with
the Buddhist monk, a Nepalese whose person radiated

calm, or so it seemed to Orlando, until he thought that perhaps he was wrong and what he took for serenity was nothing more than uneasiness with a language that was as odd and uncomfortable as these immense flat spaces. In any case, Daya spoke, monosyllabically, to Orlando, saying how he was *so please* to be here, and *interest to know Jesus*, a desire he thought would follow naturally from the clarity of the sky. Orlando, who knew something about Buddhism—not much of course, but then he could comfort himself with the thought that knowing anything at all was better than ignorance, that the shroud of unknowing had never been to his liking—was able to coax from Daya a few words about *dukkha*, the deeply paradoxical Buddhist view that life is suffering.

—It is change that make us suffer, said Daya.

—But change is all that there is. Nothing remains the same, ever.

Daya smiled and nodded, yes. Orlando found this exchange either infuriating or illuminating, he wasn't sure which; it was as if he were the disciple of a Zen master who had revealed that the tea was tea and then slapped him across the face. Then again, maybe what eluded Orlando was the fixed thing, the still Archimedian point Descartes used to break up the logjam of the suffocating self. Was it change that made us unhappy? Certainly this hurtling toward death tinged every joy with the aroma of decay—the scent of the desert after a brief shower, hints of rosemary and warm sand, the rustle of raven wings overhead, all of life stirred Orlando, but the sensation passed in the sparse time it took for the rain to evaporate or for the ravens to disappear from sight. As he got older, Orlando knew that he clung more tenaciously to his rituals, and that much of the dislike he felt for the idea of God was rooted in the sense that what had been at his core had melted away—evaporated—in the glare of his adult life. So: *dukkha* it was. Then what would he do to overcome his remorse—if remorse was the word for what he felt? Orlando had no intention of asking a Buddhist monk for the answer to this question since he knew already what the answer would be.

Two weeks before Orlando had left Philadelphia for Albuquerque and Abiquiu in his Ford Focus he had flown to Florida to oversee the cremation and internment of his mother. She had died a month before, died, in fact, in her son's presence, but probate court had held matters up for so long that Mrs. Lisele, who had lived alone for thirty years and never compromised her belief that, having raised three difficult children, and forborne an alcoholic and adulterous husband, she was now entitled to live as she wished, had been forced to lie encased in a freezer at Goldman's Funeral Home on East Fifth Street in St. Petersburg, a town she swore she would leave before the end of her life. So much for wishes. Orlando's mother's life had been replete with disappointments and tragedies, and he felt the injustice of her cancer deeply— surely this quiet woman who wished only to watch soap operas and do the *St. Petersburg Times* crossword might have been spared a little longer the indignity of death. Nothing doing. God, in His Eternal Wisdom, couldn't do without the old woman who had been good enough to pack Orlando's lunch for twelve years, to take his temperature rectally for a decade, to listen to his complaints about his father and brother, to bear with his mediocre academic achievements, his defrocking after a year in Holy Orders, his alcoholism. The truth was, Mrs. Lisle, Polly, was too good for Orlando, and when he sat with her over that final weekend, a cruelly bright winter Saturday and Sunday, knowing even as they reminisced that he would never see her alive again, he was ashamed of the burden he had been, and would have apologized for his life if such a thing were not unseemly. In the Lisle family no one ever apologized, or thought about such things as shortcomings, or took any steps that interfered with the rituals of daily life. Orlando's father had been a captain in the Air Force when he married Polly, and after he returned from Okinawa, instead of going to college on the GI Bill or taking the train to New York to sell stocks or insurance, he kept the uniform, moved from captain to major to colonel, and drove each morning for twenty years to McGuire Air Force Base in the depressed heart of central New Jersey, to a ramshackle collection of quonset huts thrown up during the war, and worked as a liaison officer with the other services during the dull time between Hiroshima and Rolling Thunder. It was a tedious life, or at least Orlando imagined it so, allergic as he believed he was to uniforms and discipline and the uptight regimentation that so attracted his father.

Orlando hadn't loved his father. The old man knew it and didn't care. Or so it seemed now, thirty years later. Perhaps his father had adored him and Orlando had broken the old man's heart. Anything is possible when people don't speak, and Orlando wondered, not for the first time, who came up with the backward notion that silence was allied with sanctity. He was inclined to believe that the opposite was the case, *blessed are the garrulous,* those who hunger to speak their minds and take the time to listen as others unburden themselves. Orlando distrusted silence, though he was inclined toward it all his life. His first, his only, girlfriend had seldom spoken. Soon after they met and agreed to try living together, during their days in graduate school at Amherst, Samantha had whittled her communications with Orlando to the nub. She was, ironically, studying speech therapy, or maybe it wasn't ironic at all, perhaps her fixation on the things that go wrong with our voices caused her to renounce speaking, in the way medical students suffer the diseases they study. Samantha spoke to Orlando with such parsimony that he began to count her words—long autumn weekends would pass, with maple leaves ablaze and air ripe with maturing tobacco and Canada geese rising like gray stones from the pond that rimmed their apartment complex when Sam (she shortened her name, for obvious reasons) wouldn't break a hundred. On their and first and last Thanksgiving together, S, as Orlando took to calling his abbreviated girlfriend, now a waif whose stature had shrunk over the nine months of their monastic cohabitation, as if she were hoping to disappear like Sogdian or some dialect of Navaho, spoke not a word for the entire day. She nodded and gestured, and Orlando wondered if she were ill or going deaf. As it turned out S had a lover in the theatre department, a person Orlando had met at a party, a large woman whose syntax and diction were considered the equal of Sir Lawrence Olivier's, a language prodigy. So S had been saving her words, hoarding them for the evenings she claimed to be in speech therapy lab. Orlando wasn't as upset as he might have been—he didn't love S enough to marry her—but he grew to mistrust silence, to find it less a sign of profundity and more akin to dumbness.

Moving like ghosts through the early morning light, the monks and friars and nuns seemed to Orlando to be self-engrossed, wrapped up in the struggle to overcome the world and their own flesh, their silence an emblem of pride rather than modesty.

Later in the morning, after his meditation and reading—Orlando was flipping through his *Selected Kierkegaard*, thinking that this was just the book to cure him of any lingering belief in God, but he couldn't read more than a page or two before his attention wandered. Orlando knew he had never been a knight of faith. As a child, living in a pious Catholic home, prayer, Bible reading, confession of sins and regular attendance at Mass had been expected. Nothing could deter his mother from her devotions, and Orlando went along

to church on Sundays and Wednesdays and Fridays—
there was always some minor saint requiring worship,
a feast day no other Catholic had heard of, a talk given
by a visiting Jesuit. Orlando found every day pitched to
unbearable piousness: if everything were sacred, what
was profane? How many sins did he have to confess,
how many rosaries could he bear to recite? Repetition
was sanctity, or so Orlando's mother thought. His father
seldom attended church and spoke disparagingly of his
wife's overheated devotion. His father's unprincipled
disapproval, not of religion, but of his wife, was enough
to drive Orlando to even more arduous expressions of
faith, the Catholic Church a kind of black hole, an
emptiness that could never seem to be filled.

And so it was here: Christ in the Desert. Really?
And where, Orlando wondered, was He? There were
hawks and juncos and shy little prairie dogs, but no
sign of the Son of Man. He read about Abraham and
Isaac, the great leap into faith, the lovely absurdity of
belief. Orlando had been fortunate in his education.
He'd had good teachers, access to a library, motiva-
tion to be someone other than his father. He'd read
Hegel and understood how objective truth had given
way to the yearnings of the self. He was no stranger
to Kant's view of transcendental apperception—from

time to time Orlando caught himself watching himself watch himself, as if he were a figure in an Escher print or stuck in the narrow room where Vermeer apparently had spent his life. He was a reflection of someone else, a thinking thing, a substance made up of accidents, trapped in the cave—he took his time picking through the choices offered by philosophers and others he admired—bourgeoise man, an Oedipal basket case, creative unconsciousness. But in the end he was just Orlando Bascom Lisle, a young man named after a horrid town in Central Florida, a lapse in parental judgment, a child who should never have been conceived, half-loved and half-regretted. On her deathbed, Orlando's mother had mentioned her fondness for his brother and sister—neither was present at that moment—but neglected to mention how grateful she was that only one child was there to watch her arch her back, tear at her hair, and rasp through her final seconds in this world. Philosophy was of no help at such moments; no book offered real insight into the crude details of someone's dying—the stained undergarments, the look of terror. Orlando's education had served him well, had put food on his table and a roof over his head, but it had been worthless in all of the ways that counted most.

After dipping into *Fear and Trembling* and taking another walk—it was mid-morning, and the sky dropped light like rain on the little cul-de-sac of the monastery grounds. Orlando could make out the beams in the rising dust and against the white sandstone cliffs—he returned to his *casita* to find a neatly folded bit of newsprint on which was printed a tidy invitation to tea with the Prior at 11 a.m. And what did he have to say to the Reverend? It had seemed like a good idea to exchange words with a holy man, but now Orlando wondered if he should bother. It was a long drive back East, the weather was invigorating, the solitude a delight. Why diminish the simple pleasures of a monastic life—one without commitment or vows—by thinking too deeply about the reasons he was here?

The prior had a tiny office in the monastic dormitory. The floor was red sandstone. The walls were bare except for a small bookcase that contained, apart from what Orlando thought of as the standard devotional works—a Latin Bible and hymnal, the *Oxford Bible Commentary* (well thumbed), the *Rule of St. Benedict*, a couple of books by Karen Armstrong, the life of Jesus by Jack Miles, the abridged *Summa Theologiae*, and Butler's *Lives of the Saints*—half a dozen detective mysteries by Ralph McInery, a collection of poems by Wallace Stevens, and a book about Georgia O'Keefe. A small table was set with bread and fruit; there were cups of steaming tea.

The prior was perhaps eighty, deeply browned and creased by the sun. His wispy hair was the color of the mesa top, salt white, and his clothing—jeans and a work shirt—made him look like an alfalfa farmer. The only sign that he was a priest—had been for fifty-five years—was a tiny wooden cross tied with a bit of black string around his neck.

Orlando stood and bowed his head, foolishly, not knowing whether he should put out his hand or genu-flect. The prior trailed a sort of quiet power behind him, as if he were just risen from the dry river bed, a soul sent to comfort the afflicted cobbled from the barren earth. He didn't smile, but he seemed to be amused by something. Orlando had seen this look before on holy people, a look of ironic bemusement at the perplexities of the world, or of a blessed relief that he, the good padre, wasn't someone else, someone freighted with a wife and children and a real job, a sense that all he had to do was appear holy and others would acquire some elusive grace they desperately needed. His wry smile seemed to say—*I can't help you but let's go through the motions.* At least this was the thought that flitted through Orlando's head as he stood to receive—yes, here it came—an airy Latin blessing, a quick sign of the cross applied by the pink, callused fingers of the prior, just like the parting shot in Church—*ite missa est*—or the all-purpose nod to the vast emptiness that divided the material from the invisible. Orlando almost ducked. He didn't want to be crossed or sprinkled with water, or to confess his many egregious sins, or to go in peace. He wanted, he thought, not peace at all, but the sword. He yearned not for a blessing or tranquility but for turmoil, for the tearing out of his soul so that he could examine it dispassionately and discover, if it were possible, what disquieted him.

He prayed that the old man, who vaguely resembled his Uncle Herb, wouldn't offer a ring to be kissed or an embrace or call him "son." Instead Father Walters lowered himself into a stiff, functional-looking chair and swiveled around to look at Orlando. He pointed to the other, even less inviting seat and said, 'sit.' But he surprised Orlando at once.

—You have grave doubts and you have come here to resolve them. Don't say anything, please. This isn't the place to clear up your doubts or to renew your faith. What does that word, *faith* mean? I prefer those who come for some peace and quiet and a bit of vacation from their hectic lives. In my two decades here I have never met a man or a woman who found God in the desert. Can you understand that?

—No.

—What do you suppose God is?

—I don't know. I'd hoped you could tell me.

—Why?

—Why? I had that hope because you are a priest. And, if you mean why don't I know what the word means I would have to say that it is currently my view that no one does. No one. Those who proclaim knowledge of the divine are liars.

—Because there is no God?

—No, not that. Because the word has no meaning, and when people speak of God they are always speaking of something else.

—But?

—But Father, forgive me, God exists in a place that neither you nor I can comprehend. I *am* a believer, Father, and you are wrong if you think I came here so that I could believe with greater conviction. My conviction is complete. No. I am here to learn how to disbelieve, how to divest myself of the burden of God.

—I think I understand.

Father Walters poured himself a cup of tea and took a bit of bread. He looked away from Orlando, out the small window toward the chapel. Orlando followed his gaze and saw a rookery—was that the word?—of ravens had settled on the chapel roof and were complaining about the kind of things that ravens disliked.

—Do you? Do you really? Orlando didn't want to lose the thread of the conversation. He needed information.

—Yes. You and I are not so different from one another. I knew who you were from your letter of application. You wrote that your life was being undermined by feelings that you couldn't describe, of anxiety, and then you wrote, *I feel myself being overtaken by the contingent in life and yearn for a return to the eternal.* That's right isn't it?

—I didn't mean it. I wanted to come, that's all. That isn't my feeling, not at all.

—Can I tell you something? Not one us, not a single one of the brothers residing in this place believes in the way that word is used; we don't 'affirm' anything. God isn't what you think, or what I think. He's nothing. Nothing at all. We think nothing isn't important, but it—nothing—is important. Nothing is where any thought or hope can reside. It isn't already filled with the noise and the clutter of the world. God is an empty shell into which we pour our paltry human desires.

—No, that isn't right. He *is* something. He's us. Not *in us*, but *us*. It took me forever to see this clearly. And now that I do, I can't bear to think that my self, my inner being, isn't me at all but him.

—So, what? You came here to kill God?

—To kill myself.

—But why? You don't mean that in the normal way.

—The normal way?

—A gun to the head.

—I don't own a gun.

—Then, what?

—To kill the voice inside me that isn't mine.

—Augustine and Kant thought that was the moral law.

—They were wrong. It's a voice I don't recognize.

—Then I can't help you. There has to be a place to begin, a point at which we can meet and talk together. That can only be the moral point, or reason, or the God within. But it has to be someplace in you.

—It's fine. I didn't come to you for help, just to talk. When I read or walk I get confused and have to force myself to stop thinking. But if I can make up words for what I am going through I feel a sense of relief.

—Have you seen someone?

—Therapy? No Father. Shrinks don't do that. They don't divest you of your religious thoughts. Maybe they could cure me if I were schizophrenic or used drugs, but I'm not and I don't. Aside from my alcoholism, I'm normal. But the moral force—is that what you called it?—is making my life unbearable. Conscience makes me a coward, isn't that how it goes? Augustine is tedious reading. Worrying about stealing fruit. He turns his obsessions into faith. It's a terrible lie, Father, the conviction of evil within, hatred of the flesh which becomes hatred of humanity. Augustine's putrid sense of himself. Read it again Father, it isn't edifying, it's the most terrifying thing ever written, a ghost story, with the writer becoming a ghost before our eyes.

—Maybe the voice you hear is Satan's.

—What's the difference? God, Satan. What's the difference Father?

—I won't dignify that with an answer. If you don't know the difference between the loving God and the Devil then you are beyond my help.

—I know the difference well enough. I didn't ask about the difference, but about how we can know which voice is speaking to us. They might be more alike than you think, they might tell us the same things. When my parents died, both from cancer, terrible deaths, the only voice I heard in the still silence of the long nights I sat with them told me that this suffering was undeserved. But my own voice, louder and more insistent, reassured me with the thought that my turn would come in time, that this was the fate of us all and that there was nothing to feel sorrowful about. What do you make of that? Whose voices did I hear?

—Your own. Have you thought of that? When God speaks to you He does so in a voice that is unmistakable.

—You know this for a fact?

—Yes.

—He has spoken to you?

—Yes.

—Then I am lost.

—Why?

—Do you know Descartes? I read him years ago. And I've kept turning over one thing he said. No idea I have that is greater than me can have come from me; it must have come from God.

—That's foolish. We can think many things that aren't rooted in the simple truths of ordinary life.

—That doesn't sound like the view of a man living in the desert.

—What? You think I live here to escape life? To not

think about ordinary things? That's what many people assume. It's a thought that is beneath you.

—You're right. I surprise myself sometimes. So the voice I hear might be my own. That might be worse, I don't know.

—Listen to me Mr. Lisele. Be calm. We are in a tranquil place here. Go back to your room and rest. Go for a walk. Think about what you have been saying to me. You have exhausted me with your ideas. I am an old man and now I must pray and rest. I'll pray for you if you would like.

—Thank you Father. I apologize for tiring you.

The priest said nothing. He left the room. Orlando sat drinking cold tea and feeling as if he had behaved badly. He realized, too late, that he hadn't asked the questions he wanted to ask. He had wanted to ask for forgiveness, or at least be given some hope. As often happened when he spoke his thoughts to anyone, Orlando felt worse, not unburdened, but full of self-recrimination. He finished his tea and left the room. Instead of returning to his casita, or walking yet again in the desert—he was sick of the desert—he went to his car, got in and drove away from the monastery. He didn't think about where he was going, but when he came in a swirl of red dust to the paved road he turned north, toward Abiquiqu

Lake and the empty plain that reached up the northeastern part of New Mexico, all the way to Shiprock and the Four Corners and beyond. He drove all day and most of the night on roads as straight and flat as the paradoxes of geometry—the shortest distance from no place to no place. He didn't think about anything; he didn't listen to the radio—there was nothing to listen to but Navaho-language stations broadcasting from Farmington—nor did he consider what he would do when he ran out of gas—he no wallet with him, no money—he simply drove into the black, freezing afternoon and the deepening gloom of night, peering out his side window to marvel as the broad band of stars made themselves visible, first one by one, and then, as the moonless night blackened, in great white swirls of faint light. When the car died, as he knew it would, he was in Colorado, north of Durango, a few miles away from Purgatory. He might have found this state of affairs ironic, or sad, or funny, but he was too tired to think much about it at all. He climbed into the back seat and, shivering in the bitter air, thought he might as well get some sleep.

Back East, at work again, not rejuvenated, but doing fine, Orlando received the stigmata.

His first thought, when the wounds opened in his hands and feet, was that he had contracted an infection in the desert, some avian bacterial thing that had entered the cracked dry skin that was a consequence of cold air that carried no moisture. The wounds didn't hurt and didn't bleed. A slice like a smile simply opened on the palm of each of Orlando's hands and at the top of each foot. Perhaps it was gout. It was February 16th, Ash Wednesday, when his hands opened. He was on his way home from a long day of teaching, his mind back at the monastery, or perhaps up in Colorado where he would have died had Providence (as he now thought of it) hadn't sent a state trooper.

Orlando's osteopath, a handsome older woman with steel gray hair and steel gray eyeglasses, looked at the open sores and prescribed antibiotics and a prescription cream called Bactroban. She hardly looked at him and found nothing unusual to remark in the fact that he had four two-inch openings in his appendages that didn't bleed and didn't heal. Dr. Edwards was an inattentive person by nature, which was why Orlando had used her services for a decade—he didn't much care for being examined and preferred to answer a few questions about his health and his exercise habits rather than to undergo a rigorous exam. The cream appeared to heal the wounds at once—they vanished after one application—and when the antibiotics upset his stomach—his stool turned white with the massive dose—Orlando threw them away and put the whole matter behind him.

With his honors class, Orlando was reading *Gruppenbild mit Dame* by Böll, who was his favorite writer. The German was a challenge for many of his students, but a few warmed to Böll's quietly ironic style. Böll turned Henry James upside down. Leni Pfeiffer was a mystic from the lower depths of human feeling, not a fragile "creature" but a real woman, and for that reason she appealed to Orlando. Preparing for class, rereading some of his favorite sections, the wounds reappeared—it was early in the morning, and the problem arose of how to conduct his classes with open sores. He noticed that they were larger, deeper, rawer. It was as if he had been pierced by nails—yes, that exactly. Deep in his closet, back with his old letter jacket from high school—he'd always been a packrat—Orlando located a pair of white gloves, part of his Halloween costume, the one he wore on the night he lost his virginity to the redhead whose name began with 'A' or 'F,' a nice girl he'd really liked and had been embarrassed to talk to after the party, a horrible high school party during which he had led her into a back bedroom and *furtively*—the only word for it—"had sex"—now, as he recalls the event, he says aloud the word 'cock' and 'fuck' as a test in order to see if the wounds will bleed or disappear with the blasphemy. He hates those words and never uses them, even when his high school and college friends had done so with what seemed to Orlando disgusting bonhomie. The wounds didn't disappear. He slipped on the white gloves and his father's Burberry coat and left for work.

When he arrived in the nondescript building that housed offices and classrooms and a cafeteria, Orlando had to pass through the department offices for English and Foreign Languages, and under the nose of Dr. Channa, a nose easily disjointed by any impropriety. Without preamble, he asked Orlando about the white gloves, not without the charming sub-continental twinkle of an eye that was his trademark. Channa wasn't a scholar and not much of a teacher either. He had two sections, chronically under-enrolled, of British Imperial Literature, and had once, only once, published a short note in the *Journal of Conrad Studies* on some fine point of interpretation of *Lord Jim*. Channa was one of those academics who lived for committees, for the bloodless rough and tumble of institutional politics.

He was a favorite of the Academic Dean and had been elevated to the chairmanship of English and Foreign Languages—an oddball anomaly that suited a school where the liberal arts took a decidedly back seat to math and science—raised up out of nowhere, without even a competitive search. Orlando disliked the man for his fawning manner and deadly halitosis.

"I thought they were a nice sartorial touch, Edwardian but without pretension."

"I see. An interesting idea, Doctor Lisle." Channa insisted on the absurd title, especially in his own case.

Safe in his own office, Orlando examined his hands. The sliced skin appeared redder, raw, and ached, just a little. He looked at his hands as if they belonged to someone else. He knew about stigmatics, not much, but he knew that they existed. The medieval church was rife with such things—bleeding statues of St. Sebastian, smiling icons of the Virgin, the apparitions attested to by thousands—only a little over a century ago a peasant girl, Bernadette Soubirous, had claimed to have seen the Virgin a dozen times, over several months, in a grotto on the edge of the French Pyrenees. Orlando was an educated man, a skeptic in most things, living in an American city in the 1980s—these wounds were wholly natural; the only questions worth asking had to do with their cause and the risk they posed to his health. And how the hell he was going to get through his day without anyone noticing that he appeared to be carrying the wounds of Christ on his person?

Marie Rose Ferron, "Little Rose," lived with stigmata in Woonsocket, Rhode Island, from 1925 to 1936. Not only were her hands pierced, but her head leaked blood in the shape of a crown of thorns. Other stigmatists, like the French woman Marthe Robin, bedridden most of her life, subsisted only on the Holy Eucharist. Father Zlatko Sudac, born in Serbia in 1971, is "best known for his stigmata"—indeed!—but is also a painter, presumably of religious subjects, a projected future pope, and the bearer of a cross periodically inscribed by an invisible hand, presumably God's, in the middle of his forehead.

Orlando was surprised at the numbers of stigmatics—his affliction, if affliction it was, appeared not uncommon, especially in France and the Catholic provinces of the old Austrian Empire. Though he still did not accept that he was a bearer of the stigmata of Jesus, he began to think there was some deeper meaning ascribable to the wounds that now, late in February, did not go away, even with repeated applications of Bactroban and a renewed regimen of antibiotics. He was marked—no doubt about it—and the fact of the mark (of Cain?) led him into all sorts of chains of reasoning that he had never before entertained.

E.g., Does God exist? If so, then, which one? Surely Allah hadn't visited the stigmata upon a middle-aged lapsed Catholic. Well, God's existence wasn't an especially interesting question. Everyone carried on like God was the be-all and end-all. *God this and God that, I love God and He talks to me.…* What matters more is the human: if Orlando was bearing the signs of a great sacrifice, of atonement, was he then being called upon to perform some selfless expiation on behalf of his fellow man? In the desert, at St. Thomas's, and then later on, freezing to death in his car, Orlando understood, not consciously, but with the part of his passionate mind, as Hegel would put it, that the only purpose for life was just what the monks were teaching at Abiquiu, namely, love—not *agape* and not *eros,* but the larger, inclusive *philos,* the love of one's fellow man. He had hoped this wasn't true. There was no way he would love his fellow man, even if God were to stand before him and enjoin it, he could never "love" Channa, or the dimwits who took his Introduction to German Thought class. Love for Orlando meant love of one's wife—if you had one—or children—ditto—or parents—his were dead. But surely that was the meaning of compassion—just love, nothing but that. And what of suffering? Here Orlando was stuck. Was it proper to make meaning out of the agony of history? If he were being visited in some way, if he were a surrogate for everyone else, the scapegoat, then would he need to be prepared to bear the burdens of humanity—of Channa, for certain, but also the mutts who filled the world with anger and guns and the madness of the marketplace? He wasn't Christ, but here were the wounds, right here in the palms of his hand and the smooth hairless curve of his feet, proof if there could be proof of the divine at work in this miserable world, proof that even a nobody, a lost soul, could play a role in the terrible, incomprehensible story of human life.

Orlando felt uplifted when his thoughts went in the direction of atonement, but, just as easily, they would slip the other way, and he would see his raw wounds, now regularly covered with gauze (he had burned himself with a pot of boiling water, or so he told his boss and students), as shameful, as a sign that he had been too dense and proud to think beyond his own ego until this curse was visited upon him. He prayed—for the first time since he was a boy—he asked the empty universe to forgive him, to forgive everyone, and "Let us live out our lives, unhappy as they may be, in peace and tranquility." This, Orlando thought, was the end of suffering—not its termination, but its purpose—to teach us to ask for less and to expect nothing.

At the Catholic Church on South Street, the one preferred by pious Italian ladies from the neighborhoods by the river, the youngish priest looked at Orlando's hands and feet and shook his head, then made the sign of the cross over him. Orlando wondered what this meant. The priest was saying the *Pater Noster* when Orlando interrupted.

"What does it mean Father?"

"It means nothing. You have cuts on your hands and feet. What could that mean? See a doctor. They will heal in time. But as for miracles? We are past that now."

"What are you saying? I thought the Church still verified miracles, created saints. Here in this city there is a saint awaiting canonization."

"That's politics. For some there is comfort in bleeding wounds and water flowing from the sides of crazy men. In New Mexico they actually nail men to crosses on Good Friday. But that is showmanship, not faith.

To believe is to give yourself to something greater than your ego. Nothing is more difficult. To have faith in this world is miracle enough. Go home now, please. Don't worry about this..." he was about to say, "affliction" Orlando thought, but he said nothing.

Orlando sat still.

"You seem disappointed. Were you hoping to become Christ? To die for our sins?" The priest, who was dark and good-looking, who seemed more like an actor playing a priest than a man in orders, smiled at this. "Believe me, one man being torn to pieces for the sins of us all was quite enough. We're on our own now."

"You seem. . . I don't want to say it."

"Cynical? Go ahead, say it. You're wrong. I'm no cynic—I believe. But not in this..." He gestured at Orlando's unbandaged hands, the cuts now deep lesions, gaping grotesque smiles, as if his hands had become living things, apart from Orlando's body.

"What? What do you believe? I need to know. That's why I have these stigmata. I went to the desert to find God; no, that's not true, to abrogate him, to give him up. He wasn't there. And now this. It has to be a sign of some kind, at least for me."

"And what would you like it to mean?" The priest spoke gently.

"Just that my life is all right. That I'm a decent man. That's what I want. I'm not a mystic. The others have been girls and charismatic men, tubercular like Bernadette, or children, or insane. Some were insane. The stories are grotesque Father. They make me feel not chosen but filthy, as if I were a freak in a sideshow. I don't want that. Just to know if I am a good man."

"So little? My parishioners ask me if I can promise them heaven. And if I am persuaded to say yes, then they want me to describe it. And if I tell them it is full of music and light and bodiless angels they want to know if there Uncle Sal is there already, waiting for them. They want a tour guide, not a priest. And I can lie, or I can tell them the truth, which is, I don't believe in that heaven myself. It doesn't exist. I want to tell them to go home and make dinner for their husband and children and be decent to the neighbors you dislike and don't call the poor black family on the corner any names. But I don't do that. I lie. It's much easier. But you are asking so little."

"No heaven. I agree. But I am asking a great deal. Will you hear my confession? Will you forgive me?"

"For what? Have you done something terrible? Are you a murderer, or a thief like the two who were crucified with Him?"

"Worse. Much worse."

"Worse than murder? I don't believe it. Perhaps your conscience is too finely tuned. I'm in no mood for a confession now. May I simply forgive you, forgive whatever it is that has made you split your own body open?"

Orlando didn't say anything.

The priest again made the sign of the cross and spoke some Latin words—"*Lavabo inter innocentes manus meas: et circumdabo altare tuum, Domine. Ut audiam vocem laudis: et enarrem universa mirabila tua. Domine, dilexi decorem domus tuae: et locum habitationis gloriae tuae.*" Again with the Latin words—what was it with this dead language, why was it so moving to him? Orlando wasn't forgiven, but he was blessed.

Orlando did not visit any other priests or rabbis or ministers or imams. What were these men but people like him? He went about his life, going to work, teaching his classes, attending meetings, all with his hands heavily bandaged. Some of his colleagues were sorry for him, and sent casseroles prepared by their wives or coupons for meals in second-tier City establishments. A few dropped by his office—none came to his house—and told stories of their burns and cuts and concussions, of auto accidents that could have ended much worse than they did, or of an botched gall bladder surgery that killed the second cousin of the senior professor of medieval history. The visits were well meant, but tedious. Most of his colleagues continued, as they had always done, to ignore Orlando completely. He was a minor member of an unimportant department—who cared about Mann or Bernhard or Handke?—and if he had been burned or scalded or if his hands had been chopped off in a sausage grinder, well, what could one do? Tenure cases were coming up, promotions, class reductions, research grants. Orlando was grateful for the men and women who felt no interest in him, just as he felt no interest in them. Imagine, he thought, if anyone knew, if any of these rational humanists, with a smattering of lib-eral Protestants and couple of Philadelphia birthright Quakers thrown in, had suspected that their silent, Germanic junior colleague had received the mark of redemption—wouldn't that cause a fuss?

In late March, as suddenly as they had appeared, the wounds were healed. Or, healed themselves. Or, were no longer imagined by him to exist. He admitted to himself that he was disappointed. He didn't want them back, but he wanted to know what they meant. Probably nothing at all. But then again, what if they had been a *sign* of something portentous? What if he were a *vessel?* Orlando was a modest man, an underachiever, but he rather liked the thought of being the bearer of glad tidings, a John the Baptist for an age of unbelief. But he knew that whatever the marks had meant would never be revealed to him—to him, least of all, was clarity promised. That was the trouble with being a harbinger: you were too far out in front of the meaning you bore to see what it was. He knew he would never know, and that, after a while, seemed just as it should be.

An Artist in Vermont

When she was young, in college, her paintings had been done in the style of Cezanne. At RISD, she had fallen in love with her Painting III teacher, a disheveled older man who lived most of the year in a small northern Vermont town, painting meticulous landscapes—autumnal, vaguely melancholy, unpeopled—on tiny canvases. The man whose name she could no longer speak even silently to herself had been married, of course, but lived alone in dismal north Providence for five months of the year to support his painting during the other seven months. It hadn't been difficult for her to get him to bed. She posed nude for him once or twice, at her suggestion, and that was that. Never would she have thought that she used sex to advance her career—what career? She was twenty-three, a senior in college, about to earn a B.F.A. in painting that would be about as valuable as a semester of shorthand—less actually. She was Jewish. Her parents lived in Center City Philadelphia, in a lovely Federal home a block from the oldest lending library in America. She had grown up in Ann Arbor where her father and mother had gone to college and graduate school and then spent nearly thirty years teaching at the Stephan Ross School of Business. Now that they were retired they spent most of the year traveling. When she thought about it, she realized that her favorite painters—Cezanne, Derain, Pissarro—were the painters her parents had loved and shown her at the Metropolitan, the Louve, the Art Institute. She wondered why it was that her tastes had been fixed when she was nine years old; she still couldn't abide the abstract expressionists, painters her parents had also disliked. Her canvases looked like knock-offs. If she were a poet she would have been a plagiarist, but as a painter she appeared to be a copyist, like those lifelong students who carted their easels into the Art Institute and spend months attempting to recreate Poussin or Rembrandt or Caravaggio, painters whose familiar style seems ripe for theft or pastiche.

The older painter with whom she had slept—he wasn't that old, sixty or so, about the same age as her father—shared a small farmhouse with his bedridden wife, a lovely woman who had multiple sclerosis and whose activities were confined to her studio—she too was a painter—and her garden. The woman who was sleeping with the artist whose name she now pretends to forget had asked if she could go to Vermont with him when he returned home in May. The woman's parents were trekking in North India and she did not wish to spend a hot summer in Philadelphia, jobless, wondering what she would do now that her college career was over. She told the older man that she loved him, and it is likely that she did. Or perhaps she was a *disciple*—she liked the image of herself following her mentor to the Northeast Kingdom, absorbing his boundless knowledge of art history, and in her fantasies she was a seeker attached to this distinguished genius, learning at last how to draw and use color, how to see nature the way an artist might.

The truth was he wasn't a genius, and she wasn't especially attached to him, and she had no interest, really, in following anyone, though a summer in Vermont did seem appealing.

Hers was a passionate nature, and like many women who are serious, if not talented, she found men her own age dull. In high school, though awkward and over-wrought, she had been a favorite of her male teachers.

Full of life was a phrase used in her evaluations, as if there were legions of dour sixteen-year-olds walking the halls of Mary Clayton Academy. But it was true, she had something even as a young woman, a fire in her eyes, an eagerness to attach herself to various projects, many of them dubious. For example, learning the harp or earning a black belt in Tai Kwan Do (she did neither). She joined the film club and later broke away from it to found a David Lynch Appreciation Society, a group of self-styled *cineasts* dedicated to screening and deconstructing *Blue Velvet* and *Twin Peaks*. Her interests came and went with seasons and friendships and boyfriends. Her teachers and advisers thought she might be sexually active, but this was mere speculation, or wishful thinking on their part. She did well at MCA and was accepted to her first-choice school, the Rhode Island School of Design, even though art had been more of a sideline than a passion. You never know, she would say, where and when you would find your vocation.

The old painter was delighted to take the young woman with him to St. Johnsbury, actually to a quite rural area west of the town, to a clapboard farmhouse that was half-toppled into Nestor's Creek, to his three tick-infested labradors, his goats and feral cats and studio stacked with half-finished canvases. And of course to his wife. He introduced the young woman to Margaret, to the woman he had married thirty years before, courted and wooed and wed at the height of his struggle to sell a painting, *one fucking painting*, as he had chanted over and over, *a lousy fucking painting*, and then, happily married, before he'd had a taste of success, he and his wife had settled into poverty in a grim downstate mill town—he'd been born in Nashua to a family of textile workers—and, once settled, he began to paint in a new way, with joyful disregard for the formal considerations that had inhibited his expressiveness (he would later write in his unpublished memoir, *The Gloom of Northern Spaces*, that he had to *transcend* his formal, European training, though in fact he'd left UNH in his sophomore year and never studied in Europe), with a brighter palette, with thicker applications of paint, working on a smaller scale, without second guessing his *inspiration* or going back to his work once he felt (momentarily) satisfied. His work began to sell. A gallery in Burlington, then one in Albany, and then, just as he hit forty, the Linbach Gallery in Boston, with branches in Philadelphia, Austin, and Santa Fe, took up his work, old Mr. Linbach championing what were called in the catalogues *visceral evocations of the cold beauty of New England landscapes*. It would have been a stretch to call the painter *great* or influential, but he was good enough to make a profit for Linbach, and to pay his own and his increasingly disabled wife's expenses— the medical bills were high, and the money went quickly, so the artist took an annual half-year appointment in Providence, brought his wife along for solace, but she hated the city, the humid air and the ugly triple-deckers, loathed college life, his colleagues of course, and in particular the shallow small talk of administrators and the smug would-be-artists from top prep schools who expected her to be as personable as her garrulous husband. So after a few months he drove her back to Vermont where, she said, she would prefer solitude and the risk of accidental death—e.g. falling down the stairs or into the creek, or starving if the grocery boy couldn't get down their road in winter, or freezing to death if her weak hands weren't up to stoking the fireplace every half-hour. She was serious, or at least the artist believed her to be so. He couldn't allow her to die. But he needed the few months away from her, from their hermetic life together. He liked the college, the students, the bourbon that the Dean poured so liberally at the weekly faculty party. The salary wasn't bad either. Twenty-five grand plus health insurance for a semester; two classes and studio time. He shared a sublet with another visiting painter—a falling-down ruin of a house off Hope in the Portuguese part of town—so he could afford to pay the guy who cut his firewood to check on Margaret every day or so. Plenty of people lacked steady employment in St. Johnsbury; Gabe was glad for the extra hundred a week and Margaret came to enjoy his sullen company. Apparently they played gin for an hour every afternoon, or so Margaret wrote in her weekly letter—there was no phone—and the artist, who could be easily lured into complacency when it came to his wife's well being—congratulated himself on the arrangement.

Now, in the first week of May, he drove home with his protégé in the seat next to him—rubbing his leg, stroking his shriveled cock. The artist enjoyed the attentions of the young woman. Though he couldn't pretend that, a) she wasn't dull company, aside from the sex, b) he wasn't impotent most of the time and unwilling to go the chemical route to produce an erection and, c) he wasn't going to fool Margaret for even one second as to what was going on. The plan he had devised was to lie to his wife. The girl was there to help out around the house, to work on her art, to take instruction from both the artist and his frankly more talented wife. He would mention how gifted the girl was, how much potential she would have once her technique matured—Margaret wouldn't believe this, and she would see at once the red-head with the lovely breasts and long legs didn't know the first thing about composition or color and that she was there to boost her husband's ego. Margaret wasn't a fool. Her own body was quitting on her and she could feel pity for anyone who wanted to push back against dying. Anything that would ease this dread was welcome, and Margaret, with her enlarged sensibilities and good heart, couldn't condemn her husband's futile affairs.

When the artist and the young woman arrived they made a point of behaving formally with one another, as if they were father and daughter. Margaret was cordial, gave the young woman a glass of cider, homemade bread with blueberry jam, and showed her a small but tidy room on the second floor of the house, the room that would have been the baby's had the boy not died after only a few hours, twenty years before.

—You'll like this room, the view toward the hills is calming, and the finches love the oak so you'll wake up to their chatter. We eat early in the morning, at six o'clock, and work until noon. After lunch I go to the garden and that might be a good time for you and my husband to work together. We don't have electricity so we dine early and read before the sun goes down. There is hot water and a shower down the hall; try to be brisk since our solar heater only warms fifty gallons a day. And flush the toilet with the bucket. Sorry about the privations. When we bought this house we were quite poor, and then when we weren't poor we decided we liked things the way they were. Winters are hard but you're here for the best time. If you go for a walk take a stick with you—there are several near the front door. The neighbors don't corral their dogs and they might run toward you if you pass north along the road. Just wave the stick. There are a lot of snakes around the house but don't be alarmed, they're harmless and do a nice job of eating the mice.

Margaret gave the girl her best fake smile—Margaret thought of her as a *girl*, she was just that, a little dull looking to the older woman's way of thinking, with the lost look she had seen in so many young women in the village; even her body odor was childish, soapy, with an undercurrent of sex, 'coltish' came to mind, but that wasn't right, Lolita maybe, but more subdued. Yes, Margaret could see the attraction her husband felt. It would be guilt-free sex, no possible strings attached, no feeling, at least on his side, though she imagined the girl thought she was in love with the great artist and would save him from his sexless, loveless marriage. Just like in the movies. Margaret thought about how often she had read about this kind of thing, all the tedious novels on which she had wasted her time—she no longer wasted a moment—so many of them obsessed with matters of the heart. The good thing about a degenerative disease is that its 'progress'—was that the word?—allowed time to consider one's priorities. She was an old woman, or, perhaps not so old, but no matter, she had come to see that tidying up her own self was of greater concern than fretting about the untidy selves around her, including her husband's. Yes, she loved him still, and not only nostalgically. He was a good man. His talent was minimal and being rapidly depleted—Margaret thought that teaching had hastened her husband's artistic demise, but she knew he longed for an audience. She would have loved him had he given up his art, as he had threatened to do many times over the years. He was good with his hands, and he might have built furniture for the leaf-browsing tourists—he might have chosen *techne*, instead of the pointless fine art of oil painting—but he loved to sit for hours, smoking his cigarettes, drinking Scotch and staring at his half-finished canvases. Margaret enjoyed watching her husband, though not when he was painting—his technique and mode of working struck her as uninspiring—but she loved to watch him when he was unaware of her, which was often, when he was lost in thought, thinking, she guessed, of his lost illusions, or his futile dreams of success and happiness. She was, she knew, a disappointment to him. Unsociable, plain, more talented as an artist, and now, worst of all, a cripple. Well, they were almost done with one another. He might marry this young fawn who sat on the bed before her, wondering, Margaret thought, when the old lady with the two wooden canes would leave her alone.

—What do you think of my husband?

—What do you mean?

—I mean, what do you think of him as an artist, a teacher, a human being. It isn't a difficult question.

—I like him. He's nice. I like his paintings very much.

—What do you like about them?

—Everything. The colors, the subjects, the composition.

—Good. That's a good answer. And the rest?

—The rest?

—As a teacher, as a man.

—He's a wonderful teacher. He's patient with me, with all of us. And he's a nice man.

—You like the word *nice*?

—I guess. Why are you asking me these questions?

—You're my guest. I want to know you, what you think. The only connection we have is my husband. He brought you to me. So I ask.

—Yes, I like the word. It means something specific to me.

—And what is that?

—That someone cares. They have feelings.

—Feelings? And not everyone does? Have feelings?

—Of course they do. But not everyone has the right feelings. Some people are mean and impatient and wish bad things for others. He isn't like that.

—I see.

—Do you? Perhaps we aren't talking about the same thing. Or maybe you want to say something you aren't saying.

Margaret thought: she's smarter than I thought. And, of course, she was. Everyone is smarter than we give them credit for being; knowing this is one of the most important lessons we can learn. She wanted to say: *go away*. But she was too polite.

—No, I don't want to say anything else. Not now. We'll have dinner in about an hour, if that is convenient for you.

—Yes, that is convenient for me, thank you.

With this the young woman turned away from her

hostess and began unpacking her oversized suitcase. It looked like she was planning to remain all summer. Or maybe stick around until Margaret's heart gave out. Neither woman knew what would transpire, but both understood that events would come to pass that would make each of them remember this awkward interlude in the small, stuffy bedroom for the rest of her life. How long these lives would last neither one knew at that moment, of course. Margaret was sure that her memory only need operate a short time more before it was consumed in the foreordained fire. The young woman saw herself at the beginning of an exciting life full of art and love and adventure. Both women were wrong about their prospects, but that was to be expected. Nothing is more likely to derail a life than the sense that its boundaries and trajectory are fixed by fate. There is no fate, only contingencies and luck, and most luck, it seems, is bad.

After a surprisingly relaxed dinner—Margaret and her husband exchanged news and gossip while the young woman concentrated on her food—the three of them went to their respective rooms to rest. Margaret and her husband had not shared a bed in many years, not since Margaret's illness began to sap her strength and to require that she spend many hours of each day resting. She thought it ironic that her body, for which she had once had such a high regard, not in a mere aesthetic sense, but architecturally and formally, had turned against her during the prime of her life. She thought the death of her infant son had been the precipitating event that brought on her disease, but this was speculation. Margaret suffered most from ataxia and occasional nystagmus; she might be in the garden, tired but functioning reasonably well, and suddenly topple over. Reading was difficult for her, but her paintings, on which she still was able to work for an hour or two a day, had shifted toward fields of color that reflected the difficulties she experienced with her vision. She was beginning to see the world differently, and it was clear to her as the MS progressed that the world we inhabit is indeed the creation of our minds rather than of our senses. She had promised herself not to whine about being ill, not to drag her husband into a depressing cycle that corresponded with the tidal push and pull of her symptoms. She had been mostly successful. He had been upset with her when she left Providence, feeling that her efforts to make small adjustments to the life of a faculty wife had been half-hearted. She felt a little guilty about her behavior, but not much. She hadn't asked him to look for a job. He certainly could have found one closer to their home. He didn't like the long, isolated winters. During the years when he saw himself as De Kooning, living far from the temptations of the city so that he could work, he had loved Vermont. He could go for days speaking only a few words, weeks without going into town, months without listening to NPR or reading even the local newspaper. But then his paintings stopped selling—there was a recession, or perhaps it was inflation, she couldn't recall—and little by little he began to spend less time in his studio and more time in town, sitting, she knew, in the One Horse Tavern, drinking whiskey and imagining that he was one of those romantic figures from the 1950's whom they both admired so much—Pollock or Rothko—exhausted from creating art and recovering with alcohol. Margaret stayed home. She been staying home for the most part for twenty years and had no intention of doing anything else. She'd travelled enough. One place was the same as another, and when you were ill, when each day brought some as yet unexpected nuance to the palette of suffering a body could endure, it was just as well to be at home.

The young woman left her room first. Margaret could hear the door close, her soft tread on the uncarpeted floor. The front door opened and closed. The light was fading. Even in May the evenings were cool, the nights cold. Snow was in the forecast, a last gray day and white morning before the spring thaw. After a few minutes Margaret's husband opened the door to his room, right across the hall, and tapped on the door.

—Margaret. Are you all right? I'm just out for a stroll, maybe go to go into the studio to plan tomorrow's work. Do you want tea?

She did not. She thought of suggesting he sit down to talk, but didn't have the stamina for a scene. Let him go.

Margaret lay back in bed and put her novel on the table. She was rereading books that she had loved when she was young. She hoped to be able to keep her eyesight long enough to go through Jane Austen again, *Daniel Deronda* and then Proust if she could manage it. Why not? Painting was no longer the passion it had been; gardening soothed her but was becoming difficult. She closed here eyes and imagined her husband embracing the young woman, fondling her, whispering—what? Margaret didn't care. After a short time she fell asleep and dreamed of the ocean.

The pretense that there were painting lessons being conducted lasted less than seventy-two hours. Margaret saw nothing—they were careful—but her husband's manner around the young woman made it clear that they were lovers. Margaret wondered if she cared. The sex was inconsequential, having the woman in her home was an affront. Margaret had too much time to think about things; it was too soon for any gardening. She was tired most of the time, and she missed talking to *the wood-man*, the boy named Gabe, his neutral remarks and kindness. Thinking of Gabe made her laugh—now she was a character in a play by Chekov, a lonely countess, abandoned by her husband (a physician or journalist) and falling in love with the estate's caretaker. Of course with her husband home the young man was no longer needed. Margaret didn't want a nurse or a companion or even a friend—an indifferent acquaintance seemed just right, someone about whom she might have vague fan-tasies. Solitude, banter, convivial meals with her spouse, George Eliot and the bluebirds—just arriving—that would do. This woman, this interloper, she interfered with the simple welcome Margaret had always reserved for her favorite season.

—She doesn't have as much potential as you told me. Margaret said to her husband.

This was an understatement. Margaret had slipped into her oblique mode of address, as she thought of it.

Her husband said that he did not like being spoken to 'ironically' as he put it, but his wife pointed out that irony had a different meaning than he supposed.

—Well, what does it mean then to be ironic? Enlighten me.

—Irony is when you recognize a shift in meaning, when words could mean what they usually mean, or something else. Or when you communicate something while implicitly knowing that you aren't saying what you mean, not because you don't want to, but because you can't.

—You've gotten pedantic in the few months since I saw you.

—And you've grown naïve.

The artist did not like being thought of as naïve, and became angry.

—I can see you don't like me saying that, and I'm sorry I did. I would never hurt you, though you appear not to have the same scruples about me.

—Because of the girl? Are you saying this because of the girl, because you think we are having an affair?

—Please, let's not discuss it. All I wished to say, really, is that she doesn't appear to me to have much of a gift for drafting or color. Her paintings, the ones you two have been working on, look like the work of an undergraduate, a beginner. Your *protégés* have been more talented in the past.

—That's why she needs a teacher. And what *protégés* are you referring to?

—Evelyn for one. Don't tell me you've forgotten her?

—No. I haven't forgotten her. The word seemed wrong to me is all.

—I know you sleep with them. Please don't bother yourself about it.

—It's my own fault.

—It isn't anyone's fault. It's the way of things.

—I love you, you know that.

—I suppose I do. You know, my legs are weaker than they were in the winter, my eyes keep darting about, and I'm forgetting things. I never used to forget anything.

—No, you never have.

—But I do forgive.

—Maybe, I'm not so sure. But you're wrong this time. Wrong about her. We did try, once, back in Providence. It was my doing. But I couldn't. I think that's over for me. And, it's strange, but I feel relief. All of those of years of obsessing about bodies.

—I did it too. Not like you, I never acted on my feelings, though you know I could have. I suppose if we think about other people enough we lose one another.

—Have we?

—I think so. Yes, I think we have, or I have. I haven't been able to care about you and the girl. Just that she's in the way. I found myself yesterday thinking maybe you two should go someplace for a while, to Key West. See how it goes.

—Jesus Christ.

—It *has* occurred to you.

He got up and went to the sideboard. There were many bottles of whiskey. He poured a drink and toasted his wife.

—I'll drive her to Burlington and put her on the train for home. And we'll be fine. It was just that she thought so highly of me.

—You're afraid, aren't you?

—Of what"

—You *know* what.

—You're the only person I've known who isn't. Margaret laughed at this.

—Don't send her away. I'm trying like her.

—Believe me, it's nothing. I don't feel anything for her.

—That's worse. Not to feel anything.

—No, it isn't.

High summer arrived. Margaret had good days and bad. Her legs would work well enough to carry her to her studio or to the garden, and then, for several days in a row, she would be forced to remain in bed, or in her rocking chair. Her husband was attentive, then, after a tumultuous Fourth of July celebration—he'd been drunk and abusive—he'd withdrawn into himself, remaining all day and much of each night in his studio, painting, he said, with a new-found passion. The young woman borrowed the Volvo and drove to Philadelphia to visit friends. It was a relief to Margaret to have her gone, but also unsettling. She found that she no longer wanted to be alone with her husband. There was nothing she wanted to say to him. They avoided each other, and an oppressive silence settled over the ramshackle farmhouse. Margaret was rereading *Jane Eyre* and realized she was the madwoman in the attic, a captive of someone else's history. In the middle of July, on Bastille Day, Margaret went into her husband's studio—something she never did—to look at the work he had been doing. There was only one canvas, large and loosely stretched, leaning against the wall near the work table. It was blank.

The Funhouse

Nihil sibi ipsi praesentius quam anima.
["Nothing is more present to us than our soul."]
Augustine

❋

Wednesday
December 6, 2000

❋

Now, the week before what he was calling "the final indignity," Garber was mumbling, half lucid, sedated on hydromorphone, a little crazy in any case, worked up and depressed, in pain and beyond all feeling— who could blame him for being irate? The millennium had arrived with a vengeance—Y2K, the Rapture, the Decline of the West. The pundits had a field day those final months of '99, no disaster was unthinkable, no scenario too absurd—the best seller lists were topped by books with titles that included the phrase "the end of"—history, literacy, physics, love—you name it, Americans wanted it to end so that something new—Jesus arriving on a surfboard, Elvis and Walt Disney and Richard Nixon risen from the dead—could save them from the boredom of being rich and fat and stupid—this was Garber's view of the matter, bitter—of course—but not unreasonable. The sitting president—absurdly "Bill," like Garber's uncle who'd died in a boating accident—now would have to button up his fly and go back to the sticks, lick his wounds, then get busy making a bundle, which, Garber knew, had been his plan all along. How fortuitous that the millennium had come fast on the heels of a sex scandal—the self-righteous (nearly everyone!) were beside themselves with indignation—a *blowjob* in the White House! Cheat the taxpayers, screw the poor, order cruise missile attacks, but Jesus, don't let an intern suck your dick! At first Garber had found the farce of the past three years funny, but when he realized the moralizing was for real he grew melancholy. How could people be such *schmucks*? Garber knew people who threw up their hands—"It's tragic", they said. And, "*Get me out of here!*" Garber had read stories in the *Times* about people who'd finally thrown in the towel, progressives and reactionaries, liberals and conservatives, all of whom had given up on the Republic—on the guns and crime and abortions, on the Jesus Freaks and robber barons, on the drugs and crappy schools and crooks in Congress—everyone had a gripe whose content and ferocity depended on their political views, on whether they followed Rush or Rachel, urban cosmopolitans and hicks from Iowa who'd decided to cast their lot with the Irish or Portuguese, to finish their lives in Dublin or Lisbon, Nogales or Tijuana, anyplace but the US of A with its unremitting spectacles. Garber had thought about leaving himself, dreamed of finishing his life on the Costa Brava, but of course he was poor and, to be honest, he hadn't wanted to miss what he called the "finale" of national decline. Dying now, Garber realized that some dope from the Bible Belt would probably buy his little Capitol Hill townhouse and use it for screwing Congressional pages—*Goddamn it.*

And: no more sex, or red wine, or dinners at Ruth Chris; no sunsets or detective novels or movies with Meryl Streep; no politics or sleeping in, no phone calls to his children, no fights with his ex-. *Never again.* One of the better things about dying, Garber believed, was that he had at long last outgrown his piggish male ego. A brainy man, not bad looking, with charm to spare (he thought), Garber had loved seduction more than books or ideas or even his beloved political battles. He flirted with his students when he was teaching, with the wives of colleagues, with strangers at parties. He'd been married twice and would have considered a third Mrs. Garber until he was diagnosed with liver cancer the year before.

Inept in love, he said aloud, and thought: *like my hero* William Jennings Bryan, not really Garber's hero, but an interesting specimen, a Bible-beating fool who thought a man could serve the people and maintain his principles, an orator, large and lachrymose, ambitious enough to seek the presidency three times in order (Garber believed) to repair his soul. Garber was himself unattached—detached—untethered like a balloon about to float away for good. He had enjoyed deathbed (that ghastly term, whose deep meaning he finally perceived) meetings with both of his ex-wives and half-a-dozen of his female friends. The wives—Barbara whom he met in grad school and been married to, on and off, for twenty years, and Bernice (Bernie) whom he had married and divorced in the time it took the previous president to get himself impeached by self-righteous Congressmen who did their intramural screwing at the Hay-Adams or the Mayflower and not in the Oval Office. Many a person had been screwed in the White House, but this dalliance with an intern somehow upset the Nation in a way that bombing innocent people never had. Anyway, Bernie, the one-year wonder, had been good enough to drop by Garber's little row house to ask after his health. Two children with Barbara, no time for any with Bernie. Garber, never a dutiful husband or father, was now wistful about his children, his daughter and son, fully grown up, accomplished and normal—who knew how they'd done it? An LA filmmaker and some kind of computer person in San Jose, handsome kids with lots of friends and probably many lovers. As far away from their Old Man as they could get. Garber was proud that they seemed so much saner than he had ever been, less prone to obsession and not at all attracted to the darker side of things. It wasn't his doing; Barbara had a gift for living—if that's what it was—he had lacked. One of his women friends, what's her name, had said that *he* was a child, a comment which struck Garber as dopey. *Childish*, he had said, but not a child. Big difference.

Yes, he had behaved badly. Was selfish, vain, unreliable, loquacious (vapidly so), thoughtless, megalomaniacal, a bad listener and personally sloppy—but still. There were the many good qualities, and as he lay on his bed—sore in his buttocks and legs and back from being flat for so long, mournful in the morning light (he dreaded night and hoped he would 'pass away'—he liked the phrase, suggesting as it did the turning of the leaves or the arrival of the New Year—during lunch time, which for Garber, with his workaholic habits, had always been the most pointless time of day. He never ate lunch and hated not being able to get anyone on the phone for the two-hours that official Washington set aside for schmoozing)....

This was how it was going for Garber. His mind would not settle. He was thinking in parentheses. He was restless and unfocused and jittery. His good qualities were as follows: funny and serious. Maybe not as funny as he thought. Serious then. Which, in his own cancer-addled mind was a redemptive quality, given the stupidity of the age. Seventy-percent of Americans believed in heaven. Sixty-percent denied evolution and almost that same number believed the Bible was literally true. Eighty-percent thought they had a guardian angel! Under the circumstances a sense of humor helped.

Yes, his brain now resembled one of those flighty warblers whose spring songs had thrilled Garber on cool summer mornings in Vermont. He had loved waking up in his austere bedroom on the third floor of the falling- down farmhouse purchased with the advance for his second, his most successful book, a sensationalized history of the devastating strikes of labor's formative period—Homestead, Pullman, and the Great Railroad Strike of 1877—a book he wasn't proud of, a potboiler he had written because he was broke, saddled with child-care payments and a monstrous credit card nut occasioned by a spur-of-the-moment trip to India and Pakistan, a trip that nearly killed him but which led to his "conversion"—using the word loosely—to no-frills Theravada Buddhism, the only religion that had ever appealed to Garber, an agnostic who bitterly denounced any so-called faith that didn't advance the interests of the working class.

"'The working class'—what a joke," Garber hadn't failed to notice that his beloved proletarians had gone over wholeheartedly to the Republican Party. The world turned upside down.

"*Gott in Himmel*," Garber shouted—a curse, a prayer. Mr. Samuels glanced over at Garber's bedroom window and frowned. Mr. Samuels, (Garber wasn't sure what his first name was and never would have addressed him without the formal Mister in any case), his neighbor of many years, a man no older but far more active than Garber, a G-13 at Labor whose job apparently was managing the compilation of statistics for the Congressional Budget Office—a meta-job, Garber believed, which must have had the Zen quality of inducing boredom so intense as to either drive one mad or to take one, as it apparently had the benign Mr. Samuels, to a plane of Being equivalent to that of a Bodhisattva, a serenity derived from columns of numbers, percentages, growth factors, labor mobility vectors, potential employment indices, actuarial computational models—these were, Mr. Samuels had assured Garber, important concepts, and he had often brought up the details of his job over the back fence on autumn Sunday afternoons right after the weekly Redskin's loss had propelled him, Samuels, a still-rangy black man who had been a tight end on Dunbar's 1969 City Championship team and who bled Redskin maroon, out into the cleansing light and crisp air to clear his head and curse the owners who had decimated a once-proud franchise—yes, Mr. Samuels, who now turned away from Garber's window, accustomed as he was to outbursts originating from the crazy socialist who never mowed his lawn or shoveled his walk or decorated his porch for the holidays but who was, nonetheless, not a bad sort for a white man, not the kind of neighbor who made a big deal out of pioneering on an all-black block east of the Capitol, just a regular guy who kept to himself, mostly worked at home, and never borrowed tools that he didn't return. That his neighbor was fatally ill was unknown to Mr. Samuels. Had he known, he would have had Mrs. Samuels make a ham and potato casserole and he would have come to sit with Mr. Garber each evening to chat about sports and weather—not politics. Mr. Samuels was an Eisenhower Republican and had no patience with his neighbor's soft-hearted view of the world. But he didn't know of the cancer, and he wouldn't, not until the following Wednesday when, returned from a day of meetings with the House Labor Subcommittee on Regulation, he saw the ambulance, fire truck, and two police cruisers parked next door. Later on, a black family from Savannah would rent the house from the real estate company deputized by the executor of Garber's will to discharge his obligations—the socialist had died insolvent, not that this surprised Mr. Samuels—and the man of the house, who came and went, was a Falcons fan with whom Mr. Samuels had a loud argument concerning reimbursement for the damage done by the branch of an oak tree that had crushed a section of his, Samuels', porch. There came a day when Samuels would rue the passing of Garber, but such things, in the great skein of time, are of no importance.

Garber saw all of this clearly. He found it remarkable, as he was dying, that the future came to him mixed with the past. If time were compressed to a point, if all living things were God, if the world was existent all at once, if a man's mind was made transparent by the act of dying—if these things were true, then Garber, the most cerebral of men, could see clearly into the future. Mr. Samuels would miss him; his wives would not. His daughter would mourn her father for many years, discovering his good qualities when it was too late; his son would not share his sister's nostalgia for the past and would promptly forget the Old Man as he pursued his first ten million. Garber's damaged ex-vet friend Wallace—the person who, it transpired, would come to Garber's aid when the dying man was most in need of a friend and who would offer him a gift that eased his passing—Wallace would at last become a writer, as he so sincerely wished, but would never publish anything. His many friends would raise their glasses at Garber's favorite watering-holes, toasting his memory, and then they would forget why they had been fond of a man so self-absorbed; but, a little later on, would remember that he had been witty and easy with cash, and so they would miss him for a while, with all the sincerity that anyone can muster for a ghost. This is the way it goes with the dead. They are useful as a means of bringing the living together, but quickly forgotten.

"Though a round portal I saw appear/Some of the beautiful things that heaven bears, /Where we emerged, and once more saw the stars."

Garber, somewhat precocious, had read Dante when he was in ninth grade. Only Hell, as that was the part that featured suffering. His interest in Dante never waned. In college he'd learned Italian so he could read the great Florentine in the original. His master's thesis was written on Dante's politics, comparing Dante to Machiavelli, and later on, with much revision, the book had been picked up by a small Massachusetts publisher, but it never sold and wasn't reviewed. It was on the strength of this little book that Garber had secured his first teaching job at a second-tier liberal arts college in Vermont. He'd hated teaching. He disliked his students, found them dull and disinterested, too privileged to understand the value of an education. And he'd been a terrible teacher. On class days he would get headaches, and his vision would grow blurry in anticipation of the moment he had to walk into the seminar room with its buzzing florescent lights and smell of chalk dust and disinfectant to talk about pronouns and dependent clauses and the use of the comma. He had no firm grasp of English. He had majored in history in college and was close to finishing his degree, but the job market was saturated with academic job seekers, Sixties idealists who weren't into money, at least not yet. So he taught English composition for a few years and was unhappy but channeled his unhappiness into political work, writing mostly, with some forays into union organizing in the Burlington and Albany areas. His doctoral dissertation at Amherst was on the repression of workers under Mussolini in the early years of fascism. It took him years to finish—he was a methodical thinker but a disorganized researcher. He collected thousands of notecards with quotations and citations, scattering them around his workroom, and then desperately scrambled to find what he needed as he wrote. He was hopeless. Barbara helped him finish—without her he never would have ordered his life at all—and when he was done with the dissertation, which was picked up by Columbia and won the Garibaldi Award in 1974, she was worn out and done with him. She left Garber for a colleague of hers, a fellow lawyer, but returned with only minimal recriminations (on both sides) after a few months. It turned out that she loved her husband's annoying and obsessive personality, his 'maniac character,' more than she'd known. Or she didn't enjoy Carson Welles— "the most boring man who's ever lived"—as much as the *idea* of a "settled existence with a mature man." Garber was happy to have Barbara back. He loved her hard-assed way of dealing with the world, her red hair and freckles, the way she got what he was saying, even if, as was often the case, she disagreed with it. "You're against everything," she'd informed Garber, "and I'm only against a few things, that's the difference between us." This kind of talk irked Garber, but here was something he had to agree with. In those days, the mid-70's, post-Vietnam, post-Watergate, post-prosperity, Garber was against everything. He was "sick of the fucking fandango" that had unfolded since '69, "the year the country went to shit." When he'd make those sorts of pronouncements, when he'd tell Barbara that he wanted to move to Canada to get away from the nut jobs in Washington, when he'd go so far as to apply for a Fulbright in a God-forsaken place like Nigeria, he was in earnest, but a day or so later he'd think of some reason he couldn't leave, some cause he had to address or some piece of work he had to do. He loved the fray; enjoyed being pissed off at the stupidity of his fellow Americans, and not often, but sometimes, was touched by their generosity.

When he thought about his life, drifting on his hospital bed ($200 per day, paid for with Medicare, God bless LBJ), watching with some sadness the progress of the day—Mr. Samuels was practicing the saxophone now, as he did each morning before work, Garber felt irked that he was dying. *Irked.* He wasn't bad, Art Pepper it sounded like, short bursts of 'Straight Life,' not exactly Pepper's signature tune, but ironic and lovely—Mr. Samuels had taught Garber to appreciate jazz during the years of their distant acquaintanceship, especially, of course, the music of the great alto players—where was he? Oh yes, every book had cost him a wife or a girlfriend. When he'd finally left St. Johnsbury, left his cronies and girlfriends behind, ran out on the Green Mountain State, and been hired (after a bitter negotiation) at American University to teach history, he'd discovered he had a knack for exactly two things—writing books about politics and talking about politics. At everything else in life, including friendship and love, Garber had to admit—and why not admit it, now that the game was up? —he was a flop. When he was engaged in a project, writing about the Wobblies for example, a project that took him three years, or when he was traveling regularly from Washington to Detroit, putting together an oral history of the UAW with a couple of union guys, or when he was organizing the American Committee to Defend Universities—against corporate control, rapacious administrators, federal budget cuts, the Defense Department, and, before long, computerization—Garber displayed his fundamental monomania, his resolute, single-minded, unselfishness—his best side. But he also displayed indifference to everything else. Friends left him alone, and then, after a while, drifted away. Girlfriends hung around his messy Capitol Hill townhouse for a while, waiting for the phone to ring, and when it didn't, they packed up and left. Barbara, who had hung on, left him and returned half-a-dozen times, flew to Detroit or Chicago or St. Louis or wherever Garber was agitating, researching, or organizing, and tried to find a niche in his life, a fingerhold into which she might insinuate herself. But it was no good. He'd be upset rather than pleased to see her, wonder why she had left home to crash with him in some Motel 6 outside of Dallas when he was busy meeting with the Graduate Student Association of UT-Dallas, persuading them to go on strike against the university for higher TA salaries or more comprehensive health care—demands that no university would ever meet since the pool of hungry grad students was as limitless as the ocean, especially as the country shed jobs in the name of 'competitiveness.' Barbara would hang around for a while, feeling foolish.

Now, too late, Garber was embarrassed by his behavior, near tears as urine leaked into the adult diaper he had reluctantly begun to wear at night as he lost control of his bladder. Losing control: that was the name of the game—his bladder, his hands, his thoughts—one by one the world he had carefully made and comfortably inhabited was lost. Garber cried quietly for a few minutes—what the hell, he hadn't cried when he'd been diagnosed, or, stoically, as he moved from an active life to being housebound to nearly bedridden—at each station of his cross Garber had remained dry-eyed, but now, a week away (he sensed the time but hoped for months of life, at least), he let himself weep. He was helpless against the onslaught of the past, and while he had forgiven himself—had he not, like Dante, entered the circles of hell to be shriven? —he couldn't forget. He wept, and then he slept.

In his cancer sleep, the little buggers multiplying in Garber's weary self—if he had a self and wasn't a

Cartesian robot, a ghost tucked away in his pineal gland, watching the ship of the body go down but confident of floating off into the sea of souls, perhaps to be given another ship to command (Garber, in his Buddhist moments, really did believe this)—as he sank deeply down into addled dreams, Garber watched himself lying in bed, and decided, or so it seemed, to dream his childhood into being.

What he wanted to dream was of his mornings, the time he had loved the most through those early years of school and summers and holidays. He remembered his mother coming in to wake him, just as the sun was pushing up out of the Atlantic and the oaks that rimmed the yard had begun to lighten. He would open his eyes and see his mother there, fully dressed—she had been up for an hour, packing lunches, setting out clothes, perhaps finishing the ironing from the night before—and although he would grumble about the time, he was happy to rise and wash and join her in the steaming kitchen for oatmeal and toast and, once he was ten, milky-sweet coffee. His mother insisted on coffee because it promoted 'alertness,' a trait she valued among all others. To be 'bright-eyed' was the sum of virtue; there was work to be done, a world to be conquered— the laggards would be left behind. And then Garber, just plain David in those days—never Dave or Davie— would dress in his school uniform and gather his books and walk with his mother to the bus stop. What had they talked about on those mornings? Garber, drifting up slowly from his nap, couldn't recall.

(Should he let go now, or should he hang on? He'd begun to feel that his departure was a matter of choice. No, not yet, there was still some life in him).

Garber wanted to enjoy the panorama of his existence, a wide-angled view of his time on earth, past and present and maybe the future compressed to a point. That would be his peace. The things he'd be leaving behind, including those winter mornings walking hand in hand with his mother to the bus, those things were gone forever, as extinct as democracy and good manners.

Awake now, Garber passed from dream to consciousness without missing a beat. She's long dead, he thinks, and he remembered that he had held her hand as she died— the same one he'd held on the way to the bus, or as he walked, frightened, into the ocean, or that he'd held when he was in the hospital, many years before, half dead with pneumonia. She was energetic and bright-eyed right up to the last week of her life—Garber was surprised at the depth of the void her passing left. And now it was his turn, he had come to the head of the line, the great long line of the dying he had stood in for so many years. Garber smiled, thinking about how life was waiting for something you wanted never to happen.

He'd been born in New Jersey. Smack dab in the middle of the Garden State. In Asbury Park, lovely when he was a boy, with its boardwalk and Casino, but as he grew up an increasingly forlorn and seedy city. He was the spawn of what had come in the 90's to be thought of—thanks to a movie and a book and the public's yearning for something to grasp onto as the President went down in erotic flames—as the "Greatest Generation," a description which Garber considered laughable. He'd written a book on *The Overrated Generation*, a tilt at windmills intended to show that people like his father and his mother had been the beneficiaries of the self-sacrifice of a small percentage of the population of the United States—fewer than three hundred thousand American dead, which wasn't nothing, but how did this compare to twenty million Russians, six million Jews, untold, uncounted millions of Poles and Slovaks and Czechs? Sixteen million Americans served—but neither of his parents had joined up. Garber's father had gotten out on his eyesight and the fact that he was the sole custodian of his demented mother. *The Overrated Generation* asserted that the Depression/World War II generation had played its grasping hand skillfully and received far more in benefits than it had deserved. Cheap houses, free university educations, jobs—actual jobs! —social programs that the ingrates had turned on once they had milked them dry, plus endless adulation, the icing on the cake. Movies and books and parades and monuments filling the National Mall from end to end. "Where," Garber had written, knowing he was stepping in shit, "was the monument to the Freedom Riders, the pacifists, the union men and women who'd fought the real fight, the one for the crumbs left over once the 'greatest generation' had had its fill?" And this: "Nowadays a Vietnam vet is more likely to blow his brains out than find work. And it's the dinosaurs praised by the faddists of 'greatness' who reap the benefits of the war and who keep on collecting, decade after decade." Yes, he was looking for trouble. The *Times*, which had studiously ignored his other books, handed the review of *The Overrated Generation* to a hack from *The New Republic*, a professor whose version of red-baiting had been refined during the Nixon years, The reviewer noted that "David Graber [sic] was well-known for his perverse attacks on all conventions, liberal and conservative, and was a spokesman for those who blame America for all the ills of the present," a comment that had nothing to do with what Garber had written but which achieved its intended purpose—Garber's publisher cut him loose, citing poor sales. That was to be expected. In Eastern Europe in the 80's he'd have been put in jail or worse. Losing his publisher was one thing—he found another—but being accused of hating America—that pissed him off. Garber loved the old bitch with the passion of a critic: "Lighting fireworks one day a year hardly makes you a patriot," became a line he used often, in defense of his perverse brand of loyalty, if not to the actual government, at least to the ideals it professed.

What had irked Garber was that this same generation—his old man—became the tax evaders, Proposition 13 supporters, the critics of Headstart, shills for Goldwater, Reagan lovers, Billy Graham revivalists, benign neglect theorists, trickle-down freaks. His father had read a book by David Stockman—that *schlemiel*—maybe the only book his father had ever opened. The book argued that giving money to the rich was the best thing for the country—the so-called producers—the same people who came back to Uncle Sam year after year for bailouts and starter capital and tax breaks and who sat in the Congress and on the Court—Stockman wanted to give them *more,* those who had it all needed more of the hard-earned dollars of the union guys, the truckers, hotel maids, assembly-line workers (the few who were left), cops and firemen and teachers. For Garber's father there was one proposition in the catechism: Once you got your dough, no matter how, figure out how to keep it. Garber remembered bitter arguments with his father over taxes: a duty, said Garber; *socialism* proclaimed his father. "What do they do with it?" his old man asked, meaning, of course, the black people. "They waste it on God knows what." Meanwhile Garber's father hid his earnings by taking payment in cash when he could, and spent it on Cadillacs, sport coats, and golf games. How did this happen? How had his father, a Methodist turned Roman Catholic—he'd converted to marry Garber's mother—a man who had sat in the austere First Methodist Church of Asbury Park or in the Rococo cathedral of St. Mary's to atone for his sins, who tithed the church and claimed to have read the Bible every day, a man who had adored FDR and Henry Wallace, voted for Stevenson twice, eventually became, through the alchemy of greed, a Goldwater Republican, a *Nixon supporter* (Garber shuddered to think of the signed photos of Nixon and Agnew—those crooks—in his father's "library," the room where the old man smoked cigars and flipped through *Fortune*), and finally, near the end of his life, a Reaganite. Garber still couldn't believe it—that his Papa, his good and decent father, the man who drove him to his Little League games and left work early for years to watch Garber sit on the bench during football and basketball season, his handsome and charming old man who smelled of Aqua Velva and Right Guard, who dressed like a mobster, that his father had become a selfish old man, a bigot, a delegate to the 1984 Republican Convention. It had broken Garber's heart when his father, deep into his eighties, living on Social Security in a wretched Florida condo and sucking up millions in Medicare after his colon was removed, spent his final weeks on earth enthralled by Ken Starr's attempt to destroy Clinton.

How had his mother stood it? His parents' marriage hadn't done much to prepare Garber for the relationships he'd stumbled into as an adult. His mother had been unhappy—anyone but his father could have seen it—but she'd stuck it out for her kids' sake. Or was that just Garber's take on half-a-lifetime of devotion? Maybe Ellen—he'd always called his mother by her first name— had adored her husband. Apparently, the Old Man had been a handsome fellow in high school, a cheerleader and junior jock, too small to be a star, but with a competitive streak that could be cruel. Well-dressed and groomed, a man who got his haircut every Saturday morning, who bought his suits at Robert Hall and wore Italian loafers he picked up on Madison Avenue each Christmas, a ladies man, a liar who'd claim to work late and showed up at three in the morning smelling like perfume and bourbon. He started life as a salesman, peddling fire and life policies, working door-to-door "among the coloreds", a hard worker who eventually became a general agent, and, for the last twenty years of his life, worked at Metropolitan Life in Newark as some sort of low-level VP, a commuter, photogenic (Garber had a box of pictures of his father, posing with gray-faced corporate executives, trucking association VIP's, mobsters), a man with "prospects," a fine catch (Garber imagined) in Ellen's eyes, and a way to escape her own crazy family, her alcoholic father and depressive mother.

"He didn't pan out," she had said, as if he were a household appliance or an investment, which, Garber supposed, was what he'd been. On the other hand, his mother hadn't been easy to live with; a perfectionist and neat-freak, loyal to her nutty mother, cold as ice if you crossed her—Garber could half-understand why his father had run around on her, why he stayed at the office as much as he could and grew fond of Old Fashioneds.

Garber knew that it takes two people to ruin a marriage, but he wasn't about to put his mother through the pain of self-examination on her deathbed. He let her go on about how George had ruined her life. Maybe he had. Or maybe they'd ruined each other's lives, or maybe they were happy as clams all those years that they fought like feral dogs and then, for weeks at a time, never spoke a word to one another. Who knew? Garber's own experiences with women were hardly a study in mental health or conjugal happiness. He went out for coffee and donuts for his mother the final weekend of her life, sweet milky coffee she sipped throughout the day, and instead of confessions they reminisced about the good years—and there had been many back in the fifties and early sixties, before things had gotten too crazy. Garber had played home movies for her—carefully threading the brittle film through her forty-year-old projector— films of family vacations in Florida in the days before there was anything to it aside from sand and ocean and a few cut-rate motels. The ancient, yellowed 8mm film whirled through the reels and flickered on the bed sheet that Garber had spread across the living room. His mother was propped up on the couch with her coffee and glazed donut, almost happy, relieved in any case to be getting it over with. Garber's father had died two years before and since then she had spoken more often of her own "departure." Garber would have none of it— he reminded her that his father had been a smoker, a drinker, and someone who never exercised or "took care of himself." In fact, he'd treated his body as if it were disposable—bacon and eggs for breakfast every day, burgers for lunch, steak for dinner. When Garber's mother had served salads or pasta or chicken for dinner her husband had complained of being hungry— "Chicken is an appetizer"—he'd proclaim, and the minute he finished his meal he lit up a Tareyton, dumping the ashes on his plate and pushing the butt in his mashed potatoes. He'd been a boorish man, yet, during that last weekend of her life, all Ellen could see was the nice-looking boy she'd fallen for, and herself a good Catholic girl who'd won the Latin Prize at St. Rose, a virginal teenager who'd landed a war-time job a Ft. Monmouth as a telephone operator, lonely in the way everyone was in those days, friendly with boys but never able to say what she needed from them, never expecting much more than a house and kids who would "fail to appreciate her," this was what she said to her son that last night—a Saturday, right before Mothers' Day—"no one appreciated me," but it wasn't true, Garber had adored her.

As Garber rolled on his walker—the humiliation!

—out of the bedroom and down the hall to the cluttered living room so that he could stretch out on his ratty couch, it occurred to him that his most vivid image from childhood was of his father asleep on the family's big blue couch (bought using his Diners Club card) and of Mom drinking coffee at the kitchen table. His parents hadn't occupied the same room too often—his father only went into the kitchen for meals—and his mother spent her living room time on her feet, ironing. His family had seemed to be pulled apart by forces that operated in the way black holes (it appears) pull all matter inward, toward some cold conflagration; there was never an explosion in the Garber house, but a continuous collapse of feeling.

"That's you, it must have been when I went to college, 1964, and there's Pop all trim and tan, and you with your pearl sunglasses, always afraid of the sun, and I'm nervous here about meeting my roommate who turned out to be okay in his way, and…." Garber had gone on and, on that weekend, nervous at the fact of his mother's departure—he'd never understood the privacy of death before—he babbled about the past as if he could stop time.

Her greatest pleasure had been going to the beach thought Garber, as he reclined on the couch, half-asleep, wrapped in the warmth of memory. This was common ground. When he was little, Garber's mother had walked him across the street from the boarding house to the Palace where she'd given him nickels to play Skee-ball or to ride the Merry-Go-Round—the best in New Jersey—and, when he was older, she would stand next to him as he played pinball, gently nudging the machine enough so the ball would carom off the top bumpers and add to his score. The Palace was either cold or hot—it was an open, airport hanger of a building, snot-green, with the grotesque face of "Tillie" stenciled on the outside. Garber had nightmares about the clownish face of Tillie. His bedroom window had faced the Palace and the Lyric Theater, both were brightly lit (on rare, quiet nights Garber had been able to hear the neon tubes buzzing, an unearthly hum that had put him to sleep). Garber's room had curtains, but the green and red lights pulsed against his ceiling, and if he looked through the curtains, there was the demented grin of Tillie.

Garber looked into the future, into the wreckage of the city he'd grown up in, the empty buildings, the porn theatre, also shuttered, where the Lyric had been—he'd seen "Irma La Douce" there, and "I Am Curious, Yellow"—the broken glass in the once-majestic doors of the Convention Center where he'd gone with his friends to listen to the Four Seasons. Close to death himself, Garber's glimpsed the abyss, a blackness that approximated the silence at the beginning of time, as in the dioramas his parents had taken him to see at the Hayden Planetarium, the dome filled with stars and planets, the dizzying feeling of leaving his body and traveling back to the beginning. He let himself dream, and he saw images that belonged to his past and to the future. Why not? Time wasn't linear—it had taken Garber until now to understand that the world wasn't moving through time but was within it, that time was the origin of everything, the ether in which matter and mind were embedded. He *was* time, and his mind contained it, and, as he approached his end, he could at last see the source and ending of himself, of all things, as clearly as he saw the vanishing present. As a half-baked Buddhist, Garber was skeptical of the ego, and in his cancer mind he could clearly see that dissolving of the past into the future, proof that he was no one, and that his dying was no more meaningful than a sunset, and far less beautiful.

He thought, "I've become quite the philosopher," and laughed at himself for spinning out theories, when it was too late. A theory of life is valuable at the onset of adulthood, as a guide to making the most of one's

time, but it hardly mattered what anything meant—
meaning had come to an end. Here was Garber, addled
and drugged, still a sentimental cynic, wondering how
it could have been that the smiling brunette dressed
in a blue sailor suit—with great legs and a stunning
figure—had become his mother, had carried him in her
body, had suffered his birth, then had dragged herself
through four tedious decades as a homemaker and wife
to a flim-flam man, who had, in her late 60's, at last
found the courage to live alone, to push her children
away so that she might finish her life as she wished—
how could she be gone, vanished? With both his parents
dead, with their bodies turned to dust and stored in fake
marble lockers among the live oak and tupelo draped
in Spanish moss in separate south Florida towns, only
now did Garber understand religious belief—at last he
knew that not his immortality but theirs was the point.
William James was right: the "will to believe" could be
conjured up out of grief or love. But real belief was more
akin to freckles or a clubfoot—a birthright.

Later in the morning—if it was morning—his watch had
stopped and didn't own any clocks—he rose refreshed.

"Up you bum," Garber felt, all in all, not bad. This
had been part of the disease. No need to be hasty: once

he'd perished they'd be done for as well, perfectly honed engines of destruction, rather like the Republic, allowing another blow against a democracy which had never been much in the first place.

"We never believed in it," this made Garber sad, though he couldn't imagine that he had a single illusion left about his country. He'd spent his life arguing in favor of something no one wanted—accountability. The politicians weren't much for telling the truth or doing what was right, that was to be expected, but the people themselves—his neighbors—what had they been thinking these past four decades as they put one crook after another into power? Not Jimmy, incompetence wasn't a crime, but the rest of them, and this time around was the worst of all. A stolen election. He'd seen it coming. He'd written a piece for the *Nation* a month before, his last journalistic effort, on how the election was too close too call not because Bush and Gore were equally liked or despised—Bush was a nonentity and Gore was stiff as a board—but because the Republicans had figured out once and for all how to game the system, how to keep minorities from voting, how to divvy up the key states so that pluralities didn't matter. Sure enough, here was a story in the *Post*, the last paper Garber would ever read, saying that the Court would decide whether or not to allow the recount to continue. That did it. Garber knew how the Court would vote—no doubt about it. He could only imagine the arm twisting going on a couple of blocks from where he sat at his desk, flipping through old pictures. Nine Justices, all bought and sold. How Garber would like to believe again! He jotted a note to himself— "Call the kids...call Wallace. Will?"

He thought, *It was a relief all those years to have faith.* He had believed in many things when he was younger—in God, in his country's probity, in his fellow man. Not much left of those fancies. He could remember now, fingering a picture of himself as a high school freshman—tie and jacket, hair slicked back, slightly crooked teeth (his parents hadn't believed that orthodontics was a necessary component of a happy life)—that it was at fifteen that he'd renounced God in favor of reason, or now, "reason" in quotes since he'd given up on that as well.

"It suffices to say that the issuance of the stay suggests that a majority of the Court, while not deciding the issues presented, believe that the petitioner has a substantial probability of success. The issue is not, as the dissent puts it, whether '[c]ounting every legally cast vote ca[n] constitute

irreparable harm.' One of the principal issues in the appeal we have accepted is precisely whether the votes that have been ordered to be counted are, under a reasonable interpretation of Florida law, 'legally cast vote[s].' The counting of votes that are of questionable legality does in my view threaten irreparable harm to petitioner Bush, and to the country, by casting a cloud upon what he claims to be the legitimacy of his election."

It was 'reason' that had allowed sophistry such as this to exist. To the country? Garber laughed when he read these words in the 'National Section.' Best to laugh. No, Garber had quit reason, though not at fifteen. At fifteen he'd begun to devote himself to getting laid, to reading every book ever written, and to purging his soul of Catholicism. Now, at fifty-six, he'd decided to devote himself to writing down what he did believe in, hoping there was something he could leave for his children, some evidence that he wasn't an a nihilist—far from it, he still believed in too many things for his own good.

Time to sort through the papers. To impose order on what was chaotic—or to create chaos out of disorder. At this point it was difficult to tell what made sense. Ideas of order were always, Garber knew, a cover-up, a way of hiding the truth. He'd learned from reading serious books that the unvarnished truth was far more difficult to come by than riches or power or sex appeal. "In case of doubt, let truth be told," one of Garber's authorities had written. Then he reached for another of his authors, close by, well-thumbed: "The maker's rage to order words of the sea,/Words of the fragrant portals, dimly starred,/And of ourselves and of our origins,/In ghostlier demarcations, keener sounds." Garber remembered walking on the orange sand of Key West with Barbara a lifetime before—it had been early summer and the sweetness of hibiscus and bourgenvilla filled the air and the warmth of the ocean and its briny, viscous rush across his feet and legs—how happy he had been at that moment, how little the world had weighed on them, no children yet, intense heat and the heavy feeling of mid-day, when time stopped. Garber closed his eyes and tipped back in his desk chair, focusing all of his diminished powers on the task of evoking that moment, pulling it up from the depths of memory as one might pull up an enormous fish, felt below the surface but invisible, brought to clarity after a struggle. It was impossible. He couldn't keep his flighty mind on the task; the memory slipped away. And then another thought came to him, less comforting. He daydreamed a conversation among his children and wives, they were gathered in a nondescript room, framing their relief that he was gone at last. A hard truth: they would be quietly pleased to see him go. Yes, it was true. He'd been aloof, and before that meddlesome—he'd wandered in and out of his children's lives since they were little; he'd left Barbara and returned half-a-dozen times. He'd sent checks home, but was seldom present. He'd lived apart in Vermont and Washington as often as he could, valuing his time too much to waste it on those who loved him. And what had been so important that he couldn't be with his children? Had his books made any difference? Did the political causes he'd thrown himself into make the world a better place?

"Look around you fool, does the world seem any better for you being in it?"

Maybe, Garber thought now, he'd made things worse, the battles, the lawsuits, the arguments with colleagues—he'd been impossible to work with, contentious, opinionated, uncompromising. He'd called decent people with whom he'd worked names—to their faces, behind their backs—"idiot, fascist, dope!" He tried his preferred terms of abuse out on himself. It hurt to think now of how he'd behaved in the name of his beloved truth and his narrow version of justice. He'd been a bigot, a Puritan. Oh, how good it felt now that it was too late to make amends to sit at his desk, with a skim of light pushing the motes of dust around the room, and to beat himself up! Garber hated to think so, but maybe Freud was right, maybe we wish for death just as much as for life. This possibility would explain why nobody could solve any collective problems, why families were so often unhappy, why love affairs were seldom sustained, why people (those Garber happened to know) seemed to take a perverse satisfaction in their own failures. There it was, love and death, merged into one thing, the life-force, the yearning to be, and the just-as-compelling urge not to bother. The perennial question; the only question according to Camus and Hamlet and what's his name in *Magic Mountain*— Garber had literary support for his views, he'd read a lot of novels so he could prop up his opinions with high-minded precedents. Settembrini. Or Peeperkorn. Garber moaned and got up from his desk—he was moping. He put a CD in his player, the Brahms B-Major Trio, and sat on the couch to listen to the Beaux Arts version, music he loved more than any other. The music of the spheres—such a lovely notion, the universe, blank and black, suffused with Brahms as ordered by the fingers of Bernard Greenhouse which were in turn ordered by the harmonies of the world. An unbreakable circle of beauty. Garber supposed that like Mann, or rather like Hans Castorp, "Music moved him more deeply than anything else," that it was his form of worship, and had been since he had first shut his mouth and opened his ears long enough to hear what he was listening to. He'd started with the easy stuff, with Chopin's waltzes and polonaises and Beethoven's symphonies, and then moved on to more demanding works by Schubert and Stravinsky, landing, for several years, in the ethereal realms of late works—Schubert's last songs, Beethoven's last quartets, the haunting B major trio of Brahms. The only reliable way for Garber to pull himself together— he was frazzled and wrapped up in memories—was to sit still and listen to these thirty minutes of harmonic beauty, so full of yearning (as it seemed to Garber), a negotiation among piano, cello, and violin over which of the three voices could fully approximate the real thing—Beauty Itself. And what was that? Garber had spent his life as a pragmatist, a supporter of lost causes, a bad historian but in truth he preferred the restful cadences of poetry and music. What was beauty? He had no idea. There, that passage, the piano galloping along ahead of the others, the cellist answering back, the violin calming the other two—he wasn't a music critic, but this was exquisite. He felt calm and whole—healthy. Beauty, he supposed, was like this—a bargain or perhaps an argument, among creator, object, and consumer. There could be no "theory" of beauty since theories assume a limited number of variables, or at least variables whose limits can be precisely described. But with this Brahms there was much to consider aside from the genius of the composer, the talent of the performers, and the mood of a dying man. What if Brahms had changed a single measure? He did in fact revise the work late in life, and it was the revision to which Garber was listening now. Did this fact alter its aesthetics? And if the performers were less talented, would that diminish the beauty of the piece? Was there a calculus of such things, where any change could be plotted on a graph approaching zero aesthetic pleasure, and each incremental error in performance—a slip by the cellist, or a tempo slightly too fast (here!) by the pianist—would detract in some small fashion from the integrity of what Brahms's had envisioned way back in 1854? These questions had puzzled Garber for years, ever since he began to listen to music "with both ears open." He had wondered what the camp inmates at Auschwitz had felt, aesthetically speaking, when the camp orchestra had been compelled to play Wagner at "concerts" organized by *SS-Obersturmbannfuhrer* Hoss. What "laws" of aesthetics applied then? Was "beauty" what the orchestra created, or another form of terror? Hoss, Garber knew, had been a Catholic, a man obsessed not only with duty, but with sin and penance. He'd had an intense fixation on purity as a young man—the "sins of the flesh" had been especially troubling to him—perhaps he'd overseen the murder of a million people to cleanse himself of desire. The body, after all, was the source of all beauty for the Greeks and Romans. When the Christians came along with their mad ideas of otherworldliness those glorious male and female figures became diabolical, temptations to be destroyed through mortification. Even nature lost its beauty in those early Christian centuries; the pastorals of Vergil and Theocritus became just another of God's mysterious hieroglyphs—a texts to be deciphered rather than enjoyed. Christianity insured that all pleasure became suspect, forms of temptation, so that beauty was reduced to the single function of inducing transcendence, of lifting the mind upward to God. Even the cathedrals, monuments to otherworldliness, were to be *seen through* rather than *marveled at*—they were, after all, stone and mortar, and, like flesh and blood could have no standing in a spiritualized world. Garber had written all this out years before; now, listening to Brahms with tears in his eyes, he marveled again at the success of religion's campaign to devalue all of the things that mattered most. What was beauty? The core of life, all of the things that had made Garber happy, the things which he had believed in, the things that he now yearned to hold on to for as long as possible. Death was oblivion—he would cease to exist, it would be as if he never had lived—but for now, on this cloudy-bright day, this music cemented his bond to the earth, the only earth there was, the only place he would ever live. Had lived. Garber thought he might begin to refer to himself in the past tense, get used to his absence. He was like this rest in the adagio, a meditative silence as the cello faded before the violin's *glissando*. Not quite a silence—a pause between passages—a shift from major to minor keys. Had Brahms been embarrassed by the exuberance of this music written when he was twenty? Teary-eyed, Garber thought about this question. Though he was no artist—he had been on his best days no more than a polemicist, a man who, as one hostile reviewer had written, "a two-bit intellectual with a chip on his shoulder"—Garber had enough intelligence to recognize his own failings, and to be embarrassed by many of the things he had written and said over the years.

Maybe it was time to go.

Being right: this had been his great failing. Why not own up to it now, sitting here in his musty sweatpants, feeling less well by the minute—hungry, but with no energy to prepare any food—he'd always wanted to be the one who knew best, ever since he'd been a child he'd insisted that he was the authority on everything. He'd been thought clever when he corrected his father, and then he began to correct his mother, his brother and sister, his friends and teachers. He'd lectured everyone on every topic—from the cultural significance of *Mad Magazine* to the reasons why no real baseball fan could care for the Mets. He had been, he knew now, a pedant, a bore, one of those tedious know-it-all's who mistook certitude for knowledge. He'd been an indifferent son, an unmotivated student, an incompetent teacher, a shrill and inconsequential political journalist, a diffident husband, a disengaged father, a cynical citizen, and a poor excuse of a man. He was, he knew, at the end of the line, and what he had been, what he was, was what he would be from now until whatever proximate date he finally left this world. And in a second of clarity, of selfless recognition, Garber realized that nothing he'd done wrong, or right, had made the slightest difference.

When the Brahms ended, the CD player shifted to the next tray and Garber was surprised to hear Wagner—arias from *Tristan und Isolde*, performed by Deborah Voigt and Placido Domingo. When had he listened to this? He couldn't recall putting this music on the player, so perhaps Manuel had done so, or one of his visitors, Barbara might have done so as she admired the great tenor and could still stomach Wagner. Since he was too tired to get up, Garber closed his eyes and listened—this was music he knew well, romantic decadence he had once listened to avidly.

In dem wogenden Schwall, in dem tönenden Schall, in des Welt-Atems wehendem All —-ertrinken, versinken — unbewußt -höchste Lust!

When Garber took the time to think about it, he found such sentiments embarrassing. Holy desire? Really? And those Wagnerian actors, poached in their costumes, rambling on for hours about feelings pitched to the highest octave of madness. He'd enjoyed such romantic goings-on as a young man, but later on in life, when a bar of Wagner wafted into his sonic space, all Garber could think of was Hitler and Goebbels weeping at Bayreuth—*Das Judebthum in der Musik*—Aryans sailing to Valhalla over the corpses of millions. But sitting in his college philosophy class listening to his professor explain Freud's ideas, nineteen-year-old Garber had believed that all feelings could expand indefinitely. Wasn't this the point of feeling? To focus on sexual desire—the sum of what Garber felt as a young man—until it consumed his consciousness, Isolde dying for Tristan—wasn't this the idea? Garber thought that nothing in his life had mattered so much as passion. Not love necessarily, but a continually unfolding myopic fixation on the people that circumstance threw in his path. He'd lived fully, no doubt about it, never held back his foolish "heart," trusted it to people who had mostly treated it as a poor gift, who had other concerns and who had found other hearts more to their liking. Was he a romantic? Trusting feeling over reason? He thought not. His method had always been to leaven his thoughts with feeling, not to go blindly into anything but, once he'd thought things through, to be passionate about them—he disliked the lukewarm in people, ironic detachment appeared to him to be a fear of life, hedging bets against an uncertain fate. Garber took risks and he'd paid the price for doing so—lost jobs, wives, children, and friends. But loss was the rule of things, wasn't it? Garber remembered how he had started to write things down, believing that by doing so the events of his life would be preserved forever—now, sunk into the silence of the morning, no one nearby to confide in, he saw the folly of his hope.

"Suppose," he said aloud, "the Word really was eternal, the alpha and omega. Then if you wrote out your life something would endure, something of you would live on." And he'd written about his life for decades—he had boxes of notebooks full of the *minutia* of everyday life—but these transcribed events were lifeless, pointless. It was only in memory that Garber had any reality—but then memory was notoriously unreliable. Here he was in the midst of his sixth decade, the victim of some oddball genetic mischance, cancerous through no fault of his own, growing (while he thought about it) deadening cells that were pushing out the living, taking their jobs, undermining the Garber way of life. Like, Garber had to smile, capitalism itself—a great social cancer—pushing the life from the body-politic one cell, job, family, community, at a time. Fattening a few and starving everyone else; destroying in order to rebuild and destroy again. Strip mall tumors that had poxed the landscape Garber loved.

Melanomas—Wal-Marts and K-Marts and Valu-Marts—boxy lesions full of festering junk, warehouses metastasizing across the world, all stuffed with the effluvia of greed—with shit. He was rolling now, writing down the many ways in which the world was afflicted, in his element once more, polemicist to the masses who could care less, who only wanted bigger TV's so they could watch porn and football while they ingested supersized burgers and cokes and fries that would, in their turn, produce cancers. Would computers come to rule the world? Of course not, the world belonged to cancer. Cancer was the only God, now and forever, world without end, Amen. Garber was willing to concede that cancer was a pretty interesting example of human suffering, all things considered. It made excellent metaphors, it killed through excess and indirection—here it was in the liver, and then it's there, in the lungs—cancer reminded Garber (since he was, in the immediate warm aftermath of Placido's "*O wüßtest du, Lust der Welt,*" not inclined to mince feelings) of politics, of how power killed with great delicacy and with gross brutality. Power was the real cancer; or was it the other way around—had we had it backwards all this time? Cancer was power—it made people rich, the giving of it and the "curing of it" and the writing about it, and the worry it caused. Cancer was the urge to believe that ruling this world insulated one from death. Or maybe this was too simple, maybe the elixir of power was more subtle, maybe the point of power was not to push back against the inevitable, but to embrace it, to go up in flames as Tristan and Isolde chose to do, to transcend power by embracing it. We needed cancer to remind us of death—"We might forget otherwise," Garber sang in his own scratchy tenor—"*We might forget we're mortal*," a line for a duet—he saw himself on stage at the Met, dressed for Valhalla, his arm around the lovely Cecelia Bartoli, singing "*Potremmo dimenticare siamo mortali*," Italian being the most operatic language. He sang it now, on his feet, his eyes closed, buffoonish, but happy—"*Potremmo dimenticare siamo mortali*." The opera—he would write the libretto—would be called *Cancer*. The *Times* might rave: "We applaud the courage of Mr. Garber in staging a five-hour spectacle dedicated to the dreaded scourge of cancer: who has seen such a thing since Mimi expired ("*Sono andanti*?") or Isolde wept over the body of her beloved?" Who could say? It might be a hit; after all, soon enough everyone would be terminal, or in (temporary) remission. The few remaining cancer-free Americans might be appalled, but their turn would come—the opera would have legs, the CD's would sell out—Mobile Oil could play it on Saturdays before college football. Garber suddenly felt dizzy and sat down. Maybe not. Watching others burn up was its own reward, but reveling in disease was in bad taste. And romanticism was dead. All that had come of Garber's own fling with romantic art and poetry, aside from the discovery of the universal impulse toward self-destruction and a fondness for fellatio, was what he came to think of as the "turning toward the past," toward the study of history. Hegel replaced Wagner as his go-to German, and the idea that history had a purpose, and that the purpose had something to do with "freedom"—whatever that meant—began to take shape as a formative idea, a direction and purpose for a life that might otherwise drift out of control. Not opera, but politics, not irony—he loathed it—but sincerity.

Garber pushed his *carcass* (as he now referred to his body, which seemed an alien presence, unrecognizable, without muscle tone, gray and splotchy, all the hair suddenly gone from his legs and arms, as if it too had read the writing on the wall and preferred the comfort of his bed linen, which was now thick with curly black follicles, to the coming fire; also on his sheets, apart from spots of blood and piss stains, were what appeared to be flakes of white paint—actually bits of dry skin that were peeling from his torso like fish scales) up from the couch and slouched into the kitchen. He was hungry. If he ate he'd probably throw up, but he had to take that chance. He pulled two slices of white bread out of the bag and found a couple of plastic-wrapped pieces of American cheese in the fridge as well as a nearly-empty jar of Gulden's Mustard—his favorite. Nothing better, Garber knew, than a cheese sandwich on generic white bread. The fetish for whole grains never made sense to Garber. He ate a couple of bites of his sandwich and then gagged—the drugs had destroyed his sense of taste, part of the medical campaign to wean him from life. He couldn't drink anymore, or taste food, or get an erection, or go for a walk—so what was the point? Pachomius and the other Desert Fathers lived off locusts and scorpions, approximating death through starvation; they lived in dugouts in the hot sands of Ethiopia, batting away the devils that beleaguered them. This sort of renunciation mystified Garber: if the taste of food or wine or the sweat on the woman's neck were evil, why not just blow your brains out? Well, of course, there were no firearms, so maybe Jerome would have had to jump into the sea, or into a pit of vipers, or have himself buried alive in the Sahara. As long as you are renouncing, why not go all the way? But then, that was *wanhope*, the deadliest sin of all, believing you were beyond saving—but saving from what? From life. None of this had ever made sense to Garber, even in his years of studying Dante, reading the Fathers, delving into the history of Dante's religious beliefs. Garber had been high-minded when he was younger—a disciple of Rousseau and Marx and Saint-Simon and the other dreamers. He'd lived for ideas and schemed at making the world a better place for the poor and downtrodden—for much of his life he'd believed in justice and peace and brotherly love. Now, sitting at his kitchen table, he fought off the biliousness that came with ingesting his bland cheese sandwich—he could still sip a little bourbon each day, and now that his liver was shot he could do so with impunity, and he could sometime keep down a handful of rice, but that was all. He was an alcoholic Buddha, Jim Beam and basmati, more than a grain a day, but still, not enough to keep a man alive, even a man who was half-dead. What had happened to him, to his noble dreams for mankind? Must idealists grow cynical, give up on truth and justice, start reading *Fortune* instead of *The Progressive*, obsess about the stock market and their fucking portfolio? Years before, during the period when he had been committed to *praxis*—he wanted to move mankind along on the road to the terrestrial paradise, which he envisioned as a perpetual summer vacation, lounging on the beach, drinking good rum, screwing beautiful women, and reading novels. He hadn't ever worked out the details of supply and demand—he hadn't a pragmatic bone in his body—but he wanted to try out direct involvement in the struggle (in those days he used no quotation marks around this word, and why should he? Was there *not* a struggle?), and so he flew off to Nicaragua for a year. Right here above his stained Formica table, the one with red trim that he'd inherited from his mother, an old wreck of a table at which he'd eaten 20,000 meals, a relic of his boyhood that was still circled with brown lines of nicotine like flattened worms—where was he?—yeah, anyway, above it hung a photograph of boy named Edwin, twelve when the picture was taken, almost certainly dead now, a cadre in the FSLN army, a dark-haired kid carrying an AR-15 who'd told Garber that already he'd killed three *contras* and hoped to kill many more. Garber had met Edwin outside of Ocotal, a small pueblo in the north-ernmost part of Nicaragua. The Sandinistas were there to defend the provinces bordering Honduras against incursions by counterrevolutionaries—by thugs and bandits who raped and pillaged in the name of freedom, whose boots were made in San Diego and whose guns came from the Springfield Armory. Garber was with a group of Quakers, building a health clinic that would be destroyed within a few months of its completion. It didn't matter. There were no doctors or medicine so the clinic might as well have been a hostel. Sitting there gagging on his sandwich, Garber could remember in stark detail the broiling hot sun, the stench of the open sewer that poured green down the hills toward the river, the shrieks of the grackles and the waves of parrots who rose as a green cloak from the acacia trees that encircled the pueblo. At sunset there was gunfire from west of the pueblo, occasionally a mortar round landed in the center of town, but the *contras* mostly remained on the Honduran side of the Rio Coco, enjoying the largesse of the CIA. Garber knew he'd done little good for anyone that year, least of all for himself. It was the end of his illusions about his power.

Garber left his sandwich on the table and put on the kettle for tea. Clio was looking out for him—she was pushing on without him. Fair enough. No point in wanting to be immortal—Garber was well-versed in the arguments in favor of dying, its metaphysical significance, its contributions to ethics, its central role in politics. How it sharpened the will to live, or, in Garber's case, illuminated the things that existed beyond his control. This was what Garber believed—that events had careened past human imagining. Since the modern era had arrived in the eighteenth century—since the *serment de jeu de paume*—from the insistence on bourgeois rights, the collapse of the old order (never mind that the *ancien regime* had returned, though as a shadow of its former self, diminished by successive revolutions), time had sped up past Garber's ability to comprehend or control it, inevitability had replaced deliberation, the masses of men and women who were no longer invisible had no choice but to destroy everything that had come before—*après nous, le déluge*—none of the corrupt institutions of the past could be allowed to exist, and so history and its victims rushed forward into an unknowable future. Garber, of course, wasn't in the front of the pack, but he was there, limping among those least able to keep up.

Though he didn't know it, Garber had been born on a Wednesday, fifty-six years before. Born in the early morning, a time of day he'd enjoyed throughout his life. He'd always been an early riser, enjoying his coffee and the day's bad news while watching the sun creep over the Chesapeake if he were in Washington or over the green hills that surrounded his house in Vermont.

His mother had said it was an easy birth, but she had been a stoic and wouldn't have complained no matter how much she had suffered. He was her third child, but the first to live; his older brother and sister, buried in a vast sea of gravestones just west of Asbury Park, survived only a few hours—their lungs had been weak, their hearts frail.

Mornings were when Garber's brain had worked best; he did his serious thinking before noon and, if he weren't teaching or saddled with some other job he would use the afternoons to take walks around the city or, if he were in Vermont, in the lush woods surrounding St. Johnsbury. During a year he spent between jobs—he was fired from the Smithsonian for "insubordination", Garber took his three-month's severance and retired for a mini-sabbatical to his run-down house in the woods overlooking Crow Hill in northern Vermont.

It was autumn when he arrived.

After the disaster at the Smithsonian, when, ordinarily, he would have stuck around to fight his firing, wage a hopeless lawsuit for breach of contract, Garber decided to take the easy way out and go for a long vacation up north. He'd never spent the autumn in Vermont, and his plan was to lease his house on Capitol Hill to an intern or visiting scholar working at the Folger Library, easy in those days—it must have been the Carter era since thinking about it now (Garber was still in bed, staring at the cracks in the ceiling) he recalled his tenant, a middle-aged lawyer from Georgia had come to Washington for a stint as a consultant at the Department of Education. Ken or Kirby—there he was, projected onto the water-stained ceiling above his bed, in the corner by the dead philodendron that hung out of its pot like the tentacles of a jellyfish. K Something. He'd been six-seven, with a protruding Adam's apple and enormous feet. A pale Abe Lincoln, maybe also with Asperger's, or maybe just a country boy who'd had too much protein or a Vitamin A deficiency. Garber had every northerner's prejudices—he hadn't minded Carter (at first) aside from the *aw shucks* manner and the absurd religious beliefs. But after Nixon and no-account Ford everybody wanted a competent choirboy in the Oval Office. "'The city upon a hill'" Garber intoned, "'lest we lose God's grace.' What is it with us?" Of the many paradoxes embraced unwittingly by his fellow countrymen, the most witless of all was the notion that an entire nation could be at one and the same time obsessed with money and beloved by God—and still maintain a presumption of innocence. Karl Driscoll.

Or Bissell. Not a bad sort for a southerner. Probably priggish, a small-town bumpkin who'd gone to Yale. That was one problem with Garber's mind—it was full of tidy boxes into which he had to jam everything and everybody. It had been Bissell, "Damn it," a memory glitch, and at once Garber feared he'd start forgetting everything. "But it was, what, 1979? Twenty-one years ago?" Karl had paid Garber six months up-front—four grand in cash—and asked if Garber minded pets. "Dogs?" No. Karl wasn't a dog or a cat man. He'd had fish—tanks full of rare tropical fish—beautiful things—plecostomus, angels, corydoras, gars and lung-fish—Garber still remembered them, their names, and it was easy to do so since Karl left the lot, the tanks, the pumps, the whole complex world of rare fish, right there in the living room along with a note apologizing for any inconvenience, but he, Karl Driscoll or Bissell, was off to London for a year and just couldn't deal with it—the whole mess worth, he said, three grand—and he hoped Garber would find them as "rewarding and relaxing a pastime" as he had. Which Garber did, for a few weeks, until the lovely blue and yellow and red tetras and mollies began to float, belly-up, to the top of the tank and, one by one, he netted them out and dropped them in the toilet. Something about the pH of the water, or maybe he was feeding them too much. Little fishy-smelling flakes, vile stuff, funny how the senses stay sharp, sense memory, he could still smell the water, tap water distilled or softened so it wasn't deadly to the fish, but then it hadn't mattered. Their connection to life that seemed ephemeral, tiny hearts and a tube that ran from mouth to anus that you could see in the lighter angels, the black speck of the brain, no larger than the point of a pen, nothing stored there but instincts dating back to the watery Devonian. The brain in us—Garber thought—not much more than a larger, newer bundle of instincts, but not so different from that which drove the pretty tetras toward the surface to gobble little bits of fish meal and corn and minerals, the stew that kept them swirling through the murky water for a few weeks until, one by one, they expired. Anyway, after a month Garber had been stuck with three large tanks full of fishy-smelling water, slimy sunken ships, and blackened sea plants. He'd sold the equipment for fifty bucks to a kid he knew from AU—*Karl Bristol.* "Bastard."

Those months, that autumn and winter, up to mid-March, the mud season in Vermont, had been among the best of Garber's life. The house was silent and empty and, beginning in mid-September, very cold. He had to spend a part of each day doing chores—chopping wood, bringing water up from the creek and boiling it, stoking the fires for cooking and heating, dealing with the stench from the outhouse, sealing the unaccountably large windows that did nothing to keep out the cold air, patching a leak in one of the dormers, cleaning up mouse dropping that filled each room and imparted an acrid smell of paraffin and rot to the house. It snowed heavily in October, catching Garber unawares, so he had to force his way through snowdrifts in his low-slung sedan to lay in supplies—fifty pounds of rice, fifty of beans, cans of soup and vegetables, oil and coffee and sugar and beer. He dropped two hundred dollars at the Safeway, filling the trunk and backseat of his ancient Skylark and guaranteeing that he wouldn't make it back home without running off the road into a ditch—he'd nearly gotten frostbite walking back to town to hire a tow truck. His thumb hadn't fallen off, but it might have—"Me without a thumb!" Garber wondered what he would have done if he'd lost his fingers, or if he'd passed out in the cold that dark frozen Thursday before Halloween, trudging through thigh-high drifts to get Mel Cummings to drag his overladen car out of the ditch across from the round barn. After this episode he mostly stayed put. From October until February he took walks on clear days, temperatures hovering around zero, wondering how anyone could endure living under these conditions year after year. So Garber read Dickens and plowed through *Capital*—dull reading—and reread his favorite books by John McDonald and Zane Grey—he wasn't a snob—and practiced the recorder for an hour each day. The snow covered half of his living room windows by Christmas, a day he celebrated with a bottle of wine and a can of corned-beef hash. He did some serious thinking during those months, writing out what he later referred to as his "prison notebooks" on legal pads for later transcription (he never looked at them again, and now, twenty years later, they were still in Vermont, someplace in the house, and would be discovered by Barbara as she cleaned the place up prior to selling it. She read some of what her husband had written all those years before, but most of it wasn't compelling or legible). Half of the mornings he'd been awakened by howling wind and heavy snow. On clear mornings the rooms would be so cold the insides of the windows would be thick with ice. Garber would wrap up in his ancient woolen bathrobe and trot downstairs to relight the fires in the kitchen and living room—the rest of the downstairs was blocked off with polyurethane—and while he waited for the water to boil and the rooms to warm he'd put on his battery-powered short wave radio and hope to pick up Morning Pro Musica out of Boston.

Looking back on those months, Garber had to admit that he hadn't realized how lucky he was, how happy. Not quite Thoreau—he couldn't walk to town—but in his Emersonian mode, self-reliant, untethered to the world, disconnected. At first he missed the newspapers, but that feeling passed. Conversation was more difficult to give up, but he found the sound of his own voice comfort enough. He got into the habit of reading his books aloud, and of arguing with himself, dissecting his character. "I'm rebuilding," he would announce, "making myself a new man." Each day he'd "venture forth like Shackleton," into the sub-zero afternoon, the light dimming early, the firs and spruces bent double under the accumulation of snow—a hundred inches by early February—crossbills and juncos and white-crowned sparrows the only birds, and of course the ravens, big flocks of the socialist birds stoically perched high atop the oaks that edged his property—Garber had marveled at the raven's ability to endure blizzards, sub-zero temperatures, and snow-covered landscape (what did they eat?). His creek was iced over but he could see the slow seething of water beneath the ice, red maple leaves frozen an inch below the surface, probably trout suspended in mid-thrust, and he'd crunch up the creek to the property next to his, half-a-mile north, the Rupert's place, a gray double-wide with an enormous satellite dish out front, ruined trucks pillaged for their parts scattered around the front, three chimneys burning hardwood full time. Tim Rupert liked the cold, snow-shoed up the hill to poach deer and jackrabbit, but his wife Eunice was cold averse, "a Florida girl" and had to have the place well-heated. Tim went through five, six cords in a winter and collecting that much wood kept him busy summers. He was a mechanic, a hunter, a fisherman, father of four, all six of the Ruperts tidy in their sheet metal home on the banks of Slow Creek, eight miles from town. Tim Rupert's life persuaded Garber that his learned stereotype of the common man was bunk. In retrospect, or in the clarity of his dying, Garber understood he'd missed the essential person, missed what he could have seen had he not been so eager to reduce the world to categories—the great failing of intellectuals, Garber knew. And he could see in Tim and in his other misanthropic neighbors—the ones with tall fences and Dobermans who lived down three more dirt roads from Garber, people already unfindable who felt they needed more insulation from the rest of humanity—what it was the Founders had been so afraid of, what they had needed to shut out—the "common man," the truly self-reliant, the man who needed no slaves, whose market was his neighborhood, who owed no one money and did business, what business he did, in cash. As Garber trudged through the deep snow that winter—all alone, disconnected from the world—it came to him as a kind of revelation (angels with golden tablets) that his country was nothing but land, vast expanses of hills and snow and plains stretching west beyond imagining. *There was no country.* Tocqueville was right—the thing was impossible to imagine. Garber saw his neighbors as separate nations, disunited and opposed both to one another (and especially to him, the seasonal interloper), and lacking the means or inclination to act civilly, aside, of course, for their occasional vote. But the Founders—those phonies—had insured that voting would merely confirm the *status quo*. It had bothered Garber a little that his idyll in the Northeast Kingdom had merely confirmed his city cynicism, but what could he do? The truth was plain to see, especially in the emptiness of a January in Peacham. By Presidents Day Garber had gone around the bend. He talked to himself all day long. At the end of the month, during a brief thaw, he'd had enough.

His plan had been to remain in his house until May, but in March he drove south on I-91, down through Amherst and Springfield and Hartford, coming to rest, temporarily, in a hotel he couldn't afford in mid-town Manhattan, from his bucolic retreat to Tenth Avenue, the Buckingham Hotel on 47th, a derelict warren of tiny rooms with a view of an airshaft, a place Garber often stayed when he was in New York, not cheap, and not comfortable or altogether safe, but it would do for a week or two while he regained his equilibrium. He walked through Times Square feeling like a tourist, jostled by the crowds. His mission in the city was connected to his firing from the Smithsonian—he needed money, and that meant he had to talk to his editors, "his" was wishful thinking—he'd been out of touch for a few years and was never highly regarded in any case. Garber hadn't been much of a journalist. He liked to stretch his legs, take the long view. His articles had always come in over budget, five thousand words meant nothing to Garber, he had a story to tell, too much research to squeeze into a paltry three pages; he gave his editors hell if they tried to cut his articles. Progressive journals paid nothing anyway. Five cents a word? Garber had shaken his head in disbelief when a twenty-five-year-old Harvard kid at *The Nation* offered him two hundred bucks for a "short piece" on SALT II. What could you say about nuclear disarmament in five hundred words? He couldn't write another book, not now, and he wasn't going to make a living writing for the three magazines who were inclined to publish his stuff, so instead of looking for work he spent his two weeks sitting in the 42nd Street library reading, and at the Met looking at art he'd not seen in years. He had a vacation from his Vermont sabbatical, "came back down to earth," read the *Times* every morning, ate eggs and bacon "at a dive on 52nd Street," then walked to the main reading room where he read at random—the history of the Ottomans, novels by John Williams, poetry magazines, back issues of *The New Yorker*. And he'd walked the streets—what was better than walking in New York City? From Riverside Park to Battery Park was nothing for Garber—he'd always been an epic walker, a hiker in the hills of Vermont, a trekker down Broadway from Harlem to Washington Square and the Strand. He'd played chess in the parks—Bryant was his favorite—and had beer in half-a-dozen watering holes he knew from earlier visits. Oh he loved the city all right, even late at night, sipping Jim Beam or ice tea in his hotel room he'd felt comforted by the teeming millions outside his dirty windows—the copulations going on around him, the meals being consumed—life.

Now, too late, Garber had an impulse to rise up—
life!—and to go into the bathroom to look in the
mirror. Was he still here? His face was the one he'd
always had. Of course it was worn, frayed at the edges,
deeply lined around the eyes and mouth, but his twice
broken nose was recognizably the one he'd had as
teenager—a fall from a bike and a ground ball to the
face—and his eyes were identical to those he recalled
from his childhood, murky and unwilling to be either
blue or brown, not soft, but not hard either, undefined, unfinished. There was no mistaking his pallor,
the unnatural sagging of his face, as if it were melting,
Garber peered into his eyes, tried to penetrate through
the iris and lenses and vitreous fluids—he was looking
for his soul. It had to be in there, if it were anywhere
at all. He'd lived at times as though his soul were in
his guts or his cock, lived crudely, justifying his appe-
tites with the excuse that the day would come when
he would no longer have them, or, if they hung on,
he would be incapable of doing anything about them.
But he'd always known the soul was in his head, right
behind his eyes, in that exact spot where he'd looked
for the words that would describe how he felt or what
he wanted. Copious hairs grew from his ears and nose

and above his eyes—he had a startled looked that he didn't care for so he opened the cabinet above the sink and took out a pair of scissors so he could chop away at his eyebrows. "This is folly." What was the point? Soon the annoying hairs would be burned up in the fire—it was all arranged—Garber had the foresight to have his corpse incinerated down the block at French's Mortuary, the ashes given to his ex-wife for scattering. Everything was arranged, and as he looked into his eyes now—flecks of brown danced on the mirror—Garber felt nostalgic for his body, sorry that it would soon be reduced to nothing. He'd enjoyed being Garber this past half century, enjoyed the farce of being someone with his name and history, but in truth he was just a body that looked like this, and a mind that had these thoughts—an English-speaking myopic white male born right after World War II who had lived a life not unusual for his type. The world had moved on. Those who'd been ignored were now, at last, getting their due. Bush and Gore were dinosaurs—what did it matter which one of them was anointed to run the country? The old bitch was dead—Garber smiled at this and noticed that his teeth were coated with pink blood— the future belonged to those who'd been screwed by the White Races—Garber washed his mouth out with Listerine—his spit was bloody—the European imperialists were reaping the whirlwind—their once lily-white capitals were now full of Nigerians and Bangladeshis and Sri Lankans and Vietnamese and Muslims who made their women wear black burkas and high-cast Hindis who worked harder than whites and would soon dominate the economies of northern Europe. Served them right. Garber thought of flossing, but he hated the way the taut string cut into his mouth, so he gargled again and then shaved his sad chin with his old Norelco electric. He was a tidy man, one who had always gone off to his jobs in clean clothes and polished shoes. He liked cologne and hair gel, a monthly trim at Korey's on Georgia Avenue, starched shirts and underwear without holes. His father had admonished him to dress well—"Clothes make the man"—and while Garber had scoffed at the crudity of this formulation, he'd believed it, and had always sought to make good impressions on his friends and to avoid giving his enemies reason to mock him as a typical slovenly leftist.

(He needed to call the Veterans so they could pick his clothes and furniture—he'd already distributed his liquid assets to his favorite charities—to Martha's Table and the Sierra Club—and his books would go to the DC public library, and his house, well, that would be the bank's. And his face and bleeding gums and sagging gut would end up in the crematorium, a vapor, his life gone up in smoke.)

(He'd read in Raul Hillberg or someplace else that it took the Nazi's 30 minutes to kill 2000 Jews with Zyklon B in the fake showers at Auschwitz and then another half hour to reduce the body to ashes in the crematoria. Near the end, with the Red Army only miles away, the SS maniacs had sped up the killing of Hungarian Jews, burning the bodies in pits piled high with trunks of oak and ash cut from the nearby forests of Silesia.)

He couldn't look at himself any longer. In a moment of rage, Garber smashed his ancient metal Norelco against the mirror, shattering it and cutting his hand. Fragments of glass filled the sink and flew into the shower and onto the floor. "Fuck it," Garber shouted, "fuck them," whoever they were. He wasn't sure why he was angry or whose faces he wished to smash—Nazi thugs certainly, but it occurred to him that there was no end to thugs so what was the point? Maybe it was best to lash out against death, against the unfairness of his own and against the impossibility of understanding how dying could be at once horrifying and comforting. He was angry because he wasn't angry enough—he felt so little that he thought he might already be dead.

His Salvadorian nurse arrived at noon. Manuel, with whom Garber spoke Spanish, gave him a sponge bath, and listened to the *chero* go on about the Phillies. Garber was passionate about baseball, and like most lovers of the game, his admiration was really nostalgia for the past, for baseball of all games was the most intimately connected to memory, to its own history. Those who, like Manuel, thought the game was slow were unaware that the games unfolded at the pace of ordinary life and not with the frenzy of lesser sports like football, or the pointlessness of soccer, with its third world stagnation, pushing a ball back and forth for half-a-day only to end the thing in the final *golpe* of the tie-breaker. Garber nattered on about the trades the Phillies had made that month, wondering if the team would gel—"chemistry being more important than talent." Manuel could have cared less—he had four children and three jobs—but he liked that the old gringo spoke Spanish well enough to be understood. Garber enjoyed anyone's company, and he liked showing off the little bit of Spanish he'd picked up during the year he spent in Nicaragua—it was a beautiful language, full of colorful slang and capable of expressing crudities an English speaker couldn't even imagine. And it was the language of Vallejo and Neruda.

"They call it the 'death gene,' a nucleotide that effects our waking time or sleeping time, like if you go to bed at midnight and wake up at 7 that's programmed, it's your circadian rhythm. You've heard of that," Garber was sitting up, temporarily lively after his third nap of the day, stimulated by Manuel's genial presence. No, Manuel hadn't heard of his circadian rhythm or of nucleotides and wasn't entirely sure what a gene might be, but Garber didn't care.

"And so you know that now scientists can predict the time of day you'll die based on this gene, and by extension approximately when, all things considered, not if you get hit by a bus or end up like me, but if you die of 'natural causes,' there's a point beyond which your organism cannot continue. And what I begin to wonder about is what's left, what's under our power? When you come right down to it there isn't any individual will. We're stuck between genetic determinism and history—all of its decided for us, and if you believe in

God," Manuel did, fervently, but had lost the thread of his patient's chatter, "then there's that to consider as well. God knows everything, is the force behind everything, so how can you have free will? I know, this is an old problem, solved centuries ago by Augustine and Aquinas, but still, saying there's a difference between time and eternity doesn't seem to me to let God off the hook, or us. And you have to see things from the point of view of DNA and bacteria. Mostly that's what you are Manuel, you've got like eight bacteria, bacterium, per cell, and then there's these things called prions which are untethered proteins—and they kill you as well—and you're coded for diseases like diabetes," Manuel had diabetes, the kind where you have to inject yourself with insulin three times a day, and he didn't like the word "coded," which he had immediately translated (as he did with the Old Gringo, simultaneously moving from English to Spanish, or, if the old man spoke to him in bad Spanish, Manuel had to fix the words so he could make sense of them), as *contraseña* which didn't make a lot of sense, "and," Garber continued, "there's everything around us—the GMO corn the FDA lets Monsanto serve up, the homone-laced beef, second-hand smoke, carbon monoxide and sulphur dioxide from the power-plants— you name it. We ate boiled peas and margarine when

I was a kid, packaged bologna, white bread with mayo slathered on it, blue Italian ice and a thousand pizzas. My father smoked two packs a day in the house. What chance did I have Manuel? I'm reaping what was sown years ago…"

Garber ran out of gas. His conversational riffs erupted spontaneously—it didn't matter if there was an audience or not. Garber had always talked to himself as he thought about something or when he was writing—monologue or dialogue, it made no difference. His brain was busy shutting down his somatic systems like one of those cinematic submarine captains who issued dozens of orders to get the damn ship to dive just as the enemy depth-charges sped toward the half-submerged hulk—in Garber's case his toes appeared to be going first, icy oblivion creeping up his limbs toward his vital parts—balls and heart (Garber's hierarchy) until, unless he were to hasten things along, he would "pass away."

"Do you need to crap?"

"Not a chance."

"Tomorrow we can fix that."

Garber had Manuel push him down the ramp (also paid for with public dollars) that joined his kitchen to the tiny rectangle of packed dirt and dead roses that constituted his backyard. Not one to spend hours growing grass or flowers, Garber had let his yard go, and his neighbors on both sides who took pride in their thickly groomed lawns, azaleas, and cultivated beds of roses, gladiolas, daisies, and various annuals, regarded with ill-concealed contempt the assault on property values that Garber's house and yard represented.

A surprisingly warm late fall afternoon, pleasant in the sun. Manuel would be back in an hour to wheel Garber inside and back to bed. The taciturn Salvadorian had another client down the road, off North Capitol, a woman with diabetes and incipient kidney failure named Emma Johnson whom Garber knew in passing from the block association, a black woman whose grandmother had been a slave on a plantation outside of Norfolk. Garber was a grassroots man, always had been. The block association had organized to persuade the City Council to repair the basketball court in Gleason Park, the only place local kids could stretch their legs after school. That battle took a year. Money was tight in D.C., not because there wasn't money but because the wealthier Northwestern section of the city along Rock Creek Park got most of it. Just before his diagnosis the Capitol Hill Association (of which Garber was Secretary) had collected four hundred signatures in opposition to the closing of the Senior Center. That one would be tougher to win as a big-shot developer had his eye on the property for upscale condos. The neighborhood was changing. Young white staffers who worked on the Hill were buying into the neighborhood, pushing up real estate values. Garber hated gentrification. Better for a neighborhood to be run down than for the residents to be run out—that was a slogan he'd come up with for a campaign he had hoped to run—Defending Our Neighborhoods. Democracy begins on your block, in your corner of the city. That sort of thing. Garber believed it. But nothing was going to stop the sharks from transforming the old cities into enclaves for the rich. And the residents—black and poor, Manuel and his family, those with the misfortune to have just arrived in the land of missed opportunity—would be shunted off to nursing homes and prison and sleazy exurbs out beyond the jobs and pleasures of the city. "A man should learn to detect and watch the gleam of light that flashes across his mind from within…" Emerson, that old pisser, had been right about that.

Just then the sun burned through the thin clouds and touched Garber's face. The pressure of heat and light brought tears to his eyes. It was difficult not to see this as a sign, ninety-six million miles was a long way, a *shaft*—"Roy G Biv", came to mind from someplace far removed from the moment—touching his forehead and cheeks lightly, warm—a blessing. "*Vade in pace,*" Garber recalled from the Latin Mass of his youth, the priest turning at last—having tidied up the altar and put the chalices in the gold box, what was it? the *ciborium*—the moment when the sanctified hand that had turned bread to flesh and wine to blood was raised from the ghostly robes with the final blessing, go in peace, and Garber had, clear-headed and chastened but relieved to be out of the stuffy church, back to the world in which he felt comfortable, the one where the sun struck one's face with the force of a blow. Garber realized that he had been neglecting simple pleasures for weeks, so enthralled had he been with his own death. He hadn't sat in the yard since Election Day. Hadn't allowed his mind to drift with quite the freedom that it required. He'd voted early at the Sherwood Rec Center and driven to the newsstand on Connecticut to buy half-a-dozen newspapers and magazines. He was sick, but he'd gone for coffee and read *Le Monde* and *The Guardian*, speculated about the outcome of the election with the regulars. He had been feeling well enough to get on with his life. He wasn't teaching—he'd taken a leave of absence—and the days had started to seem almost hopeful. Though

Garber wouldn't have said so, all through October and November he had believed that he was in remission, that the latest, horrible six weeks of chemo had cured him.

Garber found a comfortable spot between dreaming and waking, a shadowy realm in which he seemed to float a few feet above his dozing body. He belched to ease the pressure in his chest and tasted bile. He was too weak to move the chair more than a few feet, but he wanted to turn toward his neighbor on the east side, facing the back porch of Ivana Janko, the latest arrival to the neighborhood. Ivana—maybe forties, a translator at the State Department, a refugee from Milosz's Serbia, vivacious and sexy, fleshy in the way Garber had always preferred women to be—heroin chic, or *New York Times* Style-Section homage to the misogyny of *haut couture*, had never appealed to him—Ivana had cascades of black hair pinned in an elaborate architecture that threatened to topple at any moment. Would that it toppled in Garber's presence; he could only imagine (and that barely) the pleasure of running his fingers through Ivana's *tresses*—nothing more than dead follicles, coated in summer, he knew, with a sheen of oil from Ivana's scalp, perhaps some flaking skin, who knew what else. Since his cancer Garber saw mostly the flaws in bodies.

Every beautiful face was a skull, mortised bones carrying about a few pounds of vital tissue. Garber had read a great deal about the death cults of the Middle Ages, the Dance of Death, the push and pull of living and dying at a time when plague and famine were the norm. He'd done the reading out of curiosity and as part of one of his projects, but until now he hadn't understood the burden of the body in the way almost all pre-modern people had understood it. He was rotting—that's what it felt like—and Ivana's hair and neck and breasts (unconstrained, he was certain, as he watched her standing on her back porch, smoking) were a momentary reprieve from that fact. Standing there puffing on her Gitanes (Garber knew the aroma), looking unfocused in her privacy, Ivana appeared to be a figure from Sargent, an artist well represented just down the road in the National Gallery. Ivana retired into her kitchen, pretending, Garber believed, not to have seen him, preparing her evening meal of *pasulj*, beans in sauce, a dish she had cooked for Garber each time (of two) he had been invited to her home for a meal. Her house was tidy and, Garber thought, feminine, filled with books and newspapers written in Cyrillic script, with thick drapes covering the windows and coverlets—or was it duvets?—thickly piled on the couches and chairs, paintings of Balkan peasants hoeing turnips or drinking Rijeka, fruity booze that had once caused Garber to experience a horrible hangover. Ivana had served tiny glasses of the poison in her smoky kitchen—Garber, familiar with its toxic properties, took demure sips and poured it down the sink when Ivan turned her back. Both dinners had occurred two years before, within a week of one another. Garber believed at the time that he was being auditioned for the role of lover or boyfriend. He must have failed whatever test Ivana had set for him because aside from a chaste kiss nothing came of their lingering conversation over *krempita* and strong coffee—maybe she was repulsed by Garber's admission of a failed marriage, or his political views. It appeared Ivana, newly arrived from a nation where children had been bayoneted and old Albanian men and women had been tossed into shallow graves by Serbian teenagers, beautiful, sensual Ivanaita (as Garber called her in an excess of unreciprocated affection), was a fan of law and order, of "unlimiting executive powers," of Reagan and Bush but not of Clinton and Gore—and who could blame her? It was Ivana who introduced Garber to Jasenovac concentration camp and who related to him the story of Croatian atrocities against Serbians. For his part, and as a guest, he kept his mouth shut about

Sarajevo—this was 1998 and war criminals from Ivana's country were still being rounded up and sent to the Hague—it was, Garber knew, bad taste to start comparing atrocities.

Waiting impatiently now for the return of Manuel, ready to go inside and lie down, maybe toke his medical marijuana before the evening news—he'd need something to prepare himself for the latest from Florida, the shenanigans coming out of Pensacola, tales of chads and dimples that had allowed the Sectarian Court to award the country to that bubblehead from Texas—a disaster—but he'd watch as he had his entire life, wherever he was, Walter Cronkite, now Dan Rather, the sober reading of the news which Garber could no more ignore then he could ignore the beating of his own heart. Even as a young man, obsessed with sex and literature, Garber had found himself curious about what went on in the places he'd never visit. Later on it was power that intrigued him—how it was procured and how it was used; then, after 1970 and the horrors of Vietnam, Garber's obsession was propaganda, with the conspiracy that was government, the myth of democracy and justice belied by the reality of corruption. The stinkers! Garber's anger would outlive him. Though he aspired to

Buddhist calm and stoical acceptance of fate, the truth was Garber's soul was toxic with rage at the crimes he'd witnessed. How must God feel looking down on these *gonifs* who were stealing the country?

To calm himself, Garber changed directions, back to Ivana and Sargent, and thought for nearly five minutes about the art that was on display down the hill—the Rembrandt portraits, the Eakins' picture of the boy playing his banjo, Gilbert Stuart's iconic founders arrayed on one wall of a single room—a shrine to the mythic American past. Adams next to Jefferson, that odd couple, reconciled as old men, full of gripes about Monroe and Adams and the upstart Jackson, dead on the same day, the Fourth, fifty years after publishing those immortal if disingenuous words—*inalienable rights*—The Founders still made Garber querulous. On the other hand, the paintings, monuments, equestrian statutes (Bolivar!) and marble palaces that lined L'Enfant's imperial boulevards roused him—he was a patriot in his own way, an odd duck who hated what he loved and loved what he hated. Dripping with sweat on a June Saturday, between marriages or girlfriends or resolutely alone, the once hale and energetic Garber would march from Third Street down Capitol Hill (admiring bronze Liberty atop the Latrobe's Capital building) and head for the National Gallery or the East Wing, sidestepping tourists who would be gray with sweat—whatever state or nation or continent they had arrived from the visitors would be unready for the murky swamp atop which America's capital was perched, atop the confluence of the Potomac and the Anacostia, so ripe with black flies and mosquitoes that the wealthy built summer homes a few miles north in Chevy Chase or Bethesda. Nobody remained in town during August even in Garber's day—except Garber himself. He'd always loved the city in summer, the surreal feeling of living in a sweltering southern town that had somehow become the nexus of the world. And now, coming on Christmas, the national tree set to be illuminated in two days, balmy for December, a few scraps of snow in his backyard from a Thanksgiving storm, his final run up to the holidays.

Here was Manuel. Garber hadn't noticed his coming. The sun was near to setting, blurred orange against the commuter smog and low-hanging clouds. The nurse was saying something, but Garber wasn't listening. It had come to him a few moments ago, as he watched Ivana toss her cigarette into the backyard, open her door and disappear into her house—just then Garber understood how little time he had left. How he was, despite all attempts to maintain the pretense of going on, done with it. With the pain and indignity, the unbearable sense of loss. A wave—it felt like a wave—of fatigue washed over him, fatigue and grief and perhaps relief as well. Whatever remained to be done needed to be done soon. But what was there to do? Garber, a man who had spent his life engaged, active with causes and busy with work, now had nothing on his schedule. He was free at last. As Manuel, mumbling into his cell phone in Spanish, wheeled him up the makeshift ramp into the kitchen, Garber wondered if he had lived a decent life. He had longed to know the answer to this question, but as he watched the sun ease into the Potomac, he realized he no longer was interested—what I've done is irredeemably lost, he thought. The world would get on without him.

While Garber napped for the final time that day, late in the afternoon, a day that had passed unremarkably and, for Garber, with an unmistakable sense of finality, his friend Wallace came to the house and let himself in the back door. He'd taken the train down from Philadelphia, arrived early in the afternoon, and then taken the Red Line north to Silver Spring to see an old Army buddy. They'd sat for a while in a ratty kitchen a block from the train tracks, smoking and reminiscing. They avoided two subjects: the fiasco then occurring on Capitol Hill and in Tallahassee, and, even more deliberately, the reason for Wallace's trip to Washington. Butch wasn't a friend, but he was a survivor of the same war that Wallace had survived, and he was a person who could get things for people he trusted, and when Wallace had phoned and asked for a favor Butch hadn't asked any questions, just set a price and a meeting time, and that was that. Wallace left Butch's house, took two trains to Capitol Hill, and walked to Garber's house. He had no wish to visit with his dying friend—he'd already said his goodbyes. In fact, he would abort his mission if Garber saw him because he believed, he knew, that what he was doing for his friend was wrong. But Wallace, who was a man of deep principles, also believed that it was immoral to deny a dying man a favor, no matter what that favor might be. Garber had written Wallace a letter and laid out his reasoning, his rationale for the "heavy burden" he was placing upon a man he knew and liked, but probably wouldn't have counted as an intimate friend. Garber asked a favor "in the name of simple humanity" from the one person he believed would honor the asking and who would, even while stricken by the weight of the request, do what he had been asked to do. When

Wallace arrived at Garber's house, the living room light was on, the shades were up, and it was easy to determine that Garber wasn't there so, most likely, in his bedroom. The back door was unlocked, as Garber had promised it would be. Wallace eased his way into the kitchen, left the parcel he carried on the table, and left.

When Garber awoke he found the package that Wallace had left for him. He opened it: Wallace had done what Garber asked him to to do, but the note inside, scribbled on a piece of unlined paper, was unsettling:

> *Garber,* it read, *reluctantly and with sadness and misgivings I have done what you asked me to do. In one sense, doing you this favor was right—I was persuaded by your arguments, and, like you, I don't hold life to be good no matter what. In your position—well, I don't know. On the other hand, I can't help but think you are making a mistake. But I'm not you, and I'm not suffering, so I don't judge. Whatever you choose, may God be with you.*
>
> *W.*

❋

A week later, in the middle of the night—it was 2 a.m.—Garber was deeply asleep and dreaming of something unimportant, dreaming that he was waiting for a bus with a hundred people he'd never met, or running for a train, or sitting in an airport in an exotic city that he'd only imagined he'd ever visited, when half-a-mile west, between the Supreme Court and the Capitol, not far from where the slave market was once located, where kidnapped men, women, and children were shackled in fetid cells awaiting transport south to the cotton lands of Georgia and Alabama, there was another gathering, this one not in Garber's dreams and not a delusion or one of those metaphors of which writers and politicians are so fond, but the real thing, the nightly gathering of the ghosts of the city, the shades of the dead who assembled precisely at 2 a.m. to consider the condition of their city and of the country it governed. Ghosts aren't bursts of cold wind or flickering lights or the cause of the hair rising on the back of one's head. They don't haunt houses or the Capitol rotunda and they certainly aren't undulations arising in any of the graveyards scattered throughout the city. The ghosts of Washington are real, of course, but because they are ghosts and therefore have no existence palpable to the living, it is pointless to imbue them with form or meaning. Let's just say that the ghosts who gather nightly not far from where David Garber is snoring and wheezing (he has developed apnea in recent weeks) are what is left of dead persons when the body—that absurdity—has been laid aside. No need to visualize a little angel escaping from the nostrils or flying out of the mouth as we "give up the ghost;" the fact is, we don't "give the ghost up," it gives up on us. Surprised by our inability to continue living, the self bids us adieu (temporarily), and then, for want of employment, lingers with others of its kind until reassigned. Drawing a circle with Garber—feverish, turning onto his back, slipping briefly toward wakefulness but then dragged inexorably back into sleep—at its center, a circle with a radius of a thousand meters, taking in the heart of Capitol Hill, the observer would note that Garber is not alone in dying. Mrs. Grace Brown, sixty-four, will die before the sun rises—she and Garber aren't acquainted, though they have stood in line together at the Grubb's Pharmacy for their assorted meds, and on the far eastern edge of the city, by remarkable coincidence, an African-American man named James Garber has just had a stroke which will kill him by mid-morning on a gurney in the ER at Anacostia Hospital—apparently there was some problem with Mr. Garber's insurance that delayed his admission, though the delay wouldn't have altered the outcome. The republic of the dead grows each day. A small city like Washington sees twenty to thirty deaths every twenty-four hours, so that Garber's passing is in no way notable, though his is the only consciousness to which we have full access and so it is his story we tell.

The souls gathered within the imaginary circle are, of course, incorporeal, and therefore do not converse, though they do acknowledge one another's non-existence, and pass fragments of thoughts indiscriminately into the ether they occupy. The thinking of the dead is far clearer—perhaps we should say less cluttered—than that of the living. There would, for example, be no point in the dead feeling pride or narcissism, vanity or greed, thus much of what they think about has the clarity of innocence. This very night, when Garber joins the dead of Capitol Hill, he will be pleasantly surprised by the lack of cant among his new associates. None of them, for example, would be able to think, "The object of economics is to change the soul." Souls understand that they exist beyond accumulation, scarcity, and redistribution. Thus Garber will be far more at ease floating through the warm sea of the dead and listening to the silence of their regret then, for instance, listening on

NPR to Wall Street in Review.

The dead share one thing with the living—a yearning for life. That life has ended makes no difference. It appears—all evidence to the contrary—that attachment to life endures, indeed that it blossoms, and that while there is neither heaven nor hell, there is a middle ground—a limbo—of disappointment that life has, at least for the moment, come to an end. Souls are remnants—they aren't angels—not by a long shot. Angels are a form of wishful thinking. Young, sexless beings sheathed in white nightgowns, with long blond hair and enormous wings, Gabriel scaring the Virgin in Fra Angelico, or the cowering maiden in Rossetti's version. The ghosts of Capitol Hill are hardly angels—and they're not clothed or winged or blond or white—they're without form and are the color of slightly muddy water. There are a lot of ghosts in Washington, and seeing them, or rather feeling their presence, puts one in mind of Dante's first view of the crossing over from this world to the next. Because death is the only democracy, there's no way of telling Frederick Douglass, the great voice of abolition, from Callie Douglass, a nine-year-old girl killed in a drive-by shooting in 1986. Having shed the flesh, ghosts come at once to a far deeper understanding of what endures and what dissolves than the living—they acquire the insight Plato described in his various Socratic discussions, the insight that there are two worlds, that one, the higher, is embedded in the lower, not as a means of elevating one or degrading the other, but because everything is alive, imbued with soul, and thus mixed up with material things.

I know, this sounds like spiritualist crap or Gnosticism, a form of illusion or heresy depending on what you believe. But I have no control over how things sound, or whether or not they seem plausible. Garber was fond of saying that the truth is never easy to accept, that we are so riven by falsehoods and propaganda that we actually come to hate the truth. But he didn't know what he was saying. The truth isn't difficult or discomfiting. The truth is impossible for us to grasp—it's just the way we've been designed. The ghosts who slosh through the night of December 13th in the vicinity of David Garber's narrow three-story house on Maryland Avenue are as real as the people who live in the houses around Garber's, as real as the men and women who work down the hill in the Capitol, perhaps more real than the ghostly figures who fill the hundred thousand cubicles in the hundred blocky office buildings arrayed on both sides of the Mall—"fascist modalities" was how Garber referred to these monoliths in his *Nation* article

"Is the United States Government Destroying American Democracy?" Minutes after you have finished reading this story, Garber's opinions will melt into air and he will join the ghosts of Capitol Hill. The mode of his departure was unfortunate, possibly tragic. Garber, thoughtlessly, has burdened his friend Wallace with a sense of guilt that will haunt him for the rest of his long but unhappy life. But Garber did what he felt he had to do, and I am not in a position to judge him—I might someday do the same thing.

Like all of the newly dead, Garber will be surprised at first, but he was always a quick study and will find his place among the legions of the dead, perhaps even locate a colleague or two, an enemy—he has many—and while death is democratic, it doesn't obliterate memory. On the contrary, you might even say that death *is* memory.

In any case Garber will soon feel at home among the dead since it's dying that is natural, not living. The amount of energy Garber had consumed staying alive—the worry, the visits to the clinic, the medicines, the pain endured—all of this clinging to life will seem absurd once the moment of departure has come. He was, at the end, relieved to go.

Acknowledgments

I want to express my heartfelt appreciation to my first readers—Brigid Ovitt, David Gutierrez, and Steve Allen. To Marc Estrin and Donna Bister for their continued support of my writing and for their professionalism. To Peter Nash and Michael Keith who have, for the past twenty years, shown me the way forward. Best wishes to my long-lost friends who may or may not still live in Philadelphia, City of Dreams: John Grant, Elizabeth Nordell, and Julie Mostov. And to the memory of David F. Noble, with whom, for many years, I walked the streets of Philly.

About the Author

George Ovitt has published two novels, two books of poetry, a previous collection of short stories, and a historical work dealing with medieval history. With Peter Nash, he wrote a collection of essays, *Trotsky's Sink*. He lives in New Mexico.

Fomite

Writing a review on social media sites for readers will help the progress of independent publishing. To submit a review, go to the book page on any of the sites and follow the links for reviews. Books from independent presses rely on reader-to-reader communications.

For more information or to order any of our books, visit:
http://www.fomitepress.com/our-books.html

More story collections from Fomite...

MaryEllen Beveridge — After the Hunger
MaryEllen Beveridge — Permeable Boundaries
Jay Boyer — Flight
L. M Brown — Treading the Uneven Road
L. M Brown — Were We Awake
Michael Cocchiarale — Here Is Ware
Michael Cocchiarale — Still Time
Neil Connelly — In the Wake of Our Vows
Catherine Zobal Dent — Unfinished Stories of Girls
Zdravka Evtimova — Carts and Other Stories
John Michael Flynn — Off to the Next Wherever
Derek Furr — Semitones
Derek Furr — Suite for Three Voices
Elizabeth Genovise — Where There Are Two or More
Andrei Guriuanu — Body of Work
Zeke Jarvis — In A Family Way
Arya Jenkins — Blue Songs in an Open Key
Bobby Johnston — The Saint I Ain't
Jan English Leary — Skating on the Vertical
Julia MacDonnell— The Topography of Hidden Stories
Marjorie Maddox — What She Was Saying
William Marquess — Badtime Stories
William Marquess — Because Because Because Because Because

Fomite

William Marquess — Boom-shacka-lacka
William Marquess — Things I Want You to Do
Gary Miller — Museum of the Americas
Jennifer Anne Moses — Visiting Hours
Charles Opara — How Hamisu Survived Bad Kidneys
and a Bad Son-in-Law
Martin Ott — Interrogations
George Ovitt — The Showcase
Christopher Peterson — Amoebic Simulacra
Christopher Peterson — Scratch the Itchy Teeth
Charles Phillips — Dead South
Jack Pulaski — Love's Labours
Charles Rafferty — Saturday Night at Magellan's
Joseph Rathgeber — Bad Days on the Batso
Mohsen Rezaei — The Violet Needle
Ron Savage — What We Do For Love
Vince Sgambati — Undertow of Memory
Fred Skolnik— Americans and Other Stories
Lynn Sloan — This Far Is Not Far Enough
L.E. Smith — Views Cost Extra
Caitlin Hamilton Summie — To Lay To Rest Our Ghosts
Susan Thomas — Among Angelic Orders
Tom Walker — Signed Confessions
Silas Dent Zobal — The Inconvenience of the Wings